Benji,

~~The No One~~

~~The Loser~~

~~The Rejected~~

The Revenge Artist

By

Kimberly J Fuller

Benji, ~~The No One, The Loser, The Rejected,~~ The Revenge Artist

Digital ISBN: 978-0-9857561-4-7
Print ISBN: 978-0-9857561-5-4
Print ISBN: 978-0-9857561-6-1

For the hurting teenagers and young adults who have no place to put their pain and hurt, and no language to tell us they are hurting apart from their actions.

Benji, ~~The No One, The Loser, The Rejected~~, The Revenge Artist

Tessa

Tessa watched her sister shift around in their grandmother's overstuffed suede recliner chair. After several failed attempts to curl up sideways, Marula finally rested her head on her crossed arms on top of one knee; her other leg curled underneath her in the chair like a half bent pretzel. Earlier, at dinner, Tessa noticed the blue in Marula's eyes seemed brighter, though, maybe it was the pendulum light hanging over their grandmother's kitchen table that made them look that way.

"Are you sure you don't want to go with us to the store?" she asked Marula, who powered off the television then grabbed the book off the table next to her.

After another shift of positions, this one now a full pretzel, the same way they used to sit during elementary story time at Maman's library in Botswana, Marula answered. "No, I am fine. Really, I am. Go with dad and explore. And meet someone."

"I don't want to explore and meet "someone" without you." Tessa arose from the stool, where she had been waiting for their father to get off the phone so they could leave and made her way across the wide living room.

"Now, don't make me feel guilty…again," Marula chimed, tilting her head back against the chair to look up at Tessa.

Tessa peered down at her sister from over the back of the chair. Marula's facial features looked back at her, only upside down. "I would never do such a thing!" she faked a gasp and then kissed her sister on the top of the head. Marula's lush, golden hair tickled against her lips and chin.

Marula made a "sheesh," sound and closed her eyes. A broad, sleepy smile cracked across her lips, and she reached above her head and hugged Tessa's head as if it weren't attached to her body and was just a floating, ball-like orb.

Speaking from inside the squished head hug, Tessa said, "Okay, but don't forget that I asked, especially when you tell me later how you wished you'd romped around town with dad and me instead of hanging with the old ladies."

"Hey!" their mother's voice called from across the large, open room where she was snapping a puzzle piece into place. "I beg to differ on that "old lady" comment. I am a strapping, young forty…ish something that hiked Kilimanjaro last year."

"Oh please, you didn't even want to use the long drop toilets on the mountain," their dad said with a wink at Tessa as he came into the room, his grey jacket in one hand and snapping his phone to his belt clip with the other.

"Well, who would want to use the bathroom in a wooden box surrounding a deep hole?" Tessa's grandmother said patting the top of their mother's hand. Mikael sat on the other side of a small, square table also searching through puzzle pieces. "And I bet those huts were cold inside."

Tessa's mother shuttered at the memory. "They were! And my butt swaying over a hole in the ground was enough to make my pee change its mind and stay inside my body."

Everyone let out a laugh that echoed off the tall ceilings like a surround sound stereo.

Todd, their father, took long strides across the room and kissed Mikael. "I'm still proud of you," he said.

Mikael responded with a smile then grabbed the front of his jacket and pulled him back to her for another, longer, kiss.

When their lips met the third time, both Tessa and Marula rolled their eyes and made gagging sounds.

"Alright, you two love birds break it up," Gram said with a chuckle. "Todd, you need to go before the stores close."

With matching smiles, Tessa's parents held each other eyes. They appeared to be exchanging a secret telepathy.

Todd finally said with a quiet voice, as if Mikael was his only audience, "We'll be back in a little bit."

"Okay, Love," she said letting go of the hold she had on his jacket.

Before heading out, Todd kissed their grandmother on the cheek and then kissed Marula on the top of the head.

Tessa glanced back at Marula as she closed the front door, sealing in the image of her sister, the book open, her legs still crossed, her hair now hanging long over her face. A little brighter, she thought, but

Benji, ~~The No One, The Loser, The Rejected~~, The Revenge Artist

still not the same.

Benji
One

"You do know this nation has a blood pressure problem, right?" the girl said, sitting down in the empty booth on the other side of Benji's table. She reached over and took a fry off his plate, dipped it into his ketchup, and ate it as if it was food she had ordered.

"Hey!" he said, crumpling his napkin into a ball and resisting the urge to pound the table and make a scene. Pizza is the famous staple at Maria's Corner Café in Depot Town, but today Benji came straight from school for two things: cheese fries and a slice of apple pie.

"I saved a year of your life eating that fry. You should thank me." The stranger smiled, took another fry, sloshed it through the ketchup again and ate, mumbling, "Two years now."

The girl's hair was the color of tree bark and set high on her head in a ponytail puff of curls that fumbled and fought against each other to be set free. She wore big silver hoop earrings but no makeup that he could tell. A flash image of the gypsy street performers he sometimes sees out on Main Street— guitars in hand and singing for the people passing by—went through his mind.

"How exactly are you saving my life?" He glared at her, feeling a mix of offense and intrigue. There was a faint dimple on her chin that disappeared

5

when her smile faded.

"Well, I was over there," she pointed to the end of the long cafeteria counter, over where pies sit in a tall, spinning glass case, "and I noticed you pick up the ketchup, squirt it in several circles, mouth the count of exactly how many circles you made, and proceed to shake the salt, not over your fries, but over your circle-counted ketchup. I'm betting you're unusual, and possibly rushing yourself toward an early high-blood-pressure induced death so I thought I would lend my help and try to save you."

"Three years," she declared, her smile shining triumphantly while reaching for another fry, this one drooping under the weight of mozzarella and bacon bits. She put her other hand under her mouth in order to keep it from toppling onto the table. "Plus, I am new here and my goal is to introduce myself to someone today." She shoved the whole glob into her mouth. Chewing fast, she wiped her hand on a napkin and extended it across the table. "Hi, I'm Contessa, Contessa Knightly."

Cautiously, questioningly he extended his hand and shook hers. "Benji."

"Short for Benjamin, right? You did count those circles, didn't you?"

His face warmed as if caught on hidden camera doing something personal and embarrassing. Tilting his whole head down toward the plate of fries, he proceeded to separate the area she touched, pushing it to the outer rim.

"Well, did you?" She seized another fry, this one from the fringes of the plate as if he separated them

6

for her to share.

Stiffening his back, he met her eyes head on and slowly nodded his head.

She helped herself to a fry and a stray bacon bit piece. "There's four years."

"If you are counting one fry per year of my life saved then shouldn't I be near death? You know, for all the times I've already eaten here, *with* salt in my ketchup. If that's how you are counting."

She smiled so big and genuine it made his stomach do a peculiar flip flop. Her teeth were absurdly straight and white, and he bizarrely imagined she must have a great dental plan and is past the braces phase of her life.

"I can always pick the strange ones, no matter where I go. It's a type of art." She crinkled her nose. "Wait, I'm not insulting you, am I? I mean "strange" as a compliment, not an insult. I'm saying you're *unique* but in a good way."

After taking a gulp of his soda, he pushed the plate over to her. "I'm not insulted," he said.

She accepted the offering with a wink of her eye. "Good. I would hate to start a friendship with an insult. I save the insults for later." She shoved three fries into her mouth at one time. Minus the ketchup.

"Later on," he thought, thoroughly confused. There would be no later.

"Well, I hate to not be insulted and run but...," He opened his wallet and tossed a ten dollar bill on the table, forgoing the slice of pie.

She picked up the money and held it in the air for him to take back, "I got this," she said. "Even though I did save some of your life." She swallowed, smiled again, and then lined her teeth with a fry.

It was the oddest fry smile he had ever seen. And the first.

"Okay then, take care," he said, putting his wallet back.

She scooped up what remained of his drink and took a hurried gulp. Apparently sharing germs wasn't a caution of hers. "Oh no. You are supposed to say 'See you tomorrow. I'll text you so I can help you find your way around the school.' Since I'm new and all."

From inside the neck of her shirt, she produced a little silver pen. Definitely gypsy, he thought as she pulled his hand down to the table and began to write on his palm.

"Here are my digits, Shawty," she said, though the way she enunciated it made the syllables grind against her teeth. It was the way a parent sounds when they try to speak with young slang. She sounded just as ridiculous.

She scrawled seven numbers across his hand. It tickled, but he didn't pull away.

Having no idea how to respond to her "digits," or "Shawty," comment he shrugged, said, "Okay," then grabbed his backpack off the booth and made his way through the weave of sporadic red tables— safely passing the guys he'd been listening in on— and left.

The girl waved at him through the window as he got into his car.

Benji
Two

Benji sat in his driveway studying the handwriting on his palm. The girl's writing was full of bubbles and fun, like a font used to advertise children's clothing or toys. "Two for one on bouncy balls! Today only, folks!" Even the number seven, normally a number made of straight and harsh angles, she'd written it with a swirl at the beginning and a deep concave curve in the spine.

He should rub it off. That would be the natural thing to do when a strange, all be it a beautiful and intriguing, girl unsnaps a pen from her bra strap and freely gives out her number. It's probably a fake number, anyway. He'll dial and get a voice mail announcing he's the hundredth idiot to fall for the prank. But something was genuine about her. Her eyes maybe. They danced when she spoke, the way Leah's do.

"What the hell," he said, adding the girl's name, Contessa, to his contact list of six other people. The list included work, both parents, his little sister Leah, and the widowed neighbor next door: an elderly lady with large boobs who long ago seemed to forget a bra is needed to lift them up from her stomach. Her number was "in case of emergency," according to his mother. Though, he'd hardly said more than, "Hello, Ms. Walker," to her. Besides, for emergencies he'd likely call Big Timmie at work.

Opening the front door, a nasty mix of bacon, burnt popcorn, and "clean-breeze" room freshener—his mom's favorite cover a stench smell—greeted him. Along with Rat Bastard's loud snore echoing from the living room.

"Well, look who's finally home," his mom's voice jabbed at him as he kicked off his shoes into the mud room. "As soon as you're done putting your school junk away, go clean that pigsty of a room." Camille rounded the corner of the hall heading toward the kitchen; her pants swinging against her ankles like ringing bells.

Eggplant, he thought. Back in second grade the teacher had his class draw pictures of their family. He was proud of his picture. It was a lovely picture of him and his parents. The teacher was proud too; she gave him an A. But when he got home, and his mother saw the image, she complained for weeks about how he'd drawn her to look like an eggplant. With age, he realized his depiction of her was true. She is shoulder-less with wide hips and fat ankles, and for the most part dresses in pleated pants and plain baby doll shirts. She is, literally, an eggplant in clothes, complete with short, highlighted, brown pixie-cut hair that spikes ever so slightly at the top.

When she passed him on her way to the kitchen, he knew she hadn't bothered with a mirror for a while because her makeup was cracked around her eyes and mouth. "And get your dad to call the auto repair place for that beast of a car. I heard it squeaking two houses down. What will the neighbors think?" she said, not wanting an answer.

Not bothering with a comment Benji slung his backpack over his shoulder and headed down the hall to the living room where he knew he'd find his father asleep in his old, leather-worn chair. "Please convince him to get rid of the chair," his mother had said to the interior designer she hired after they moved in. The old chair never moved and is now the weekly complaint. "That damn thing is the bane of my existence. All you ever do is sleep in it!"

His father's only reply, ever, is, "Yep."

As if his eyes were claws, Benji dragged them across the rat's body, taking in the visual of his father's tie undone and hanging on his chest, his baby blue button down shirt with half the buttons also undone and making a peep show out of the white t-shirt underneath, his grey dress slacks bunched in the groin from slouching down in the chair, and his nose making more noise than the television he'd fallen asleep to.

With a roll of his eyes, Benji moved on and headed up the stairs. *You and your pot belly can take that "bane of a chair," with you when you move out.*

Up in his room, Benji tossed his "junk," on the desk then sat down and powered up his tablet. The desk clock read three-twenty-seven. He approximated he had about thirty minutes before his mother's head exploded about his room. A half an hour is more than enough time to clean up *and* check his bank account.

His room wasn't dirty, merely messy with clothes from doing laundry two days ago. Time constraint between work and school meant he had to dig

through the unfolded basket to find things that
didn't need ironing in order to wear. In the process,
he created a littering of jeans and t-shirts around the
room. There isn't much in the room to make a mess
of anyway. A desk and chair he picked out at Ikea,
along with a clock, a desk lamp, and a picture of
Bob Marley. A tall six-drawer dresser sits next to
the closet and on top sits a few books Big Timmie
gave him—one about motorcycles and the rest sci-fi
books he's never read. There are no other posters or
pictures or curtains in the room, and the only reason
he bought the Bob Marley picture was because he
liked the quote: "Some people feel the rain, others
just get wet." He had no idea which of the two types
of people he was.

On the tablet, the bank balance read another
thirteen dollars and seventy-two cents. He already
made an extra thousand dollars in interest this year
but now it was beginning to compound quickly. He
sat back with a grin and watched out the window as
the neighbor's underground sprinkler started up—
three thirty, right on cue. You can set a clock by the
sprinklers in the neighborhood. Thanks to the
required subdivision rule of underground sprinklers,
the entire neighborhood has impeccable landscaping
and a well-timed symphony of yard showers.
During the summer, early in the morning, they all
rise out of the ground like born again zombies and
spray the yards with a dew-like mist. Compared to
their old neighborhood this one screams entitled
families live here. Even the symmetrical rows of
driveways look like a car sales lot of family
vehicles. You can almost imagine a salesman

saying, "Welcome, welcome folks. We have all the latest minivans, hatchbacks, SUV's, and some trucks with inside cabs as large as a small car and able to fit a team of little league kids inside."

"Whatcha doin'?" Leah asked, startling him out of his musing.

Benji flipped his tablet face down and stood up to gather the tossed clothes into a pile on the bed.

"Laundry," he answered, turning a shirt right side out.

Leah grabbed a gob of socks from the basket and sat down on her side of the bed—her Pepto Bismol colored feather blanket fluffing up around her like a pink padded cloud. She spread the socks out in front of her.

Never once has their mother mentioned Leah's blanket in his room. Camille will holler and yell about Leah's toys being out, her play makeup left in the bathroom, her wet towel not being hung up on the hook, even her shoes lying in the middle of the floor, but the blanket, never a word. Benji assumes it's because shame will forever keep her silent.

"How was school today?" he asked. "Did you do anything fun?"

Leah held up three socks, comparing them for unity. He noticed her little fingernails were painted a glittery blue. "A dumb boy pushed Cassy off the swing and she got a big bruise on her arm. Mrs. Adams made him go to the principal's office, and we heard him crying all the way down the hall." She laid two socks down in a row then picked up two more and began another row. She looked like she was playing a memory game where you match up what's underneath the tiles until you find all the pairs.

"Is Cassy okay?"

"Yeah...Yes," she corrected herself. "Her mom said the boy pushed her because that's what boys do when they like you, but I think that's a dumb reason. Do boys really do that?" She wrinkled her nose, a look of confusion.

"Well, one time, a long time ago when I was in fourth grade this boy kissed a girl during recess and then he pushed her to the ground. So I suppose, yes, boys do act dumb when they like a girl."

Her face turned from confused to Eureka as she grabbed two of the socks and paired them, leaving the odd ones again.

"When do boys stop acting dumb? When they're grownups like daddy?" she asked, tucking a stray piece of her hair back behind the bobby pin over her ear. She'd been growing out her bangs to the protest of their mother, and now they were at an odd length—too short to do anything with and too long to let them hang haphazardly in her eyes.

At her question, his jaw pinched so hard he felt it in his ears. Turning away from her, he put the pile of folded shirts into his dresser. He righted his facial expression before turning back and answering. "Sometimes boys stay dumb forever, but not all of them. Some turn out pretty nice." Though, he couldn't think of any.

Revenge Chronicle: Color Me Neon Happy
Revenge Risk Rating: High
Revenge Date: May 23rd, 2011
Chronicle Entry Date: June 4th, 2011

Chronicle, I will have to print pictures of this one because I can't wait to see the before and after in images for myself. I'm getting better and better at this! Okay, so, Mr. Planter, yes Chronicle that is his real name, but I'll call him Mr. Nuts from now on because he really is nuts—and he's a yeller. He reminds me of the old man in the Disney movie UP, except he never turns nice. A month ago he cussed me out for crossing his yard to get to the bus stop. All I did was walk between the houses instead of going all the way around on the sidewalk. It was my first time, and I only went through his yard because I woke up late. I've heard the other kids talk about him on the bus, but I didn't think he could be that bad. "Does my yard look like a public path!" he bellowed at me from his back porch, scaring the bejesus out of me. "Come back in my yard again and I'll beat your little ass!"

Last week he threw his newspaper at a kid walking his dog past his house. He didn't hit the kid hard, but he sure scared him. From my window, I heard him yell, "You and that damn dog left crap on my lawn last week!" The poor kid, I think he was about ten-years-old, looked guilty, and he probably was, but Mr. Nut could have politely confronted him instead of beaming the kid with a newspaper.

15

Lawn obsessed; that's what I would call our neighborhood. They are all obsessed with their landscaping though Mr. Nuts seems to be at the top of the obsessed totem pole. Everyone else in the neighborhood is pleasant; they're always waving and saying hello. Even the house, where everyone catches the bus, opens their garage when it's snowing or raining so the kids can stand inside, out of the elements, and wait for the bus to arrive.

Mr. Nut's house is across the street from ours and two houses down from the small neighborhood park. There is a clear shot of his house from my bedroom window. Every day at seven A.M. and three thirty P.M., his sprinklers rise from the ground and water his lawn. Those sprinklers and his lawn obsession sparked my plan.

It began with sprinkler heads. That was the research plan; how to do something with his sprinkler heads. My first thought was to break them or dig them up in the middle of the night so he would have to have them repaired. But my research unfolded a much better plan. A plan with fire and dazzle like a Fourth of July fireworks display!

It took me three nights of sneaking out to find out what type of sprinkler system he had, and ten days to complete my mission.

<u>Night one:</u> slip out the back sliding doors, run across the street and scope out where the sprinkler attachments connect to the water supply, and also find out the brand name of the sprinkler system. I easily found the inset box on the left side of the house, covered by a rectangle top; the brand name etched largely across the cover. The moon was

16

bright the first night, so it took all of five minutes to get out, scope around the yard, and slip back into my house. Chronicle, that first night I thought my heart was going to cave in my chest with how hard it was beating.

Night two: the mission was to go back and check on what sorts of tools I would need and to locate the golden award: the fertilizer tank. (If he had one). I almost yelled, "Yes!" when I found it because I would only need a flathead screwdriver to pry the lid off. It was merely buried in another, separate, inset box right next to the main sprinkler water supply system. See, when the system is installed you can opt for a separate tank to be connected to your main watering line. That special tank releases a precision dose of "water soluble fertilizer," according to the maker's website. And that precision dose can be adjusted with a simple turn of a small lever located on the outside of the tank.

Night three: the moon was not on my side, but the fog that rolled in was. At one thirty A.M., I pried the cover open, twisted off the tank cap, and dumped a gallon of grass killer right into the fertilizer tank.

Chronicle, on the first two nights there were moments when I thought the hammering of my heart would wake up Mr. Nut, but the third night, the same way the fog rolled in and cloaked me, a calm washed over my body and mind. In fact, I was so calm that I strolled back here to the house, slid the door closed, locked it, and went up to my room and lay down. Leah never knew I left and neither did anyone else.

17

Unfortunately, I had to wait two frustrating days for the rain to stop and for those sprinklers to pop their heads up. But sure enough, the sun came out and at exactly seven and three thirty those suckers rose from the ground and did their magic trick.

By the next morning, the grass already showed signs of brown patches!

YES, YES, YES!!!

On the eighth day, when I drove up after school, I saw Mr. Nut talking with a neighbor who lives on the right side of his house. He was shaking his head and waving his arms around as if dumbfounded about why his once, greenest-grass-in-the-neighborhood was now dead grass. His whole yard, including the knee-high shrubs that lined the walkway, were a sepia brown color.

That day I watched him for a while longer from my bedroom window, and that's when it hit me. I could do one more, "up yours, Mr. Planter," thing, but I needed to head to the store first.

At one thirty A.M., I made my last trek across the street, screwdriver in hand, and opened the fertilizer tank one more time.

The next morning, I set my alarm to make sure to watch the four bottles of fabric dye I poured into the fertilizer system spray the lawn a beautiful bright neon orange.

I only wish I'd been home to see Mr. Nut's face when he walked outside.

Benji
Three

Benji sat bolt upright in bed, a knot in his stomach, a remnant smell of smoke tickled his nostrils, and he was damp with sweat. The alien green glow of his desk clock read two-twenty-two A.M. It was only a dream. He pulled off his wet t-shirt and tossed it to the floor. With his nose to the air, he inhaled, in order to be sure, but there was nothing. The smell was left over from the dream. It was all in his head, not in the house.

A small hand reached in the darkness and touched his arm. "Shhhhh, it's only a bad dream," Leah said, mimicking the way he comforts her after she has a nightmare.

He lifted her hand and kissed the back of it. "I'm okay. Go back to sleep."

It was only a dream. Dreams don't mean anything. Do they?

In the dream, he dropped a match into a can of paint thinner in the basement and watched it go up in flames. The fire bled from the can out onto the floor and surrounded him within a few minutes. He merely stood there smug, no pain, and feeling justified, as if it was his duty to burn himself and the house down.

Pulling back the covers he slipped from the bed, careful not to disturb the knot his sister's blanket made with his black sheets. Quietly, he opened his top drawer and pulled out a fresh undershirt to slip on.

Leah was already back into a sound sleep, the giant ball of fluff and flannel, light and dark fighting for space on the bed, enveloped her like a giant protective ball. Along with her blanket, no one mentions Leah's sleeping arrangements. Over the years, it simply became a habit. Each night Leah puts her pajamas on in her room, goes to brush her teeth, and then makes her way to Benji's room where he has her side of the queen bed smoothed out and her pink blanket waiting. She gets under her cover, gives him a squeeze of a hug and says, "Dear God, bless Mrs. Adam's - her teacher - bless Cassy - her best friend - and bless mommy and daddy, and most of all bless Benji. Thank you," then she curls up in a fetal position and falls asleep. Last year she ended all of her prayers by asking God to get her a puppy like Cassy's, which was a Golden Retriever. When the puppy grew from a little fun thing into a big ninety pound ball of fur that wouldn't stop jumping on people and knocking them over, including Leah, she stopped asking God for a puppy. In Leah's room, she has a different comforter on her bed, a light blue one, but she keeps the pink blanket on Benji's. He doesn't care that its bright color screams against the dark colors of his bed set; he loves her blanket being there. It means every night Leah is safe.

Not wanting to go back to sleep, Benji made his way down to the kitchen for a glass of milk. In the great room, the glow from the TV flashed like bursts of lightning. Rat Bastard lay in front of it, still snoring in his chair as if he was the missing thunder. The last Benji saw, Bob had retreated to watch TV after dinner. Apparently he was still there, sleeping soundly, his belly fat jiggling with each reverberating snore.

Benji stepped closer. A feeling of challenging the space rose in his already coiled guts—like a lion testing another for rank. One day soon, he thought. He re-ran the bank numbers and time frame in his head: *Afterward...one more year with my mother then I'm eighteen and can legally take Leah. I only need Camille for her income and job. Only one more year of saving and I'll have sixty thousand dollars. Enough for apartment rent, bus passes to save on gas, car insurance, utilities—including internet and cable—groceries, even laundry expenses, and household supplies.*

Opening his savings account with fake parental consent had been easy. First, he made sure there was no branch located in Michigan. No building to go to meant they would likely do business with him online. He was right. The Credit Union he found simply required an electronic signature—which was easy to use since his father's was programmed into the home computer for work emails—and he had to give the Credit Union permission to place two small deposits into his parents main bank account. The next day, he logged into the account, verified the deposits, then the Credit Union took them right back out. Rat never noticed the fifty-three and ninety-seven cents that came and went within a three-day period. If he did, he likely thought they were attached to one of his *live* online porn fees.

The ones Benji found out about while sneaking the bank password from the book in Rat's desk, smartly written under the title, "*Bank Password.*"

Sweat again thickened under is shirt while he stared at Bob. He had come downstairs with full force normal walking steps, but instead of getting milk he turned and tiptoed down the hall to the basement door.

Benji
Four

Twelve stairs lead down to the basement.
They are always the same, never changing, but
Benji counted them anyway. By the last step, he
was welcomed with the smell of chemicals—the
same odor that invariably conjures memories of the
medic's cabin at fifth-grade summer camp. A bunch
of sweaty kids, antiseptic sprays, and the plastic of
Band-Aids. That horrible stench had hooked itself
to his memory like a bad omen. Even the nurse's
office at school smelled the same. It's probably why
he dreamed of lighting a fire in the basement
instead of anywhere else in the house.

He shivered at the sudden remembrance of his
dream.

Early after they moved in, his dad, Bob the Rat
Bastard, decided to build a small man-cave in the
basement. The entire space takes up about ten feet
by twelve feet of the fifteen hundred square foot
basement. Rat did all of the work himself, even
hanging the drywall and painting it an ugly prison
gray. Two of the four walls are lined with waist
high work tables and overflowing with disorganized
tools. A latticed pressboard hangs along the walls
above the table, its highest hooks gripping larger
power tools, Rat's hunting rifles, a couple of
wound-up extension cords, and some mini glass jars
filled with nuts, bolts and nails. Mounted in the

corner of the room is a flat screen TV, cable and internet ready. The TV tilts and twists any direction in the room but right now faced the plaid loveseat. (Given his online secret site it doesn't stretch the imagination to assume football isn't the only thing he watches.) Next to the love seat is a square end table, hollow underneath and holding a wastebasket. On the top sits the TV remote, a box of tissue, and of all things, lotion. On the other end of the loveseat—an ironic name—is a small refrigerator. The kind found in a college dorm room. It stores the Rat's beer and alcohol. Benji gave the handle a tug to see how much alcohol was left. A six-pack of beer, two bottles of cream Vodka, and three bottles of Tequila took up the shelf space. On the door was three bottles of water and a diet Coke.

He closed the refrigerator, walked to the work table, and lined up the drill bits sitting inside a splayed box of drill parts. There were seven bits from smallest to largest and the largest looked as if it could drill a nickel sized hole. He rolled the second to the smallest between his fingers, eyeing its size and comparing it to the size of the screw in the wall socket. He hoped he didn't need to mount anything and that the industrial strength sticky tack he bought would work fine. A rough test at work on similar equipment proved good, but he was wary of its strength on the cooler basement walls. If he needs to screw anything into the wall, it will add risk. Not a good idea.

Turning in a circle, he scanned the room's wall sockets and wondered if maybe his father's taste in high school girls was because older women wouldn't want to be in a basement workroom.

He couldn't imagine how it unfolded the first time. Did he put an ad on the internet? Or on one of those lists? Advertisement: "Middle age man willing to pay with alcohol for blowjobs. Teen girls only need reply." No, that would be jail worthy. Maybe something like, "Basement refrigerator item for exchange. Perfect for eighteen and under." Either way, why anyone would willingly come to this ridiculous cave to lollipop the Rat was beyond him.

Standing in the middle of the room, Benji closed one eye and held up his hands, thumb to thumb, to make a square box as if sizing up a camera shot. Taking steps in different directions he caught the perfect angle in his sight. When he turned around, he spotted what he needed. Instead of adding an additional socket, he could cover over the existing one above the three-drawer file cabinet.

He reached for the handle on the file cabinet, anticipating what was inside. It didn't open. Rat had shown him the two pistols locked inside when he was younger. One was a nine millimeter and the other a revolver. He had liked the revolver better because it's the kind you see in old Cowboy movies. "Grandpa gave me that one when I joined the military," his dad said, motioning to the revolver. "It'll be yours one day."

But that was back when Benji thought his dad was a hero and sharing a grownup's responsibility with him. He believed his dad when he said he was, "helping him become a man," though he was only eleven. But all of that was back before life threw its gut punches, and the hero worship of Bob was replaced with a bitter tasting anger.

Benji often thought of those guns his freshmen year. "What would Leah's life be like if I end mine? Would she hate me? Would her life take a different path, a worse path?" he would ask himself while pacing the floor of his room, desperate to expel his excessive anxiety as if it were a demon infesting him. At the time, he was aware his thoughts were a bad sign. He knew people who mused about the taste of bullets and ending it all needed help, but thinking of those guns felt like a life jacket floating on top of dark water, brightly offering a way out.

Pinching the bridge of his nose, he squeezed his eyes together and forced the image of the guns to retreat from his mind.

Now focused on the fact that he found the best angle and with the least obstacle interference, he turned again to memorize the view.

Work had notified him that his equipment arrived yesterday on his day off, and he already withdrew three hundred dollars to pay Big Timmie for it—fifty percent off the retail price—now all he'll need to do is double check the angle after setup and then let life unfold its Karma.

Benji smacked the box of drill bits, disorganizing them again, and thinking about how luck had been on his side the day he found his dad's live porn information. That porn information was the catalyst for the revenge plan of all revenge plans.

Before switching off the light, standing at the bottom of the stairs, he glanced back at the cabinet, recognizing why there wasn't a need for him to think about guns anymore: He had found a different outlet for his anger. He had found revenge. And for this revenge plan, the one that would get him and Leah away from the Rat Bastard, he had named it the "Busting My Dad's Balls plan."

Benji
Five

Hovering over the toilet with one hand leaned against the wall, Benji peed and stared at his phone sitting on top of the toilet tank.

It was another hour after being in the basement before he was able to fall back to sleep. When he finally did it was restless and twitchy and filled with pre-dream moments of falling down stairs or jumping from the roof. Every time, he would jolt awake seconds before impact.

Another fire dream fully woke him for the morning, though he couldn't quite remember what was going on in that one. There was a wolf and a cliff, but other than waking with a bad feeling he couldn't put the images back together.

When he got up to brush his teeth and pee, the dream, and the anxiety had fully dissipated, and instead, thoughts of the girl at the Cafe surfaced from under the clutter. Her diamond shaped face, her light hazel eyes, the color of moss on pond water, even her fingers, which he didn't remember paying attention to. They were long and thin, and there must have been faded henna on her hand because a light reddish-brown design ran down her first finger. The image was as clear as if he'd seen her daily for months and not just met her once.

Stepping onto the cold tile of the bathroom floor, he remembered he had the girl's number in his phone.

Before he could wuss out, he took a chance and text her.

Now, he peed and stared at the blank screen and waited.

Benji
Six

At the table in the breakfast nook Leah sat with her head bowed, seemingly focused on each bite of her small dollop of yogurt and half of a banana, while their mother spoke in a formal, tight voice to someone on her cell phone. "No, they need to understand that not only is the structure unsafe but the wood chips are sharp and causing problems. My daughter came home last week with splinters. Yes, I understand the township's hands are tied but my hands are not. And Mr. Santiago, my hands can accomplish a lot."

The splinters she spoke about were a lie. Leah hadn't come home with splinters at all. It was another kid in the neighborhood. Camille, the Fake, was heading up the mob of mom's against the townships office in order to get a new play area built across the street. The mom mob's complaints: On hot summer days the metal on the structure was too hot to play on and the wood chips surrounding the play structure—the one the township built brand new two years ago—was causing injuries to the children who play there.

By Leah's posture and heavy cheeks Benji knew their mother, before getting on her blue tooth, must have lectured her about her calories for the day. When Benji is around, Camille pretends to keep her constant obsession with Leah's diet to a minimum.

Unfortunately, that also means when he's not around she pounces on Leah. A few times from upstairs he's caught her telling Leah that she's "far too chunky to be wearing," whatever she happens to be wearing and to go change her clothes.

One day, during one of Camille's rants, he should hit record on his phone, and then when the Fake least expects it play it back for her—the middle of the night would be a good time. See if she likes her tone and spiked voice jabbing her in the ears.

Leah's face, their mom on the phone with whoever, was typical for a Tuesday morning. As a rule of conscious, Benji considers Mondays and Tuesdays to be crap. Apart from his job helping to pass the time quicker, both days will go down in his history as the most miserable days of the week. Monday and Tuesday are the days when everyone from his father, to Mr. Planter, to the school cronies, are filled to the brim with testosterone. It's as if the weekend loads them all up like bull elephants and by the start of the week they are ready to explode and stampede their way through life. Getting through Monday and Tuesday is a clock watching, a-hole dodging, computer distracting, try to find ways to get Leah out of the house, sort of day. They also happen to be the days when Camille gets on a teeth grinding complaining streak and tries to push and rush and force life back into her control, as if it escaped her grasp over the weekend and somehow yelling about it, and everything else, will wield it all back under her power. Though, normally, it's Leah and the Rat who catch the brunt of her meltdowns. "Get your school crap off the table!" she yelled top volume at Leah, beginning the day with a bang last Tuesday morning before breakfast because Leah had been studying at the kitchen table the night before and forgot to pick up her homework.

"Hey," Benji said to Leah, who looked up from her plate and immediately changed her expression. Her blonde hair was parted on one side and hung in loose waves around her shoulders. Her cheeks turned into balls as she smiled.

"You okay?" he asked, tapping the edge of her plate with his finger.

She shrugged her shoulders and shook her head, "yes," but didn't speak.

Cussing out his mom in his mind, he kissed her forehead and turned to get breakfast.

Tessa

At the island in the kitchen, Tessa's mom was setting a plate of eggs, wheat toast, and a large pitcher of a strawberry, flaxseed, protein smoothie down in front of their plates.

"I put extra strawberries in this time," Mikael said to both Tessa and Marula.

When they arrived in Michigan, Mikael had been extra happy to discover the powerful blenders available in the states. Normally, she packs a small portable bullet-shaped mixer whenever they travel, but the mega blender their grandmother bought for her a "welcome," and, "it will all be okay," gift was far more of a machine than she'd ever used before. There were no more lettuce chunks in their health drinks now. Though they never minded, anyway. "Pieces of plant goodness," Marula called them once.

"You ready for this?" Marula asked Tessa, who could see her sister's eyes were, again, a dull gray blue. They were rimmed red, a sign she fell asleep crying.

"I am. Are you?"

Marula took a piece of toast from the plate and shrugged. "Trying to be."

"You'll meet people. Don't worry." Tessa leaned and shoulder to shoulder nudged her sister. "If not today then tomorrow for sure. Or, if you want, we can break the rules and I can introduce you to the "someone" I met last night? He has these huge beautiful eyes, and I think he's shy, but he passed my nice people test."

Marula tore a piece off the corner of the toast and dipped it into the small circle of honey she squeezed onto her plate. "Nope, no breaking the rules. You meet someone and I have to meet someone different. Besides I don't want a charity friend," she snorted and ate the amber dripping piece of bread.

"Charity friend," Tessa laughed. "That's a category of friend I've never heard of."

"Remember," Mikael said to Marula. "You only have the first two hours of classes then dad will pick you up at ten-thirty, sharp. The appointments will take a few hours, but your dad will be there the entire time. And you can call me at any moment, no matter what, okay? Even if it gets too hard."

With their mom, everything was sharp, or prompt, or perfectly organized and timed. Not in an overbearing way, but in a corporate executive running a large business way. Tessa and Marula knew their mother could effectively lead the world with her leadership and management skills, but long ago she had forgone her law school degree to be a mother and the wife of an adventurous world-traveling husband. She was a loving mom, but she was also their family executive and the glue that bonded them together. She was love glue.

"Ten-thirty sharp. Got it," Marula repeated.

Mikael poured part of the smoothie into a short glass. The red color of the strawberries had mixed with the green lettuces and made the drink brown. It looked like thick chocolate milk instead of a veggie and fruit drink. "Are you sure you don't want to change your mind and start school tomorrow?" she asked Marula. "You can take another day if you need."

"No, I think I would go mad with anxiety if I push it off for another day," Marula confessed, sliding her glass across the island's granite surface. Their mother poured smoothie into the glass. "I need to face it now. Just stare it all in the eyes and walk through."

A smile broke on Mikael's face, but it was heavy in the corners and not touching her eyes.

For their entire lives, Marula and Tess had been the two American kids enrolling in tiny foreign schools of less than fifty students. In other countries, they had always been welcomed and queried with great interest, like a shiny new show-and-tell toy. In those cases making friends is a fairly easy task. But their mother was worried this time. Today, they are American teenagers living in America, and as far as Tessa ever experienced U.S. kids were not easy to befriend, which was why she and Marula made up a challenge. "You must meet at least one person for the first three days of school."

Tessa already had the jump since she met a guy named Benji last night while she waited for her father to finish his meeting.

"Alright then, walk through. You got this. You can do this," Mikael encouraged. But Tessa wondered if she was speaking more to herself rather than to Marula.

Benji
Seven

While Benji stood inside the school doors, a lady with a short, blonde, spiky hairdo, a zip up work out jacket and yoga pants asked, "Hello, can I help you?" Benji vaguely remembered her being one of the new gym teachers.

"Just waiting for someone," he answered, wondering how he appeared to her in his dark blue hoodie, the hood up, jeans and steel toe boots. He was sure the way he lurked by the doors staring at the floor didn't help her suspicions.

He tried a smile and took his phone from his pocket. "I can text and see when they'll be here."

The woman scanned him up and down, pulled her eyebrows together and crossed her arms, but she didn't move along.

"Hey you," someone said from the front door. He turned to find Contessa, all smile, her teeth as pearly as last night at Maria's Cafe. Her hair was in a long braid over her shoulder, and he noticed thin strands of twine interlaced throughout the braid.

"Hi, Contessa," he blurted, jamming his phone back into his pocket and glaring at the teacher who, apparently satisfied he was telling the truth, turned to leave. "Was it easy to find?"

"You, yes, it was the big airbrushed school banner over the door like your text said. But the school, no. Why is it so far back off of the main road? And we couldn't find any signs to tell us where to go. Seems pretty uninviting."

She was right; it is an odd place for a school—three dirt road turns off the main road before you even see the compound-like building. "There used to be a couple of signs, but the school refuses to replace them," he said, pushing off his hood.

"Why?"

Benji started walking. Tessa followed. She pulled the shawl off of her shoulders, folded it into a small square, and tucked it into her bag. He kept his hands in his hoodie pockets while they walked, hoping he looked comfortable and confident though he wasn't at all. He had no idea what to say or expect—or what *she* expected from him. Apart from the teacher's suspicious questioning, he'd spent the last ten minutes swallowing down the gritty feeling in his throat and counting the square tiles on the floor. There are one hundred and fourteen squares before you reach the first classroom door. The fourteen bothered him as if they should be countable in fives, not twos.

During his tile counting, he settled on being as polite and welcoming as possible. And since he was clueless what to do with her, he figured taking her to the office was the best thing. "The seniors kept doing pranks with the signs," he said. "Two years ago they took the sign that said, Greenbrier Arbor High School—it had an arrow pointing down the road toward the school—they took the sign and hung it on the front door of a stripper bar."

She let out what he thought was a low giggle though it sounded like little breathy huffs. "Really?"

"Yeah. Two weeks went by before anyone contacted the school. And it ended up being Bishop Rockland of the First Baptist Church, who, in no uncertain terms, let them know that Top Shelf Stripper Club was not Greenbrier Arbor High School. Apparently he didn't appreciate the high school encouraging "such filth," and not taking the sign stealing seriously."

"How could he think it was the schools fault?" Her eyes squinted. Benji assumed it was a look of confusion. Or maybe disapproval. He wasn't sure. Either way, her expression jolted him and he registered that he was actually talking with her, actually making conversation.

"My thoughts exactly," he said, "The school must have been scared, though, because the next day they made a big deal about it and did a half a dozen announcements claiming if they find out who did it they would be expelled. But it wasn't a threat anyone took seriously."

She wrinkled her forehead and it made her nostrils flare the tiniest bit. "It's sort of wrong but kind of funny at the same time."

"Yeah, I thought it was more funny than wrong." He glanced at her. She didn't appear fazed in the least, so he hurried and added, "That was the last sign ever posted showing the way to the school."

"Well, I guess people can use navigation if they need, it seems fairly easy. This morning my dad used the GPS in our new car, though I still thought we would get lost in the woods and need a crumb trail to find our way back out." She made a crooked smirk with her mouth. Half her face smiled and the other half frowned. Benji decided right then that it would sting when she didn't talk to him tomorrow.

They stopped in front of an oversized glass door and window. Inside were a long counter and a wall of file cabinets. He turned square to face her and pointed at the door on his left. "This is the office. You can get your schedule inside."

"Thanks," she said. "And you can call me Tessa. Will I see you at lunch?"

He ruffled his hair. "Yep, sure, okay. See you then."

He turned away but then hesitated, questioning, and turned back. "Hey, um, I was wondering…"

"Yes," she said, her hand on the knob of the door.

"Yesterday, how did you know where I went to school? I mean, this isn't a small town so I could have gone anywhere."

She tilted her head to the side, smiled, and reached with one finger and pointed at the patch pinned with giant safety pins on the side of his backpack. Wrapped in a green circle was the school emblem, the school name and the mascot—a beaver. He had put it on his bag in order to draw on the beaver's face, but the name and emblem were still visible.

"Ah, okay," he said, touching the patch and wondering if he should take it off.

"Mystery solved?" she asked.

"Mystery solved," he said.

She kept her eyes locked with his as if waiting for him to say something more. He only managed, "Okay then. See you."

She smiled another bright smile and repeated, "Lunch then?"

"Yes. Okay."

This time, seconds went by before he made himself move. When he did, he spun quickly and trudged off.

At the corner of the hall, he determined to sneak a glance back. Tessa, of course, had already disappeared.

He tapped his forehead with is finger. Dumb, dumb, dumb, he thought, realizing he should have told her which lunch hour he had and where to find him. Something like, "You'll find me in the outside quad, I'll be over in the corner where I always sit, *alone*." His forehead tapping was enough to make a passing kid eye him as if he needed an intervention, or perhaps, a protective helmet.

As he turned and headed to his first class, the hordes of bus kids flooded through the doors.

He needed something to distract him from this girl. Something to fill time for the next few days. A small revenge would do.

Revenge Chronicle: Car Wash
Revenge Risk: High
Revenge Date: June 1st, 2013
Revenge Entry Date: June 28th, 2013

Chronicle, I can't suppress the high I still feel almost four weeks later. This one plan might carry me through the entire summer. It was a terrible plan. A risky plan. But I'm fairly satisfied.

Weeks of hypnotizing Leo, who I'm forever going to call Car Wash, with anonymous messages and risky photos of belly button piercing pictures, bare shoulders, and slits of cleavage—absent of the more risky parts he kept asking for—and I finally gave into his, "When are you going to let me feel you against me?" request.

Posing as a female turned out to be easier than I thought. It only took certain words placed in specific messages and presto...bait dangled and bait hooked. At the original message claiming to be a girl from another school, a private school, and that I saw him play at the Lacrosse game and found him, "A beast I want to tame," and, "You're far better looking than the uniform wearing, uptight guys at my school," I knew I had his attention. I simply stroked his ego and teased him long enough that on a Monday, with an image of a girl's torso and meme labeled, "no emotional strings, alright?" I sealed the date for the next day after school. (My own personal unscrew Monday and Tuesday)

Chronicle, you have no idea how on the flip I thought up the revenge location. If you were a person, instead of a journal, you'd probably slap the crap out of me for taking such a risk. But really, it was a chain of events in my thoughts that led me there: I had just written a fake fantasy to Car Wash about sex in the rain. At the same time, I remembered I needed to get gas before school the next morning. Then I was calculating the time I would need to leave in order to get gas and be on time for school, etcetera. And then, thinking of the gas I thought of Matt, the owner of Buster's Stop and Go Gas Station and Car Wash and how he called me a "faggot," when I gave my notice I was quitting last summer. And how I knew his Automatic Car Wash was never filled with the soap solution because he's too cheap and doesn't mind swindling customers.

See how it rolled, Chronicle? If I thought Karma was real, I'd chalk it up to that, but I'm sure it was just dumb luck. Until that day, when I looked at the latest message to and from Car Wash and I flippantly thought of Buster's and where their security cameras are mounted, I didn't even have a real plan on how I would conclude Leo's revenge. I had a few lame ideas, such as releasing his sex fantasies all over the school, somehow, or doing something to his car, but nothing creative and concrete. Ahhhhh, creative, that's the word I would use for this scheme. I actually had a splash of demented excitement as the pieces came together in my mind. At Buster's: I know where the security cameras are mounted from working there the summer before. Rain: the car wash stall. Timing: warm summer, late evening after school, eight P.M.

I found it quite impressive how fast Leo managed to appear through the plastic washer curtain, get his pants off, and be lollipop ready—as my confirmation message said earlier in the day. Of course he did so on the assumption he would find a naked girl dripping with water, "As if in the rain," and "A quickie so we don't get caught," I'd typed. Instead, he found a masked man lurking in the shadows and a water hose aimed directly at his pixie stick. One blast of the cold spray and Car Wash shot out of there like a booger being blown from a nose, tripping over his pants and frantically trying to pull up his soaked underwear—all strategically caught on camera, of course. I was near hysterics with laughter when I took off out of the stall and ran back to my car. (It was one time his bulk girth would be no match for my speed. Though, he never saw me anyway.)

To top the whole plan off, before he got there, I spray painted giant penises on the washer stall walls. (Giving thanks to the owner and his, "faggot," calling for that part of the idea.) Car Wash ended up being blamed for those, too.

And the best part, last week the video was leaked by an employee of the gas station onto YouTube— with blurred pixie stick and face, of course. (Lucky bastard) In the end, Car Wash is getting community service for the penis vandalism, charged with a misdemeanor, and has to pay a thousand dollar fine.

I'm quite satisfied.

Benji
Eight

"Target acquired," Benji thought, as Blue Barbie—nicknamed by the cronies because she looks like a Barbie doll and because blue is how she makes guy's danglers feel—yanked her bag off the desk next to him and turned away so hard it flipped her long blonde hair like whips on the end of a stick.

Her words bit his mind like a nasty little dog. The kind that while in their owner's arms, if you try to pet, they lunge and bite you. Not enough to cause extreme damage but enough to draw pricks of blood. Up until that moment, Blue Barbie had never been a blip on his revenge radar. But when he slipped into the empty desk next to her, which he only did because the bell was about to ring, and he was actually paying attention to the image of Tessa in his mind, not to the concrete world around him, he didn't realize he'd taken up the free seat Blue Barbie saved for the excitedly greeted friend that came in after him. One second after he sat down Blue Barbie promptly got up, shoved her face close to his, and through teeth said, "Whoever told you to be yourself couldn't have given you worse advice."

Watching the human-sized Barbie plop down four desks away with a huff of frustration and then an arm flailing wave—the signal inviting the girl who came through the door as the bell rang to sit next to her—Benji shook his head at the ridiculousness of high school. Deep inside he longed to cheer for the Blue Barbies of the world. To internally stand up for them and say, "Hey, beautiful people aren't selfish; they're only misunderstood." But people like her made it nearly impossible.

Right before Tessa began stealing his fries at Maria's, Benji was listening in on Car Wash's arrogant ramblings. "I will dominate this year. They got nothing on me," Car Wash had bragged, causing Benji to picture a gorilla beating his chest. He was all talk about the coming basketball season, but he also talked about a party he and the other guys were going to on Friday night. It so happens, the party will be at Blue Barbie's house.

Coincidence? More like divine intervention.

Benji
Nine

When lunch started, Benji was determined to push his anger about Blue Barbie to the back of his mind and fully concentrate on Tessa. Tessa: the patch observer. Tessa: a girl with henna on her hand. Tessa with a pen attached to her bra and who didn't care about germ sharing. Tessa…

"Just a small fry," he had said to the lunch lady while grabbing five packs of ketchup and plotting what things he could ask Tessa to keep a conversation easy and absent of uncomfortable silences. "Where did you get that shawl from? Who wrapped the strings in your hair? Where did you move from? Why did you move to Michigan?" He was armed with enough questions to fill the entire forty-five minute lunch.

Benji reshuffled the fries on the grass then lined them back up from shortest fry to tallest. He'd already forgone the plate and his appetite, and lined them up from straightest to most warped and from lightest to darkest. How many times can a person glance around the lunch room and the outside quad and not look like an anxious idiot? He bit into his sandwich and scanned the area again, anyway. Groups of kids assembled in their chosen packs and his eyes jumped over them, from the tables to the lunch line, to the outdoor area, searching for Tessa's face among the rainbow of kids.

When the last lunch bell rang, he'd only eaten five of the fries. The remaining twenty-one stared up at him from the grass, still lined from shortest to tallest.

He stood up to leave and kicked the left over twenty-one, abandoning them for the birds to eat.

Tessa never showed to save his fry eating life.

Benji
Ten

After school, Benji leaned against a large window across from his locker and waited for the cronies to leave. Car Wash, always the cocksure ringleader of the group, called out to a girl as she passed on her way to the busses, "Mamacita, come gimme some of that trunk junk." The girl responded by smiling, flipping her hair over her shoulder, and increasing the sway in her hips.

By some cosmic joke, the high school assigns lockers according to grade first and then alphabetically by last name. Since Benji's last name is Lockwood, and Leo's is Loehner, their lockers always end up near each other.

"I need to get in there," Benji said to one of them their freshman year, the first week of school after the third day of the cronies standing in front of his locker talking to Car Wash and blocking his way. He'd spoken to the guy he thought had the nicer face in the group, but he was mistaken because the guy dropped him to his knees with a groin shot. Hunched over and drooling in pain, Benji couldn't even answer the teacher who came to see what was wrong. And by the time he caught his breath, the cronies had slipped away and there was no use explaining to the teacher what happened. After that, he learned to pack everything in his backpack and skip his locker altogether. Only once did he wait long enough to see if they would leave, but he ended up missing his bus and needed to call his mother to come pick him up. He vowed never again. For either problem.

Now in their junior year their lockers are five apart, but the system of cliques still applies. At the end of the day, the bell rings and the cronies slowly gravitate to Car Wash's locker to banter and span their frames out far enough to cover a few other lockers. Girls sometimes join the group but mainly it's the guys who razz and rile one another before heading out like a mob of hyenas ready for a hunt.

Car Wash's heavyweight wrestler size has always been one of Benji's problems. If they were to stand side by side they'd be the visual reason you don't wrestle the lean, long distance runner against a defensive linebacker. "Watch where you're walking," Car Wash once snarled after ramming into him like a tackling dummy. Afterward, while Benji tried to catch his breath, Car Wash got so close to his face that Benji could smell his breath through his bull nostrils. It only took a couple of junk punches, elbows to the ribs, and once, Car Wash's shoe heel into his foot, breaking his second toe, and Benji learned to scope the halls and be alert. This year has tamed, comparatively, apart from the three times he had been caught off guard at his locker—the shelf inside is exactly tenth rib high, and a quick, pass-by locker jacking leaves a painful bruise.

When the halls thinned, Benji slipped away from the window and to his locker, scanning up and down to be sure. He had on his steel-toe boots, which he knew could do some damage, but a one on one fight wouldn't have odds in his favor, much less one against a pack. A flash of kids pulling out their cell phones trying to video a smash down went through his mind as he twisted the lock on his locker.

Outside of the school, Benji tilted his head back and inhaled the thick air. He could see in the distance the sky was trying to muster rain clouds, but the heavy atmosphere was all wrong for this time of the year. This was the time of the year when people gather for cider and donuts at the apple mills. A time for Halloween decor and readying kid's winter clothes to wear under their costumes. This wasn't the time of the year to line fries on warmed grass or take off your hoodie and shove it in your bag because it was too hot to wear.

Benji surveyed the school parking, which he imagined if looking from above, appeared like a painter's pallet of color and space. A dot of a car here and there and then some open parking spaces, and then another car or so. His car was in the front of the row near the one-way exit, the first black dot on the pallet of colors. Normally, he takes a space at the far end of the lot, but today, after receiving Tessa's text, he decided the front would be better. In case he saw her heading into the school before him.

After sliding into the driver's seat, he tossed his backpack on the passenger seat then leaned his head back against the headrest, taking a moment to debate whether he wanted or needed to stop at home before work.

51

This particular Tuesday began as cursed as the rest of them: Leah with her sad face, and Camille going on and on about the township and the playground, right up to the point when he slammed the door behind him on his way out, shutting her voice out of his head. Then there was a moment…the one while Tessa walked with him to the office, the one that suddenly, impossibly escalated to good. The one with her crooked smile and easy conversation. For a brief moment, she made the air of the school breathable. After though, the moment retracted back into its normal cursed, Tuesday oblivion.

Once lunch was over, he tried to refocus on a plan for Blue Barbie's revenge, but he kept coming up blank. Even during fourth-hour class, thanks to Mr. Button torturing the class with a movie on the history of politics in the U.S., he had plenty of time to ponder ideas. But still, nothing. Instead, he found himself aggravatingly, curiously thinking about Tessa. He wanted to become more familiar with her eyes, to study their color and how they were so prominent on her face, to understand how the dimple in her chin worked, and how it appeared and faded as she smiled. He couldn't stop wondering where she sat at lunch and who she decided to sit with. He searched but hadn't seen her anywhere in the lunch room or the outside areas. By fifth hour, he wished he could tear his brain out and swipe Tessa's face off, clearing her away as if she were only a mark on a dry erase board. By sixth hour, he was settled: she had been a fleeting moment of air as if blown away like a dandelion. Though, even now, he still found himself a little anxious about how he'll feel when she passes him in the halls tomorrow. Will she at least say hello? Will it hurt if she doesn't?

The buzz of his phone from inside his backpack startled him out of his musing. It stopped buzzing before he could make himself lift his head and reach into the bag. He turned the key assuming it was Leah calling to ask if he would stop and get her something on his way home, maybe a soda, sneakily, since the Fake would make a condemning red mark across her calorie counting chart on the fridge if she found out.

As he reached to put the car in gear, the phone rang again. This time he dug for it and pinched his finger trying to get it free from the page ring where it was caught inside his binder.

Seeing Contessa's name on his phone screen made his breathing pick up and his blood course through parts of his body he wasn't aware of moments ago.

He couldn't answer. He *wouldn't* answer. Though, he wasn't sure exactly why.

He kept his eyes locked on the screen, waiting for it to stop ringing. It felt like minutes before the name disappeared and his plain black background manifested, along with a banner reading, "Four missed calls."

Work would be better than home he decided, taking a deep breath and willing his blood to return to a normal temperature. His index finger twitched as it hovered over the home screen. He wasn't sure if it was curiosity or suicide that made him touch where it read, "four missed calls."

The screen came alive, declaring the name, "Contessa. Contessa. Contessa. Contessa," as if she were a type of confetti announcement at a surprise party.

Next to the missed calls icon were the text message icons, and there were four little red notices there, too.

Benji opened the texts.

Tessa here :0) don't ha8, i gonna b lates 4 canteen

food. gotta meet the counselor. hope u has 1st lunch?

Tessa here :0) its a no go on lunch...she won't stop talking...she's working hard 2 b a friend

Tessa here :0) why u no answer?? :0(meet up after school?

Tessa here :0) do i talk 2 much...does my breath stink...i promise 2 use more deo if u call me back!

Another text came through right as he began tapping a reply:

Tessa here :0) will i c u 2morrow? front door meeting spot?

He replied:

Benji here :o/ no ur breath do not stink.

His body parts warmed again as he continued...

I like ur talking. headin to work. yes...meeting spot 2morrow.

He hit send with a deep dredging breath and tilted the rearview mirror to look at himself. What does she see when looking at him? He didn't think

54

he was ugly, just normal. And few times strangers had told him that because of his height and frame he should try modeling. Every now and again he sprouted an occasional zit, especially when he drank too many sugary drinks, but right now his skin is soft and clear. His hair is the same dirty blonde color as the sand on Lake Michigan, and his eyes are bright blue and big—a little too big, which his mother says makes him appear shocked. "Don't stare with your eyes like that, Benjamin. They are too big, and you look haunted when you do," she once barked while they waited for his turn during eighth-grade parent-teacher conferences. She then grabbed his head and evaluated whether his ears were beginning to poke out like his grandfather. "Leave the boy alone, his ears are fine," his dad barked, making his mom respond with a shooting glare that would put Satan's Hellfire to shame.

"Ordinary, just ordinary," he said, finished evaluating himself and righting the mirror.

He pulled out of the parking lot with what he was sure was the biggest, dumbest grin on his face.

Revenge Chronicle: Nothing BUTT tacks
(Merry Christmas to ME!)
Revenge Risk Rating: Medium
Revenge Date: December 13th, 2011
Chronicle Entry Date: December 16th, 2011

Dumbest revenge ever! Duct tape and tacks. Ridiculous! But it worked! I think I may be on to something here. Maybe I'll become a private revenge artist, a type of equalizing justicer <— not a word, journal. Yes, that's it, an equalizer against the boneheads of the world. Too many times to count, that zit faced kid who sits behind me on the bus has thumped me with his pencil. The last time he did it the eraser band or something hit me so hard I had a spot of blood on my head. I had to corner the kid, Eddie, who sits a few seats up from me by his house in order to get him to confess that it was zit face who kept doing it.

I can just imagine an animated image of zit face behind me popping up in his seat like a prairie dog coming out of a hole, thumping me, and then back down when I turn to see who did it. Of course, everyone giggles and laughs and pretends it wasn't them, but now I know for sure. I had my suspicions all along, but Eddie finally told me. Eddie is like me, he's been tapped too, but now he gets to get on at the new bus stop so he changed his seat. I can't do that because my stop is last. That means when I get on the bus all of the seats are claimed, and I'm forced to sit in the same one every time. Once, after the second pencil snap, I asked Eddie to switch seats with me but he wouldn't, he'd already traded the pencil snap seat for the kick seat: the guys behind him push their legs and feet forward and kick his legs under the seat. Chronicle, I noticed last week when Eddie sat down, when he put his legs into the aisle, he had something on over his socks; he sat down and his pants rose high on his ankles. I think they're soccer shin guards put on backward, but I'm not sure. If they are shin guards, well, that's pretty smart of him. I don't have a guard for my head, though.

Anyway, I did it! I really did it! I stayed late after school and snuck onto the parked bus after the buses arrived back at the bus lot. It's odd that they trust the busses to be safe around the schools, but hey, it worked for me. Originally I tried to figure a way to catch the bus in the morning, before anyone else, but that wouldn't work because the pickup is too far. Plus, there was no way to get to zit face's seat before him, AND I don't want to get pummeled since he's a junior and as big around as the Pillsbury Dough Boy.

Really, the idea of how to get him wasn't born until I had to stay after school one day for my marketing class. On my way out to meet my dad for pick up, I spotted the busses pulling back in...empty of kids. Presto! Idea!

The next week I told my dad that I needed to stay after school again, and I made sure my backpack was ready with supplies: Duct tape and flat tacks. See, journal, the buses are supposed to be new in the next few years, (my mom told my dad that the *millage *whatever that is* passed to buy new buses), but that hasn't happened yet so the duct tape bus—as the kids in my school nicknamed it—bus eighty-nine, has a number of seats with duct tape across the splitting upholstery of the seats. Tape and tacks were the magic mix. I really didn't think it would work when I snuck on the bus and placed tape, slightly loose, across zit faces' seat. Under the tape, I shoved a hundred count box of tacks, lightly stuck through but not all of the way.*

I mean, who really looks at their seat when they sit down? And who cares what seats have new tape or not? Apparently not zit face. Honestly, I figured the tacks would cave under his heavy girth, but, guess what, they didn't!! They held up perfectly. Not just one tack but a bunch of them! I heard all about his, "Ouch! Shit!" scream when I got on the bus. And though I didn't get to see it, I can just imagine him shooting up out of the seat to inspect what took a bite out of his butt.

The image of him running to the bus driver and telling that someone put tacks in the seat will have me in laughter and tears for the next year! And I heard he had to hover over his seat, because of the pain for the entire ride to school, all while threatening that he would, "pound the person who did this."

I'm still laughing, even as I write. Maybe he'll need a tetanus shot now.

Stick that up your a$$, zit face!!!

Benji
Eleven

Benji sent two more texts before getting out of his car and heading for the back door of Big Timmie's shop. One text was to answer Contessa's question of why he hadn't answered his phone when she called, and a "yes, I listened to your messages," which were rambling, as if she was talking to a person rather than a message. The second, to let her know he doesn't get off work until late.

Big Timmie's store is on the west end of a strip of stores on University Street. The front is a retail store for customers and the back, behind the heavy double doors, is a workshop where he designs and builds custom security systems.

Big Timmie, Tim Stouten, the owner of Big's Custom Security, is, in fact, big and tall. Pro NFL defensive line big and tall. In his younger years, he was a strapping, firmly-toned, muscular young man. He's still muscular but carrying an extra spare tire around his waist from eating too many donuts from the bakery next door.

"Your order came in," Roderick said as Benji passed through the workshop area. "I put it under the counter."

"Thanks," he said, pushing through the double doors to the front of the store. Tommy, Timmie's younger brother and the other person who works the front of the store, greeted him with a fist-bump, and an "I'm out. I gotta get the old lady's bike to the shop before she tears me apart with her teeth." He grabbed his cell phone off the counter, slid it into the back pocket of his jeans. Then he took a cigarette from the pack in his shirt and stuck it, unlit, between his lips, and mumbled, "Again," to his comment about his wife tearing him apart with her teeth.

"Am I still covering some of your hour's week after next?" Benji asked. "And don't you dare light up or Timmie's gonna kill you."

"I know, I know." Tommy took the cigarette out of his lips and put it behind his ear. From his other chest pocket, he produced a pack of nicotine gum and popped one into his mouth. "Yeah, I still need you to cover. That is as long as her bike is fixed before we go. Damn it, how did I agree to do a ride to North Carolina and back this time of the year? My balls will be so cold I won't be able to find them."

"It's a kid's cancer ride, remember?" Benji said. The same way he'd been reminding him for the last two weeks that the motorcycle club he and his wife belong to were participating in a 'Kids Kicking Cancer' fundraiser.

"I know, I know," he sighed. "I'm not supposed to complain since by comparison to the kids I have nothing to complain about, right?" He grabbed his helmet from under the counter. "See ya, kid. Here's to making the old lady happy." His fist rose into the air in a type of power-to-the-men gesture as he stepped through the double doors.

As Tommy disappeared, a Tiger's baseball cap wearing six-foot-five man pushed through the double doors to the front. "Hey, kid," Big Timmie said, snapping a rubber band off his chin ponytail and tossing it into the garbage by the register. He let the length of his braided beard fall to his chest. Hundreds of times over the last two years of working for Big Timmie, Benji has seen him comb his fingers through the beard he's probably been growing since puberty, complain about the grays, and then braid it and roll it up into a chin ponytail. Now and then the shop will have a sudden acrid smell, that's when everyone knows Timmie forgot to tie up his beard and has singed it with the sauntering iron.

"Your shipment is under the counter," he said, bent over and rifling through the box of extra batteries he keeps underneath the computer register.

"Roderick told me." Benji punched his employee number into the computer and logged in the time on his timecard.

Timmie sat back on his heels and glared at the box of batteries as if they just offended him.

"Is it okay if I ring my own stuff into the register?"

"Yep," Timmie said then lifted his ball cap to scratch a spot on his bald head. After turning his cap beak around so that it faced the back, he re-dove deeper into the cabinet. "You gonna tell me what you got that thing for…Damn it, where are the CR-eleven-hundred batteries?"

Benji stretched across Big Timmie's hunched back and pulled a small plastic bin from the shelf next to the mounted monitor. "Button batteries up top, remember?" He put the bin under Big Timmie's face.

"Hmmm, I'd be a mess without you, kid," he said taking the bin then heading back to the double doors. "And I caught how you didn't answer my question." Timmie didn't look back before he disappeared to the back.

Big Timmie was always like that. He paid attention. He paid attention even when you would swear he wasn't paying attention. His brain simply worked that way. But he doesn't pry. He's like his security equipment; he observes but *only* observes, he never interferes.

Benji is one of the few people who know about Big Timmie's government contracts and his real money. The store does well, very well, but for Timmie it's just a place to work because he merely enjoys working. And because he doesn't want his house overrun with security toys—or customers. Timmie's "financial freedom," as he likes to call it, came when he designed and tried to patent a security system that could be wirelessly monitored on a wrist watch from anywhere in the world. He created the devices during the years when cell phones were first coming on the market, so it was tough equipment to make. One time, Timmie told him, "The government must have a key to the Patent Office," because one day during a blizzard a man dressed in a black overcoat and fur hat, and had, "the biggest nose I've ever seen," offered him a contract to make a hundred more devices, all of them for the U.S. Special Forces. Big Timmie agreed, signed on the dotted line, and has been contracted to make different sorts of government and military security devices ever since. He also explained the contract he signed included a, "I can't tell anyone how to make any of the devices, new or old, without written permission from the government," a security background check on the person, and an "I can't sell them to anyone else or I could get prison time," clause.

It was after six when Benji finally finished setting up new contracts in the computer and he could get his order from under the counter. Stuck to the top of a small, brown shipping box was a blue Post-It note with the scratch handwriting of Big Timmie. It said, "Benji's stuff." Underneath was an added "P.S." "It's illegal to make sex tapes without her consent, kid." The invoice date showed the equipment arrived yesterday.

After unwrapping the contents of the box, he pushed the bubble wrap to the side and splayed everything across the glass counter. There was one roll of low-grade adhesive tape, two face plates, one white and the other cream, a micro card, a component, and a cord for recharging the twenty-hour battery. He looked it over, touching and retouching each piece, making sure to stay grounded within the moment.

Our freedom is getting closer; he thought while running his index finger across the smooth face plate. It won't be long now, Leah. It won't be long.

Tessa

"I think Mrs. Caldwell is quite excited to have us at the school," Tessa hooked her bag and her shawl over the coat rack by the front door then went to her mother's waiting arms for a hug.

"Mrs. Caldwell. Which teacher is that?" Mikael kissed the top of her daughter's head.

"Not a teacher, a counselor," she let go of the hug and flipped off her ballet slippers into the waiting shoe tray.

"Why do you say she's excited? There is fruit on the island for you."

Tessa noticed her mother studying the shoe tray, but she left her standing by the door for the fruit in the kitchen. "She kept me through the entire lunch in her office, asking question after question about how I felt about my high test scores and how she could make me feel more welcome. I didn't even get to meet my new friend…mom, what are you staring at." Mikael was still standing in the foyer observing the shoes. There were two pairs of slippers, one pair waiting for her Gram to come home from Tuesday cards with her friends, the other pair waiting for her father's feet, one pair of her mom's running shoes, and her ballet slippers.

"I'm thinking about your shoe choices."

"My shoe choices, why?" Tessa grabbed a handful of grapes out of the bowl.

"Honey, you're going to freeze this winter. You need to get new shoes. And some warmer pants. Jeans would be best."

The front door opened and Tessa's father walked through, followed by a solemn looking Marula.

"Hi," Tessa said to them both.

Her dad greeted her mom with a kiss, holding her eyes for a moment afterward. It was another one of their mental conversations. Tessa didn't need to guess what they exchanged; she already knew.

Fixating a smile on his face, he said, "Hey, baby girl," to Tessa.

"Hi," Marula muttered while kicking off a tan pair of ballet slippers. Neither of them took ballet, but they'd grown to love the comfort of walking around in them during the summer in Mongolia.

Tessa could see her sister's sadness: her arms hung as if carrying something weighty, though there was nothing in her arms, and her eyes were shadowed by blue veins and darkness—a sign that she not only had been crying, she'd been sobbing.

"How did things go?" Mikael asked.

"Good," Todd said popping a grape into his mouth.

"Fine," Marula said, making her way to the island and sitting on a stool.

"Two days a week with the Psychiatrist plus two days a week with a group," Todd said. "She can move to one day a week with the group after attending for two months."

Tessa moved around the other side to put her arm around her sister. Marula took a grape and leaned her head against Tessa's shoulder.

Both Todd and Mikael join them, surrounding both of them with their arms.

Tessa knew Marula would be okay, but she hoped Marula knew it too.

Benji
Twelve

When the store's door chime sounded, Benji lifted his head from his equipment, expecting a customer. Instead, he saw Tessa's large hazel eyes, slim face, and a single, fat braid hanging over her shoulder, walking through the front entrance of the store.

A sudden vulnerability split him open inside when he glanced back down at his equipment. Mainly because the Busting Balls plan was displayed right on the counter for all to see, for Tessa to see, but also because the face that was forefront in his mind was walking through the door.

"Why are you here?" he asked.

Tessa paused and pulled her long shawl tighter around her shoulders. "Oh, will I get you in trouble?" She reached up and began twisting the end of her braid.

Benji moved from behind the counter. Tessa had paused by the rack of programmable door knobs. It towered over her like a tall tree with metal nubs. "No, it's fine." He scrubbed his hand through his dense hair in an effort to tame what he was sure was a ruffled mess. "What I meant was, is it purposeful that you are here? Where I work?"

"Well, yes," she said, pulling her phone from within the folds of her long skirt. "You said you had to work. See," she faced the phone to him, showing the text he sent to her answering the question where he worked. "You said Big Timmie's and I wanted to practice my navigation skills." She rocked on her feet side to side, a small but fluid motion as if at any moment she would launch into a ballet dance. "My dad needed to stop by a friend's office, so I asked him to drop me off. He's on Williams Street." She pointed to the outside as if to indicate it was right outside the window to the left, which it was, but about four blocks down University Street. "The GPS said it was close to here. He'll be back to get me in about ten minutes. I won't be a bother if you have to work."

"The GPS said. Well, that explains it," he quipped, watching her slip the phone back into her skirt. There must be a cloaked pocket blended into all the material. "You won't be a bother," he added. She smiled at him and surveyed the store.

One entire wall is a menagerie of wires and cords; all hung on protruding hooks that have no rhyme or reason. Tessa was stopped amongst the large spinning racks of hi-tech home entry and security products, including Big Timmie's programmable doggie doors with remote viewing and can unlock and lock at certain times of the day. The short wall on her left displayed a plethora of monitors, photos and posters of homes and businesses, and the Manufacture's samples of different types of security systems. In the center of that wall is a life-size poster of Big Timmie's dog, Caesar, a personal protection German Shepard that accompanies Big Timmie everywhere. When Timmie walks, Caesar walks. When Timmie sits,

Caesar lies on the floor next to him and doesn't move. "My boy, I'm licensed but I don't need to carry my gun, I got a Caesar," he once said when Benji asked him how many hours he puts in with Caesar at the canine training center. Timmie had meant his concealed carry license, and Benji almost laughed because who would ever try to mess with Big Timmie even without a gun or a dog.

He waved Contessa forward. "Please, come all the way in."

To his relief and slight fear, her feet moved her toward the display counter where he was standing. He realized she would have no idea what his equipment was for, or that it belonged to him, and yet, he still felt like a kid being caught in a lie.

He went back behind the counter and scooted his stuff away from direct eye view, closer to the wall.

"This looks entirely interesting," she said pointing to the equipment behind the glass where the smallest cameras were displayed like jewelry: royal blue velvety risers held the tiniest pieces and slotted, valor dividers lined up the eyewear.

"These are samples of different types of hidden cameras we sell." He slid the cabinet door open and brought out a tie clip. Putting on his best salesman voice he explained, "This one you clip on a tie. You can record or remote view from a computer or a smart device. The clip will appear to be an ordinary tie clip, but the sapphire in the middle is really a camera lens."

Leaning forward, she reached with her first finger and touched the bar and stone. "It's so small."

"It's supposed to be small."

"But how does it record? Where do you put the CD or the wires? Or is it like the ones in cop movies when the informant wears a wire and tucks it under their shirt?" She was still touching the bar as if exploring it for texture and realness. He noticed her fingernails were painted with a glossy, clear polish, and there was definitely faded henna on her left hand.

"A CD?" He felt his face scrunch. "Do you mean to record on?"

"Yes."

"This type of equipment hasn't needed CD's, not for a long time," He said, thinking that she just did what every other customer does, and what every employee gets tired of hearing. It's the "I saw this in a movie once," comment.

Normally, that's the point where the employees re-educate people that movies and "real life," are two different things, but she leaned back away from his hand and grabbed the end of her braid, staring at him. The look said she was waiting for an answer.

Oh," he stuttered. "Um, it either has one of these," he reached over and grabbed the micro card from his stuff and held it up. "It's a little card that goes into a box you put in your pocket, kinda like a wallet, and it wirelessly records. Or most of these record digitally and remotely to an offsite location, like a phone or a computer."

"Is it like the Bluetooth thing?" she asked. This time he tried not to furrow his face.

"Yeah, sort of, but capable of a lot longer distance."

She tucked a stray lock of hair behind her ear. "I've never seen these types of things."

"Most people haven't seen this kind of equipment. Big Timmie custom makes a lot of these. It's his specialty."

She considered the store, scanning every wall as if enthralled by the vastness of possibilities. "I'm still trying to get used to the touch screen on my phone and there are little cameras you can put on a tie." She leaned over the counter with her entire upper body. The end of her shawl draped down onto the glass like a golden waterfall, exposing her shoulders the slightest bit. "These would have come in handy in Mongolia." She tapped the glass, pointing to the camera that looked like a shirt button. There was a picture next to it, showing how to wear the device. The male model in the image was wearing an example on a blue button down shirt.

"You've been to Mongolia? Wait, why would you need hidden camera stuff?"

She kept her face close to the glass as she answered. "I've been going around the globe ever since I was born." She pointed to the sunglasses. "I saw spy glasses like those on TV the other day…no, I don't want to hide it, I mean to record what our days are like. Holding a video camera in your hand gets tiring. With these, it would be more of a first person recording, right?"

It was such an innocent reason to want a button camera. The store sold high-definition helmet cameras for sports, but Benji never thought of suggesting they use something like a shirt button camera. "Those," he meant the sunglasses, "are our best sellers, but they aren't very practical as a hidden camera. People just think they are cool looking. But yes, those would have worked for taking video of your daily life." She stood back up to face him. He wanted to reach and touch the end of her braid just to see what it felt like. "So, why did you move here? Michigan must be boring compared to Mongolia."

"My dad grew up in Michigan. Both of my parents are from here so we came to stay with my Grandma for a little while." Something about the way her eyes glanced off to the right was troubling. It was quick and unconscious, but he was sure he saw a veil of sadness cover her face and then disappear as fast. "My dad's work takes us around the world but we've mostly lived in Asia, Eastern Mongolia, and a few times in Africa. The U.S. is a place I've traveled the least."

"What I wouldn't give to live like that," he said. A quick image of packing up and moving, not just out of his house but out of the state, gave him a jolt of aspiration.

But at his statement, Tessa made another odd look. It was a fleeting, dispirited look, and then in a twinkle of a second, a fixed focused look. Or was it resigned? She pulled at a green beaded bracelet around her wrist. "Yes, I've been fortunate, but I hope we get to stay here for a while."

"Are you kidding? Why would you want that?"

The intercom chirped. "Hang on a sec." He lifted the shop phone, trying to seem aloof by leaning against the counter and crossing his feet as if it was normal for a girl to show up at his work to visit him. Gus, the only other guy who worked on Big Timmie's military contracts, explained that he left his cell phone at home, and his wife may call the front store instead.

Benji did his best gentleman impression. "No problem. I will be sure to let you know." Gus added instructions about him having to "immediately," call him over the loud speaker. And did Benji appreciate what he meant by "immediately?" Gus's wife was due with their first baby, and he was wound so tight he could hardly think.

While Gus talked, Benji tried to keep from staring at Contessa. But it was hopeless. His eyes drew back to her over and over. She waited at the counter, still looking at the display items and tucking stray curls behind her ears, which he noticed had a subtle point at the top, as if she had elf in some distant relative and the recessive gene had accidentally surfaced in her ears.

Gus gave a type of gruff sound with his breath and verified, again, that Benji understood him before hanging up.

"So what does your dad do?" he asked, with more anxiousness in his voice than he intended.

Her phone made a bird sound from inside her skirt. "That's my dad." She waded through the folds until she pulled out an iPhone encased in a tan and white Otterbox. "He said he would let me know when he was on his way." Tapping something into her phone, she put it back in her pocket. "He works for the United Nations." She said it plainly as if it was something Benji was used to hearing every day.

74

He crossed his arms, trying to act just as lax. "What sort of stuff do people do in Mongolia? And how long did you live there?"

She smiled. "My dad will be here in a minute but how about tomorrow? I can talk Mongolia with you until you tell me to stop ninnying."

Benji had no idea what the word "ninnying," meant, but there was warmth in her voice. "Sure. Tomorrow." He tried not to sigh. The idea of "tomorrow," worried him.

The light outside the store doors dimmed when a dark gray car pulled up in front, its color blending with the outside—gray car, gray clouds, gray cement streets. A man's silhouette was in the driver's seat. Benji assumed it was her father. And there was someone sitting in the back seat, their head leaned sideways against the tinted window. The mashed hair appeared lighter than Contessa's, maybe blonde instead of brown though it was hard to tell through the dark gray window tint.

"Front door meeting in the morning?" she asked, her eyes unblinking and direct, committed to having an answer.

Benji gave a single head nod. Then like that, she was out the door leaving him in a cauldron of questions. The main glaring one he said out loud to the empty store. "Why me?"

Benji
Thirteen

Benji picked up the stack of shirts in his dresser drawer, slipped his camera equipment into the space, then set the shirts back on top and closed the drawer. On top of the dresser sat a blue glass from last night. He picked it up and stared down the throat, down inside was a curdling ring of white milk left over from his nightly stomach ache.

Drumming his fingers on top of the dresser, he rehashed for the thousandth time his Busting Balls plan.

A year's worth of planning—the money, the how to's, the look on his dad's face when the cops come to the door— and now it was almost time. Soon, very soon, the Rat will be in handcuffs and the Fake's mascara will run like water color.

A memory clanged like a symbol against his brain, waking the flashback of his father yelling, "Son, I had too much to drink is all! I wasn't gonna…," after Benji charged into Leah's room and punched the rat in the side of the head.

According to science, memories can be fickle and selective, like flashes of a camera that seal a moment of time all while ignoring or forgetting things in between. The day was exactly like that for Benji. There is no memory of simple things from the day, like what he watched on YouTube or what took place at school, or even what he ate for dinner.

But then there are the solid memories, the concrete parts that burned into his mind like a soldering iron. He perfectly remembers the old house, its size much smaller than this one. He remembered the little nightlight glowing from the hallway socket and how it lit up the expanse of the area like a spotlight—that small light had served time and time again as his beacon for getting back to his room from the kitchen without turning on any other lights. He remembered it was late, and he how couldn't sleep because his stomach hurt. On that particular night, when he rounded out of his room to head to the kitchen for the milk that would settle his stomach, he heard his dad's whispered voice coming from Leah's room. "Oh, Button, it's okay…shhhh." He also clearly remembers the perception of childhood innocence. There was no sense anything was off. No intuition. No gut feeling. His thought was plain and simple: Leah probably had a bad dream and their dad was in her room comforting her.

Benji put a fist to his forehead and squeezed his eyes tight as the scene he saw in his mind came into crisp focus: Rat Bastard, pants off, bright-white hairy butt in the air, towering over Leah in her bed.

The day after, he remembers thinking: if a bee could sting a conscious that's what that moment felt like. "The scene is all wrong!" the sting said. Then there was a sudden recognition, like someone hit a zoom icon in his visual field. His mind screamed its, sudden, clear understanding. "Noooo!" he yelled then grabbed the closest thing to throw—a coloring book from Leah's dresser. It hit Rat in the back, stunning him to turn around and face Benji, the stiffness of his manhood screaming its judge, jury, and a guilty verdict. The distance to get from the door to the his father was one long stride, which he took with ease and plowed into the room punching him in the side of the head, direct contact with his temple. Rat wobbled against the shock but came back holding his hands up. Benji waited for a rebounding strike. He never hit anyone before, but he also had never been hit either. His body braced for the impact. But at the last moment, instead of raising a fist, the Rat shoved him backward into the propped open door. In his memory, the rest of the fight becomes a blur of tussling arms and hands, his father's shwong slapping at his legs while he clawed at his father's face, wanting to rip it off down to the bone.

While they fought, Leah screamed like the house fire alarm, right up to the point when their mom came rushing in and threw a mug full of cold water on them. Stunned into stopping, Benji dashed to Leah's bed to hold her, tightly cupping her ears while Rat yelled his justifications. "Son, I drank too much is all! I wasn't gonna...," stutter, stutter, justify and explain. "I didn't know what I was doing! I'm sorry!" The words crapping from his mouth like oral diarrhea made Benji want to vomit.

One of the worst things from that night was not finding out their father was a rat bastard, it wasn't the blathering language of a drunk, horny, middle-aged man who stood and begged to be understood for his perverted mistake. It was the branded memory of Camille and how she stood straight-backed, chin-up with conviction, right next to the bastard, rubbing small circles on his back as if he needed the comforting, saying, "Next time he won't drink as much," and, "It's really all fine, Benji, these things sometimes happen to men." She never once moved to comfort Leah. She didn't smack the living crap out of her husband for attempting to violate her daughter. Her disposition had been all wrong for a mother. She was choosing to comfort the bastard and not her seven-year-old daughter.

That was the night Benji said his goodbyes to the unprotecting God up there in solar system oblivion. He was no protector. He was only a phantom. It was also the very first night he slept holding Leah in a protective cocoon. And every night since.

He spent the next week Googling information about molestation victims. And for the next few months he constantly observed Leah's behaviors, trying to see if anything matched. But he didn't see any. She remained a ray of sunshine and smiles. If he would ask, "Leah, did daddy ever sleep in your bed with you before?" She would continue playing whatever she was playing and answer, "No. I like sleeping in your room, and there's no room for daddy on your bed. He's too big, silly." The only thing Benji knew for sure was he had caught his father half naked in bed with his sister, and how, after that night, Leah never slept in her bed again.

He pounded his fist on the dresser. Soon, very soon. "I *will* get her out of this house of madness," he said out loud.

It's about the goal; he reminded himself. Focus on the now, on the goal, not the past. Releasing the memory of that night to slide back and hide under more recent thoughts, he dredged a breath and ran his hand across the face of the drawer where he hid his equipment.

What if something goes wrong; he thought.

He set the glass down and scrubbed his hands over his head, ruffling his hair into a spiky mess. It was merely a whisper, as delicate as a puff on a dandelion. But he had heard the whisper before.

"No!" he responded to the intrusive, questioning thought. "I've planned for far too long."

Maybe it was anxiety caused by the cameras in his drawer and the pressure to think up a Blue Barbie plan. That must be it. A single revenge takes a lot of concentration. Two at the same time must be pushing his focus to the limit. He paced a circle on his rug, jumped up and down a few times, then rolled his head around as if loosening up for a boxing match.

Yes, that's it; he's merely antsy for ideas to come to fruition. For Rat Bastard's life to blow up and for a creative Blue Barbie scheme.

He bounced on the balls of his feet and thrust a few punches into the empty air in front of him. He'd already done more than thirty schemes, big and small, what was two more.

Glancing at his desk clock, he listened for Leah playing in the bath. He guessed he still had about fifteen minutes, minimum, to safely brainstorm. He rolled his desk chair in front of his bedroom door—in case Leah finished, or the Fake decided she wanted to come in—then went around the opposite side of the bed. Squatting, he slid Pandora out from underneath.

Benji
Fourteen

Pandora's lid fell back with ease, her nineteen-sixty's leather travel case joints old and loose. The smell of old cigars and cedar wafted into the air as her inner contents opened like a time capsule of Benji's life—a memory bank from his mind. On top, like a crown on the King, was Chronicle, his revenge journal. He thumbed through its pages and stopped on the one from when he made his mother's best friend stick to the bathroom toilet all during church home group.

Revenge Chronicle: Toilet Time Milk Swap
Revenge Risk: Easy
Revenge Date: February 10th, 2012
Chronicle Entry Date: February 11th, 2012

Journal, nothing snappy to enter, nothing clever…only made my mom's bestie sit on the toilet through the night. I switched her soy coffee creamer with milk creamer before my mom got home from work. That's it. The lactose intolerant woman was on the toilet for the entire Bible study. Easy but worth it! See if she ever tells my mother that I'm, "in need of a good spanking again." Lady, I'm too old to be spanked!

With a snicker, he closed Chronicle and began looking through last year's printed-out chats from his fake profiles on the internet. There are three accounts in all—the Belgium, the Chicago girl, and the animal rights activists. One month worth of private messages as the Belgian girl and sure enough the girls at school shared the way they get easy, top-grade liquor for parties. "The guy at 5298 Oak Harvest Lane." (His address.) And the guy is, "Quick and discreet," and wants girls "to do the down. Not guys." He had vomited when it was confirmed. But not before replying with a story about how, "We don't have to do that in Belgium," omitting keywords so he sounded less American and more foreign. "It easy here, we go to store. Drinking age sixteen for beer and eighteen for spirits. I would hate if have to do that for the drink." After that conversation, unless he needed specific information, Benji hardly bothered with the fake profiles.

He pushed the print out's off to the side; he would throw them out soon. At this point, they were boring. Even the Car Wash caught on tape conversations were old news.

Rifling under another stack of papers, he came across the Celtic cross necklace Leah gave him for his birthday last year, an old Nintendo game cartridge, the Super Mario Cart sticker worn off enough that now it was almost white. Photos of he and his old friend Jaden at the Auto Show in Detroit when they were ten, along with a ticket stub to a Piston's game Jaden's dad took them to. That day they had too many frozen cokes and hotdogs and both threw up on the way home. Before that day, Jaden always proclaimed he had an iron stomach, "Unlike Benji," he'd say. But after the puke fest, his dad began teasing him about his claimed solid stomach. "Don't eat too many pizza rolls, Mr. Iron Stomach," he'd jest. "You might not want to ride that ride, Mr. Iron Stomach," he said during a trip to an amusement park. Benji thought it was great. He has a horrible stomach…and he wasn't the only one anymore.

Under more photos, largely of him and Leah at different Holiday events when she was a baby, was a notebook with his bank information, a couple of memory jump drives with saved searches he did about famous quotes, revenge schemes and pranks, and a skeleton key. A key he stole from a display table in the church lobby. Right when you enter the church there is a long, narrow table and on top sits an open Bible and a giant sculpture of the last supper. Right in the center, underneath, dwarfed by the length of the table, is a single drawer. He merely assumed the key was left there for decoration, but he liked the way it looked, the way it protruded out past the finite line of the table top. He liked how the metal was old and distressed, the sort of key you'd see in a period movie. He liked how it invited someone to lock or unlock the drawer. One Sunday, when he was hiding in the lobby away from the boring sermon, he slinked over and let his fingers encase the key. He only planned to see what was in the drawer and if the key worked, but the very moment his fingers wrapped around the metal the doors of the sanctuary burst open and people began pouring into the lobby. So instead, his back to the table and covering the drawer, he slipped it out of its home, palmed it, and then slid his hand into his pocket.

Lifting the small key from inside Pandora, Benji twirled it in his fingers. It's the length of a normal house key, though, literally, a skeleton of a key—its parts hollowed out leaving only the essential pieces needed to unlock or lock something. For a short time, he obsessed over the key, wanting to know what was in the church drawer. But when he brought it back there was always someone waiting in the lobby where he couldn't get to the table. A few months later he won the argument not to have to go to church any longer, so the key became impractical.

He kissed the end of the key as if it were the ring on a Bishop's finger and called to mind the Scripture, "Seek and you will find, knock and it will be opened for you...."

"Ha!" he barked at the remembering of those words. I don't need to knock; he thought, I've got a key.

Sighing, he tossed the key back into Pandora and stared out the window. The sky was clear, and the moon looked like an oversized Christmas ornament hanging on the yard tree. Tessa worked her way into his mind. He glanced down at the box of stuff and then back to the moon, imagining Tessa had a box of her own. Maybe a beaded box from another country, one made special for her. Or maybe a hand weaved basket. No matter what she keeps—if she even has a box—he doubted her contents looked like his collection of sprawled keepsakes and secrets.

"So much for an idea," he huffed, tossing his stuff back into Pandora.

Tessa was now front in center in his thoughts again, and he couldn't stop imagining her in other countries walking to school with the kids, all of their faces different shades and shapes of their cultures and all smiles and joy about going to school.

After sliding Pandora back under the bed, he took the chair from the door and turned on his tablet and typed, "Mongolia," in the search bar.

Benji
Fifteen

"Homemade, warm blueberry-flaxseed muffin." Tessa's hand presented a brown paper bag; the top rolled down like a sixties lunch bag.

"You baked muffins before school?" Benji asked, taking the bag. He'd been waiting inside the door, watching her walk up. An easy smile spread across her face when she tipped her umbrella back and saw him.

"No, I'm not bright and sunny enough when I wake up to make muffins, or cook anything for that matter. My grandmother made them. She woke us up with the most amazing scent of nutty muffins. She's a gem like that." She shook the rain off of her umbrella and collapsed it.

"I'll take that too," he reached for her umbrella while she tried to untangle herself from her shawl.

"Thank you." She pulled off her wet mustard colored shawl and wrapped it around her waist, tying a knot on the side like a sarong.

As they walked and talked about muffins, and how "neat" Big Timmie's is, and how long Benji has worked there, a girl with tiny features greeted them.

"Benji, this is Padma," Tessa greeted the girl with a hug and a double cheek kiss as if they were old friends. Padma had a button nose, small, heavy-lidded angled eyes, and while her lips were plump, the width was so compact it appeared as if she was permanently puckered for a kiss. Apart from when she spoke, Padma was like a life-sized doll.

"Hi. It's nice to meet you," Padma said with a loud, projectable voice that was the exact opposite of her tininess. She extended her hand to shake Benji's.

"We have Indonesia in common," Tessa explained, causing both her and Padma's eyes to light up. "Padma moved here this year, so she's new like me. But she'll only be here for this year of school, right?"

Padma nodded her head, "Yes. My father has work here."

"Nice to meet you," Benji said filing the Indonesia information into his "things to remember about Tessa," memory file.

All three of them walked, Tessa explaining how she lived in Indonesia from fifth to seventh grade, while Padma explained that her father had lived in Michigan for a year, but their family missed him so they decided to move to be with him for his last year of work. Her entire family will return to Indonesia the summer of next year.

Tessa reached and put her arm around Padma and gave her a side squeeze hug. "Plenty of time to experience the big U.S. of A," she said, which made Padma nod ecstatically in agreement.

Padma's locker was down a different hall so they said their goodbyes—Padma's voice carrying throughout the hall and causing a few kids to glance their way—and vowed to see each other in fifth hour. Tessa laughed lightly at Padma's voice and put her finger to lips to say, "Shhh." Padma giggled, covered her mouth, and turned to go down her hall.

"Glad I wasn't the only one who thought her voice was a megaphone," Benji said. "She seems…entertaining." He laughed lightly, amused by both Padma and Tessa's interactions.

"She is quite nice," Tessa said, nodding her head and smiling.

"Mongolia and Indonesia. You realize I have more questions than before, right?"

Tessa gave him a playful nudge with her elbow and wiggled her eyebrows at him. "I'm like opening a box of mysteries."

He couldn't help but think: *like a Pandora.*

Before leaving Tessa at her locker, Benji handed back her umbrella and lifted the paper sack to his nose to inhale. "Thanks for this," he winked.

"You are very welcome, Mr. Benjamin Lockwood. See you at lunch?" she confirmed before he left.

Normally Benji carried himself stiff and ready, as if he was a tall beaker with dangerous liquid inside, but now, he walked down the hall to his locker, his body loose, head up, small smile on his face.

Wednesdays are always better than the beginning of the week, but this one—he looked down at the muffin bag in his hand—has real promise.

For lunch, Benji found Tessa waiting at the lunchroom doors, her face smiling, her arm shooting up and waving over the other kid's heads like a second grader trying to get a teacher's attention. At the sight of her, he felt the broad smile that spread across his face, cracking its normal stoic form.

In the lunch line, she told him that Padma eats lunch with her tutor. "So, sorry, you have to endure the lunch hour with only me."

"Oh, the torture," he said while he grabbed a plate of fries.

Tessa took two packs of mayonnaise and added it to the plate. "Mayo is the German way of eating Pomme Frites," she explained.

The rain had passed so they sat outside at a table in the covered area of the quad talking about Padma, what classes Tessa had, and how she liked her teachers so far. "All the teachers are very nice, but they don't smile much," she said while showing him how to dip the fries in the mayo first and then ketchup. "They also have a gravy they put on the French fries in Germany."

"Is it really *French* fries in Germany? I mean, wouldn't they be Deutsch fries?" he said dipping another fry.

"Ha! No, I think it stands for fried potato…or something like that," she said. She had a dab of the mayo-ketchup mix on the side of her mouth.

"You have some mayo…" Benji pointed to her lip then, instead, reached and gently wiped it away with a napkin.

"Thank you," she said. "My gram tells me all the time that I gobble food like a puppy, and just as messy." She then lined her smile with a fry and grinned at him. The smile made his insides flutter.

When they were done with the fries, he devoured the muffin and rambled a deluge of compliments to her grandmother on her delicious baking.

The entire lunch it was only the two of them—and plenty of staring eyes. Most of them likely wondering about Tessa, and why she was with the guy they hardly notice.

Revenge Chronicle: Swedish Fish
Revenge Risk Rating: Super Easy
Revenge Date: August 29th, 2014
Chronicle Entry Date: August 29th, 2014
and September 2nd, 2014

> *1 can of the nastiest smelling fish on earth*
> *1 kitchen sponge—the kind with a handle*
> *1 set of rubber gloves*

Chronicle, I didn't want to do the traditional fish-in-a-cronies-locker plan, mainly because I would have to be tortured by the smell when school started up on Monday. No thank you. Plus, it's been done enough times throughout schools in America. So I made some adjustments and narrowed it down to places the cronies frequent at school then matched those with places that I hardly ever go. The list consisted of the gym, the weight room, the bathroom, the office, and the school store. The winner....drum roll, please....THE WEIGHT ROOM. It's the best target: It's easy to enter and exit because there are two separate doors. It's easy to see if anyone is in there because there is a large glass window in the hall for observing. And it's an enclosed room all by itself.

Today, Friday the 29th, is the first Friday of the first week of school. To take up time after school, I stopped at Maria's for some pizza. I stayed there until six and then headed back to school—the doors are still unlocked at that time since there's open

91

*swim at the pool until nine and football practice
runs until five. I managed to slip in without anyone
giving a single glance my direction and walked
down the hall to the weight room. Except for the
jungle gym sized equipment and weights, it was
completely empty. And, as a bonus, the door was
already shut and the lights were out, which likely
meant no one would be entering that particular
room until Monday. EXCELLENT!*

*Using only the lights from the hallway, I took the
can of Surströmming from my pocket, popped the
can lid, dipped my sponge in the fish brine, and
smeared it under the bottom of two of the weight
benches. Then I tossed the sponge in the garbage
and hid the rest of the can of fish on the floor
behind the pile of barbell weights, next to the
mirror. By the time I quietly closed the door behind
me, the aroma stuck both to my nose and to the
gloves. I had to clench my teeth to keep from
gagging. As fast as possible I slipped through the
outside doors and tossed the gloves into the waiting
trash bin.*

*(Surströmming, the nastiest smelling canned fish
on earth. My special thanks go to the small, Eastern
European grocery store over on Williams Street
that sells it).*

*The weekend heat ought to make the fish brew a
bit.*

Update: Monday, September 2nd, 2014

Holy crap! I left school after homeroom! The smell didn't stick only to the weight room! I will NEVER eat fish again!

Not my best idea...

Benji
Sixteen

Blue Barbie's silver travel coffee mug must have been filled with a triple shot. Every time she took a sip and whispered to the guy sitting next to her, her breath wafted over to Benji's table. "Callie got the alcohol hookup for Friday," she said to the guy. "Her cousin is visiting from Battle Creek and he's getting us a keg."

"Nice," the guy said. "I hit up the Corner Store already."

Benji, who was pretending to stare off toward the library doors, was listening and watching them peripherally. In the last ten minutes the guy talking with Blue Barbie had made several brisk touches to her hand or arm, adjusted his shirt collar eight times, and leaned back and laughed twice, causing the library teacher to shush him. But to Benji, the most impressive thing about the guy was how he kept a complete poker face even though he was repeatedly smacked with the full impact of Blue Barbie's breath every time she spoke.

Study time in the library is one of the hours a student picks if they don't need any more credits to graduate, which meant it was either study time or nap hour for Benji. And in Blue Barbie's case it was a social hour.

Today, he sat behind Blue Barbie's table on purpose, hoping he could drum up a plan through eavesdropping. So far, a half-hour into class, he didn't have anything except a nauseating coffee stench sticking to his nose hairs.

Blue Barbie's gag-worthy coffee breath wafted again. "The Corner Store on Fourth Street? The guy who usually works there, the fat one, he's always so mean."

"Yeah," said Poker Face, "but the dude hooks me up with top shelf stuff for an extra fifty bucks and I get paid tomorrow. He already set me some Don Julio to the side."

Blue Barbie lifted her blank phone screen to her face. Using it as a mirror, she rustled her fingers through her eyebrow length bangs in the reflection. "Great. That will save one of us from doing the down in order to get some top shelf quality."

Poker Face went silent.

Blue Barbie tucked her phone into a small pouch pocket on the side of her bag and announced, "I gotta pee," then got up and headed to the teacher's desk. He assumed asking to go to the bathroom.

Poker Face rubbed the stubble on his chin and leaned back in his chair. For a few seconds, he stared at the vacant space Blue Barbie left behind, but then he lifted his arms high and to the side managing a forced stretch. He did a quick scan of his now empty table and opened the textbook sitting in front of him.

That's when it hit Benji.

He copied Poker Face's casual stretch and leaned back in his chair, tipping it onto two legs. "Hey, do you have Mr. Tubin's for that class?" he asked, pointing to Poker's book.

Poker's scrunched forehead showed he was startled to find Benji so close. But Benji's lean needed to make his jacket hang over the back of his chair and over Barbie's bag.

By the time Poker finished making sense of who was talking to him and said, "No. I have Mrs. Akin," Benji already slipped Barbie's phone out the same way he had slipped the key out of the church drawer and cupped it in his hand.

"Oh, okay. Thanks anyway," he said letting his chair fall back onto four legs. He had never pick-pocketed before but now realized he would be good at it.

He cupped the phone in his hand, slipped on his jacket—concealing the phone in his sleeve—and left his table.

The S.A.T. area of the library was the best out-of-sight section available so he pulled a random study book from the shelf and sat down in one of the lounge chairs.

Keeping the book at an angle that both faced one wall and would also be too high to see what he was doing if someone happen to approach him, he placed the phone in the book crack and pretended to point as if reading a specific page.

He touched Blue Barbie's phone screen. It lit up. It wasn't locked.

"Karmic intervention," he whispered as it displayed her main screen.

First, he flicked through a few of her text messages, which there were hundreds. It seemed she never used her deleted button. After that, he scanned her social media. It was all logged in.

That's when it hit him. He hurried through the system files and unchecked the "Hide password," and then went back to her social accounts. After taking a series of screenshots, he put them together in one file, texted them all to his burner email account, and erased the sent text. He managed snaps of her email passwords and a few of her contacts when someone slid a book into a shelf one row over, making him jump at the thud it made as it hit the back of the wood. He checked the time and stood up to peek around the corner at the table. Blue Barbie was heading back to her seat, glancing and giving smiles along the way to specific people. Until then his heart hadn't begun to register that it should speed up, but now his body felt the fast pace of rushed blood to his head, a pulse in his temples, and shallow breathing. His stomach cinched.

His hand shook as he rubbed the back of his neck. Looking at the row of books next to him, he started counting them by threes. Three, six, nine, twelve…until he felt the need to take a gorging breath. He did. And then did again. The shallow breathing ended. His chest began to rise and fall in rhythm to his counting…twenty-seven, thirty…one more breath.

He had an idea! He ripped his eyes from the bookshelf and back to the phone. With a burst of adrenaline he turned the phone over, popped off the purple, rhinestone-covered case, removed the back, took out the SIM-card, and had the back plate and the case back on in fifteen seconds.

He looked at the clock across the room. Three minutes to the bell. He slipped the phone back up his sleeve, making sure to cup it enough so it wouldn't fall out as he walked, and then headed back to his seat.

Blue Barbie was busy talking with a spiky, red-haired girl who must have gravitated to their table while he was hiding. The girl stood with her arms crossed on the opposite side of Poker Face, and in the way of the bag.

Crap.

Benji took a step, counting it. Then took another step, counting it, too. This impromptu mess is for the birds, he thought, but then quickly settled that he got what he needed so a sloppy closing would be fine.

Ten more strides and he would be to the new girl.

Ten, nine, eight, seven…he looked down, and then ran smack into her, bumping her side and making her bump into Barbie.

In stereo, they snapped, "Hey!"

"Sorry," he said, keeping his head low, not making eye contact. Then he slid down in his chair and began gathering his books.

"Can't you see the life-sized human being standing right here?" The visitor snipped.

Blue Barbie made a disgusted sound, but Benji didn't care, he was busy watching peripherally to see if Poker Face would do something. He didn't want to get pummeled. But from what he could see Poker didn't move, other than to observe the exchange.

Benji headed to the door as fast as possible, counting each step, fighting the urge to glance back.

When he heard, "Hey, Claire, is that your phone?" he knew the visitor saw Blue Barbie's phone on the floor next to her chair, as if it slipped from the side of her bag by accident.

The bell rang and he stifled his grin by biting the inside of his cheek.

Benji
Seventeen

Not caring about the cronies, Benji stood at his open locker while the halls thinned. He hummed with adrenaline and rushed blood that pulsated in his temples. With every moment, his hands shook, and he felt like he needed to use the bathroom. It was exhilarating! As if someone shoved an IV of Blue Barbie's espresso shots into his veins.

Dare the cronies mess with me right now, he thought glancing to his right and seeing only Car Wash. He appeared focused on his locker so Benji began loading the information from Blue Barbie's SIM-card into his. Now, not only did he have her contacts and passwords, he also had everything about her world: her home address, her monthly menstruation calendar, even her bathroom selfies, including the unedited ones. The ones she likely didn't post. (His favorite of those was the one with the toilet filled with pee and toilet paper.)

He knew he had limited time before Blue Barbie realized her phone wasn't working, she may have already figured it out, but he didn't care. For the moment, he was enjoying the lightheaded buzz he experienced with each moved file.

When the screen said "complete," he tucked the phone into his bag next to his SIM-card, withdrew from his locker, glanced around for any cronies, there were none, and left to go home and review his scheming high.

Benji
Eighteen

Tessa waited by the exit doors taking a bite of an apple. Benji wasn't used to having someone meet him, not on the way into school and not on the way out, so while he cocooned into his locker he'd completely forgotten.

"Hey," he said with a tense reverb in his voice.

"Hi," she replied, swallowing and raking her hand across the top of her head through her hair. It fell long past her shoulders.

The image of her at the door reminded him of a Disney character about to take a bite of the poison apple. He longed to reach out and save her from her apple.

Something must have shown on his face because her mouth pulled into a smile, drawing up more on one side than the other. The asymmetry made her look mischievous.

"I was thinking," she said. "My mom says I need jeans for the winter." She waved her hand down her legs. "Apparently my gypsy pants and wrap shirts won't do."

Benji liked her pants. They were deep purple and baggy, except at her waist and hips, and they could pass for a long skirt. Most girls at school wore jeans and a variety of tops, and clothing was the easiest way to decipher who belonged to what group, but not Contessa, her clothes didn't fit any group. Her

102

shirt was like her skirt, different. It was a teal and white-ribbed cotton material that wrapped down and around her torso like a wide ribbon and tied off on her right side. The wrapping effect accentuated her long waist and thin arms. For all Contessa's covered state, her clothing silhouetted enough of her shape to know she was curvy at the hips and narrow in her upper body.

Taking in her clothing, her shape, and those eyes, he couldn't figure how it was possible for his phone-heist adrenaline high to make him forget about her.

"I tried to tell my mom I could add boots but she said I needed more of a Michigan wardrobe. And you said you don't work tonight, correct?" She tapped her fingers on the strap of her bag. The bag's material was the same burlap as her pants, except solid teal. "What I'm asking is, and I know it's a lot to ask," she reached and lay her hand on his chest, "but will you meet me at the mall?"

Benji felt his eyes squint at the thought. He could spot a high school girl's clothes, but he doubted he could sort through a store rack and pick them out. The University of Michigan hoodie he wore with plain jeans was proof.

He blinked and cleared his throat, thrown off. "Um, I don't…," he stuttered, "I don't know anything about clothes. Or a Michigan style." He stepped back, instantly regretting moving away from her hand. "Can't you tell?" He motioned from his head to his feet.

She stepped closer again. "No, not for fashion advice, for your company. Please. I won't take long.

I'll try on things quick then we can wander the rest of the time."

"Okay," he said, "What time?"

She dropped her forehead to his chest, relieved. "Thank you, thank you."

He could smell her hair; it smelled like autumn—like the apple on her breath, and like harvested earth mixed with a touch of cinnamon and cloves. When she lifted her head, their faces were close to each other. A foreign ache pinched under his chest bone, and his right arm rose with goose bumps.

"So how do we work this?" he asked, wishing he had more thoughtful conversational insight.

She stepped away and opened the heavy school door. Benji followed, still aware of the strange ache in his chest.

"I need to make sure it's okay with my mom though I'm quite sure it will be," she said walking outside. "And my dad will want to drop me off. I don't know where a mall is, but I can text you within the next hour and inform you of the deets."

"Okay," he said, noticing the brisk slap of a chilled breeze on his face. A sign the spoils of late summer weather he felt yesterday were over, and that Tessa's mom was right, soon she would need warmer clothes.

She stopped at the car drop-off curb. "Any particular mall I should tell her?" She pulled a shawl from her bag, unfurled it with a gentle whip and then double wrapped it around her shoulders and arms.

"That depends, where do you live?"

"My grandmother's house is on…" she paused as if to search her memory. "She refers to it as the north side of town but I don't know what the area is called. It's not in a neighborhood. It's more like border-of-farm-land area. We take M14 to get here, does that help?"

"Yep, it does. Tell your mom the Oak Valley Mall. It's right off the Dexter exit. Go south on M14, and you'll see signs. Should be easy, and no navigation skills necessary."

A dark gray sedan drove up to the curb and stopped right next to her. Benji moved to go around the car toward the parking lot, but Tessa stopped him. "Wait, please meet my dad."

"Um, okay." He walked back to her as the driver's window quietly dropped down.

"Hi Dad," she said leaning in giving him a kiss on the cheek. "I want you to meet my friend Benji."

"Hi sweetheart," he said and then turned his head to hang out of the car. Her father was nothing like Benji pictured. First, he was sun-bleached blonde, not like Tessa's brown hair. Second, Benji expected a suit and tie and eyes covered with aviator glasses like an intimidating government security agent. Instead, he wore a regular, dark green, long sleeve shirt that looked straight out of Dick's Sporting Goods Golf section. Benji guessed his facial hair was two days overdue for a shave, and he was quite a bit tanner than Tessa. It seemed Tessa got her eye shape and eye color from him, but not much else.

His arm extended out of the car. "Hi, Benji, I'm Todd. It's nice to meet you. Sorry for not getting out of the car but we're late to get Marula." He gave a single head nod to the side, toward the passenger seat. Tessa followed his head gesture and walked around the front of the car to the passenger door. "Marula is my sister," she clarified over the roof.

She waved at him as she slid into the front seat. "I will text you."

"Again, pleasure to meet you, Benji." Todd pulled his arm in then gave a head nod through the window glass as they pulled away.

Benji stepped off the curb, watching them leave, his mind whispering, "When is she going to figure out she shouldn't be friends with me?"

Benji
Nineteen

Benji raced up to his room, tossed his stuff on the desk, and sat down on the edge of the bed with his phone in his hand. He knew he should read Blue Barbie's stuff and come up with a plan, but all he managed was to re-read the last message between him and Tessa and stare at the phone— waiting for her text.

Another five minutes of staring passed before he decided to grab his heating pad from the bedside drawer. Once he stretched out on his bed, he laid the pad across his stomach, turned it on high and closed his eyes, keeping his phone tight in his hand.

He just began to fall into a light sleep when a small, warm hand touched his forearm. He kept his eyes closed.

Leah whispered, "Are you in there?" he could feel the mattress tilt as she moved closer onto the bed.

His eyes popped open and he grabbed her around the waist and pulled her into a bear hug. "Whaaaaa!" He made his best Halloween scary voice.

She protested through squeals and giggles. "Don't do that!"

He kissed her cheek and she curled up next to him, leaning her head on his arm. Her hair was soft. The way the chenille blanket on the back of the living room couch feels. Her little pudgy fingers reached and curled up with his long skeletal ones.

"How is Cassy's arm?" he asked.

"It's getting better, but there's a really ugly bruise and it's all yellow and purple."

"That means it's healing," he said, lifting their twined fingers, observing their drastic differences. The blue sparkling nail polish was only small patches now.

"That's what her mom said, too."

"Do you have homework?"

"Yes, spelling words." She tilted her face up at him. "Did you know a bee is a pollinator?"

"If pollinator is a spelling word, I'm impressed you used it." He gave her a squeeze.

She smiled, set her head back down, and stretched her arm out across the heating pad. "Your tummy hurting again?"

"Yeah."

"Want me to get you some milk?"

"Naw, that's okay. It'll pass, it always does." It'll pass when his phone alerts him to Contessa's impending presence; he thought.

He remembered…phone…Contessa…but also, Blue Barbie's information. He gave Leah a little squeeze. "Wanna do me a favor?"

"Mmm, sure."

"How about you get me that glass of milk then study your spelling words, and I'll ask mom if you can go with me to the mall. I'm going in a little bit."

She shot up to a sitting position. "Really?"

"Sure, but you have to study your words first, all by yourself. I can go over them with you if you

108

study them for—" he looked at the clock, "for twenty minutes."

"And you'll ask mom?" Her eyes turned down. The last time Leah wanted to stay home on church night Camille had launched into a fit of yelling, and Leah still had to go. The next day, Leah told him the reason she didn't want to go to Bible class was because, "Patrick," the pastor's youngest son, "keeps spitting in my watercolor paints."

He kissed her forehead again. "Absolutely. She'll say yes, you'll see."

It took a few minutes for her to come back with the glass of milk and set it next to the bed. As soon as she left he began loading Blue Barbie's Sim card information from his cloud account to his Tablet.

Watching the hourglass dance around his screen, letting him know the information was transferring, he wondered what one of Big Timmie's "integrity notes," would say about him stealing her information. He is always leaving them around the shop for the employees to find; like the one he left on Benji's camera box. His most famous note was the giant, neon-green note he left on the cork board for Rob, one of the repair guys. It said, "Rob, stop worshiping women with your balls and worship them with your heart." Everyone had a week long laugh from that one. Eventually, the guys drew a Rob face on the note then moved it to the dart board. Over a month, they riddled it with darts. For every dart thrown, Rob was razzed about his women problems. They all now know more about Rob's sex life than they cared to know.

When the files finished loading, he moved them all to a folder he named, "Singing the Blues," hit save, and then turned off his tablet. It was time to convince his mom to let Leah go with him to the mall.

Rat was in his chair, the remote posted in his hand as if it was a natural extension, flipping through the channel guide. The Fake was in the kitchen dipping strawberries into chocolate and placing them on wax paper. After each dip and placement, she mumbled something about being late, and about how his dad was useless around the house, and how she still needed to do her hair. She did a dip and a mumble, then a dip and a mumble, all while Leah sat at the kitchen table with her spelling list. Leah's lips mouthed the letters of the words from the paper and then she tested herself by putting the paper face down on the table and trying to spell them again.

It was easier than he thought to convince his mother to let Leah skip church and go with him. It merely took perfect timing and extra frustration to make her say, "Fine, fine, I need to get these done and chilled, and I still have to change my clothes. Fine, she can go. It's one more thing I don't have to worry about getting ready. Now if I could get your father to move his a...." She glanced at Leah and didn't finish.

He didn't like Leah being referred to as a "thing" but he let it slide. No reason to rock what he already gotten his way. He winked at Leah and went back upstairs.

At his dresser drawer, he moved his t-shirts out of the way, took the electrical socket camera, his strip of sticky tack, and tucked them both into the front of his pants, pulling his shirt over the top to conceal everything.

With the Rat's attention toward the TV, his mom still dipping, and his sister still looking at her paper, he snuck past them all and down into the basement.

Initially, he planned to put it up after everyone went to church, but since he would be gone as well, and his mom and dad won't pay attention to anything going on around them until it was time for them to go, he might as well take a chance and do it now. This way he won't have it on his mind while he's at the mall.

While listening for movement or floor creaking, he worked quickly to peel the back off one side of the industrial sticky tack and place it on the convex back of the camera outlet. He already added the memory card at work, but it laid flush with the side of the device so he double checked when he stuck it to the wall.

After peeling off the other side of the tape, he placed the camera socket over the original wall socket above the file cabinet and pressed firmly. The socket is waist high and not near the work equipment, but looking at it now he realized the area is more shadowed than the rest of the room—the camera image may come out too dark, something he hadn't thought of yesterday. But there was no time for a test, at least not tonight, so he stepped back and admired his work. Apart from the re-set switch in the middle being a clear square—on a normal socket it is red—it was hard to tell it was a different outlet.

Hopefully, Rat won't try to plug anything into it, he thought heading back up the stairs, grabbing a screwdriver on his way in case anyone asked what he was doing in the basement. He armed the lie, "I need to tighten the toilet seat in the bathroom," just in case.

Tessa

"After I get home do you want to redo my henna?" Tessa asked, twirling a strand of Marula's hair through her fingers.

Her sister was lying face down on their grandmother's bed; one arm dangled over the edge with a book in it and the other tucked under her head. She wore black running pants and one of their dad's t-shirts.

"Sure," she said. Tessa could hear she was sleepy.

"Did you meet a 'someone' today at school?"

Marula pulled her arm up and rolled over onto her back, placing the book on her stomach, spine up and opened to save her place. "I did. There were a few nice people at school, so I met a few. Well, actually, it was one girl's doing because once she spoke to me everyone else seemed interested."

"That's great!" Tessa said, almost done with the single, tiny braid she had weaved. "And you were worried. I told you; you are the charmer in the family."

"Um…no," Marula snorted. "I couldn't compete with your magical charm skills even if I wanted too."

"Ahhh, spoken like the yin to my yang."

Marula was as charming; she simply wasn't as comfortable being an extrovert as Tessa was. They'd always been like that, each other's balancing rod. Tessa the bold one, Marula the cautious one. Tessa, the one who observes from the outside and learns, while Marula needs to plant her feet right in the center and learn firsthand through experience. Marula also felt things deeper than Tessa. It was as if her mind sucked in the vastness of the world but didn't know it should stop it from going in a direct line to her heart. "I don't want the bee to die," she'd wailed to their mother after getting stung on her eighth birthday at the Kenobi Elephant Reserve in Indonesia. The elephant attendant had tried to comfort her with the news that honey bees die after they sting you. It took another fifteen minutes for her to stop crying for the bee, rather than herself.

"How did your doctor's appointment go today? Do you like him?"

"Her. It's a woman. And Dr. Mason is very nice, actually. She doesn't come across as a psychiatrist; she's more like a college-age friend."

"Well, see, there were two bonuses to your day, a new friend, and a good doctor."

Marula smiled at Tessa, "Ms. Optimistic."

Tessa smiled and kissed her sister's head. She knew that moving to Michigan was harder on her sister than on her, but, somehow, for Marula it seemed they had moved to an entirely different planet instead of simply another country.

Tessa sighed, reached for another strand of her sister's hair and began making a basket weaving braid with it. "Do you still miss him?"

"I do, unfortunately. I know I shouldn't, but I do."

Marula yawned and stretched her legs, pointing and flexing her toes as if they'd been too crowded by shoes. "Are you still angry with him?" she asked.

"Yes," Tess said with a sigh. "But I miss him, too."

Benji
Twenty

The Oak Valley Mall is shaped like a giant star. Instead of having a clustered food court there are random restaurants, cafes, coffee shops, and fast food stops at the six-point entrances, all of them easily identifiable by their aroma dome. At the shoe store in the wing with the Asian restaurants, the smell of stir fry greeted the three of them. When they went down the wing to the card and paper store, there is a place that bakes cinnamon rolls, and another that serves imported coffee and is famous for their large selection of gluten free desserts—that wing made Benji's stomach growl and his lips taste like sugar. When they ventured to the department store, the wing with the Country Pizza Kitchen, the aroma of Italian spices, greasy cheese, and buttery crusts saturated the air. Benji was tempted to dip into his money and buy dinner when they passed through that wing. Though, he wasn't sure how Tessa would take it if he offered dinner. Would she think it was a date? Or that *he* thought it was a date?

When they first arrived, they found Tessa in the center of the mall at the information desk. She already held a shopping bag in her hand, which she said contained a pair of jeans—because they somehow "jumped off the rack at her," on her way to meet them. Now, they were on their way to the Fashion Fusion jewelry store for Leah, who was explaining to Tessa why it was her favorite store. "They have the biggest collection of headbands and an unbelievable amount of makeup to try on," she chirped. Then added that their mother never, "never, ever, never," lets her try any on when they come to the mall. "It takes too long, and there are too many germs," she quoted.

The wall of headbands was at the back of the store and on the way to it they both stopped at almost every rack of earrings, makeup, necklaces, scarves, purses, and even a rack lined with belly button jewelry. The idea of the pain it causes to get your belly button pierced made Leah scrunch her face and claim she would never have it done, even though she thought it was cute.

Occasionally the store clerk would flick her pink bangs out of her face to shoot weary eyes their direction. They weren't the only ones in the store, but they were the only ones who looked to be enjoying themselves. At least Leah and Tessa were, Benji was simply watching Tessa decorate Leah with large clip on earrings, a beret, and a teal, glitter-dusted feather scarf.

Tessa added a plastic neon microphone to Leah's outfit and declared. "Ah yes, now you are a complete rock star," which immediately made Leah raise the mic to her mouth, cock her hip to the side, and then raise her arm in the air and wave at her invisible fans.

From the counter, the clerk rolled her eyes at the rock-star comment then went back to adding tags to the products lined across her work table.

When Leah began twirling, the feather boa floating around her like a ribbon, Tessa snapped pictures with her phone, each time gasping with joy when she checked the image on the display. Benji noticed she seemed mystified by the camera, or at least in awe of what it was capable of. Ever since they arrived at the mall, she had her phone armed and ready for pictures, which to him seemed to be of random things. She took a close up of the flower designed tiles that striped the Pizza wing, the electronic directory map of the mall, the movie theatre ticket girl inside the booth, even a rack of baby shoes in the shoe store. "So cute!" she declared, snapping images from different angles and saying someone named, "Taktika," would love them.

While Leah switched her teal boa for a paisley scarf, Tessa tried adding a white sparkling hat and gloves to Benji's wardrobe. "I'm thinking those Michael Jackson knockoffs don't go with my flannel shirt," he protested, his arms outstretched blocking her from slipping the matching scarf around his neck.

"Party pooper," Leah said as he put distance between himself and them and opted instead to watch the two of them from the perch of a chair where they do ear piercings.

"Yeah, party pooper," Tessa laughed, mimicking Leah, but then went back to moving from rack to rack and draping Leah with whatever she could find.

When Tessa clipped on a belt made of beads that hung down to her knees and began to twirl along with Leah, making the beads flow outward like ruffled waves of water, Leah clapped with glee.

"May I have this dance?" Tessa asked Benji at the end of her last spin; her hand outstretched and one leg behind in a type of royal curtsey.

He shook his head emphatically. There was no way he was leaving his chair to dance in the middle of the store.

Tessa looked at Leah and whispered, "I dub him the king of party poopers," which made Leah break into a fit of giggles.

While winking at him, she reached her hand out to Leah and said, "Will you, my dear, dance with me?"

"Why yes, yes I will," Leah said, taking Tessa's offered hand.

Tessa lifted their clasped hands in the air and let Leah twirl under her arm, the feather boa floating around her again.

Watching them, Benji couldn't help his smile. The dazzling wonderment in Tessa's eyes, as she watched Leah twirl and giggle and fill with joy, was contagious.

When Leah finally stopped dancing and flung herself into Tessa's open arms, an alarming thought crashed into Benji. Was this allowed? Had this happiness only come to tease them? Images of a possible future flickered through his thoughts: Leah as a teenager walking by a new set of cronies, swaying her hips at their cat calls. Leah storming through the house with measures of overflowing attitude. Leah having her phone taken for texting inappropriate things. Could he even prevent that type of path from consuming her?

He tried to refocus on Tessa and Leah, who were newly adding hat upon hat until they were stacked six high on each of their heads, but the intrusive thoughts kept coming. How does life weave its bitter trap? Would Leah be smiling one day and then suddenly, when he least expects it, like his father prowling in the night, her pink Pepto-colored blanket will disappear from his protection and be replaced with distrust, pain, and anger? Anger for a world that devours human inner light and leaves in its wake a hole so big the deluge can only be satisfied with thoughts of pistols and revenge, and ways to escape it all.

"Smell that?" Tessa said, now decorated with a fuzzy, tangerine-colored beret, a couple sets of clip on earrings, four watches per arm, a long wiry necklace that hung navel length, and a red bejeweled microphone to match Leah's neon one.

Leah lifted her nose in the air, as did Benji. It was the smell of hot pretzels fresh from the oven.

"Let's get pretzels." She leaned down to Leah's fake microphone. "With oohey, gooey cheeese," she crooned in a raspy singing voice.

Leah's cheeks rounded big and plump with a smile that matched her eyes. A fit of clapping burst out of her like a bullet leaving a chamber, taking over her whole little body, even making the feathers on the boa around her neck clap their ovation.

"Dibs on pretzel sticks," he called.

"Dibs on…" Leah paused, her face settling long and sad. "I can't have any," she said looking to

Benji. "I already had chocolate strawberries and I don't have any more calories for today." She'd eaten the strawberries earlier, paired with a lecture from the fake on how it was a much better choice than the crap she usually wants to eat.

"Order what you want," he said to Leah, whose face twisted in conflict. Benji knelt down to be eye to eye and took her hands. "We'll only eat a little bit, okay? And we'll enjoy them."

Kissing the top of her hand, he reminded himself that soon he won't need to worry about their mom, and then he led her to the pretzel counter.

Benji
Twenty One

After ordering, they sat down at a small table across from the movie theater and play area. Leah inhaled her half of the pretzel bites as if they were her last meal while Tessa and Benji took their time and talked about the things she bought that were "Michigan weather appropriate." Fashionable, furry snow boots included.

Benji was half done with his sticks when the draw of the play area became too much for Leah. "Can I go over there?" she asked, pointing to a short, walled-in area where parents hover over their children from benches surrounding colorful play structures shaped like caricature animals.

Picturing a bunch of snot covered toddlers taking their snot covered hands and gooping up the playthings, he stifled a shiver. The whole area must be a petri dish of amoebas.

Tessa surveyed the area. A childish joy glazed over her eyes. Her expression made him bypass his horrified thought and say, "Sure," to Leah, who first squealed then hopped a few steps before slowing down to appear casual as she walked through the opening of the play area.

For the most part, it was empty. Other than a few little ones who walked around like wobbling dolls trying to go from a turtle to a lady bug, to a sleeping dog. All while parents toddle behind them making sure they don't fall. Leah was the biggest kid in the area, but she didn't seem to mind. So he shouldn't either. He refocused on Tessa.

"She is quite sweet. And bright. I love how she knew all about the matching games at the Brain Game store," Tessa said, still watching Leah for a moment before looking back to him. "Can I ask you something?"

He nodded since his mouth was full.

"What did she mean about the strawberries and calories?"

Benji swallowed his chunk of pretzel with a gulp of water. "My mom does that to her."

Tessa's eyebrows drew together, and her head tilted. She looked like a curious puppy who didn't understand the sound she heard.

"She counts her calories and keeps track of her food." He spit the words out like he tasted something nasty. "She's stupid."

"You mean your mom, right? Not your sister."

"Oh no. Definitely not my sister. I meant my mom. She's crazy," he clarified. "She digs at Leah about her food and her weight, calling her chunky or telling her how boys don't like fat girls. She'll say anything to make her feel terrible. I guess she thinks it will motivate Leah to lose weight—weight she doesn't even need to lose."

Tessa had been reaching for a pretzel but now her hand paused, dangling over her tray as if she forgot what she was doing. She pulled her head back, and her eyebrows drew in further.

"She's a jacked up bitch," he said, shrugging his shoulders and popping another pretzel bite into his mouth.

The declaration caused an abrupt reaction in Tessa's body language. She dropped her hand, absent of the pretzel bite she'd been reaching for, and shifted in her chair. Her head tilted down, looking at him through the tops of her eyes, staring at him as if inspecting an alien species.

He swallowed, both to empty his mouth of the pretzel and to swallow the freshly formed knot in his throat. What?" he said defensively. "She is."

But he was already nipped by a sudden worry whether he had invoked a spiral down in their new found friendship. So in a softer tone he added, "Both of my parents are jacked." Leaving off the profanity this time. "Aren't your parents?"

She shook her head. "No, not at all. My parents are great."

"Well, you're rare. And lucky," he said. "Because my parents will never be in the…," he made a flicking gesture with his hand as if to wave off the thought, "great parents category."

She wiped her mouth and sat back in her chair, crossing her arms around her waist as if to hug herself. "I'm sorry."

"For what? You didn't do anything."

"I guess I'm sorry for asking. And for your parents. And for you." She glanced over at Leah, who sat on top of the ladybug waving at a curly haired little boy who stared up at her wide-eyed. "And for Leah."

"Yeah, well…," he shrugged, crumpled his napkin, and tossed it onto the tray. "My dad is a rat and my mom is fake and I'm a realist, so happy or great won't be stopping by our life anytime soon." He glanced at Leah. "My sister and I will be fine…eventually."

Tessa's saddened face spoke volumes about her ability to empathize, but it made him wish she knew the truth. He hated the idea of his parents receiving any portion of her sympathy, even if given innocently.

Her eyes met his. They were heavier than a moment ago as if her lids had become weighty and sleepy. "You know," she said. "There is this small town in Kenya, and every morning before the kids leave for school the dads take their sons for a walk so they can talk?"

"Talk about what?"

"About life, friends, good things that happen, bad things that happen. Anything."

"Is this your way of hinting that I should take walks with my dad?"

She shrugged her shoulders. "It couldn't hurt, but no, what I was thinking is maybe the two of you can find something in common. Something you both like. Then maybe you could focus on those things."

Benji leaned back in his chair and crossed his arms. "Not gonna happen," he said, thinking how he wouldn't want anything in common with Rat Bastard. How could he explain about him? About what he's like or about those girls. Or what he's probably done to Leah. He couldn't.

Could I?

125

The thought was flat and strange, like someone speaking a foreign language. No, he needed concrete video evidence to speak for him and Leah.

In the time it took Tessa to wipe her fingers on a napkin, pull her hair up out of her face and slide a hair band from her wrist over it to make a sloppy up do, he was settled. There was no one to tell until the proof was in his hands.

She fluffed her hair bun and tucked stray strands behind her ears. "You know, my dad got into a lot of trouble as a teenager."

The tiny point of her ears drew his attention. Between the little dip in her chin, her ears, her hair now cascading down from the top of her head, the mall lights catching little flecks of glitter still trapped in her curls from the jewelry store scarves, he was enthralled and completely disarmed. He didn't want to be, but he couldn't help himself. Tessa was, without a doubt, something breathable. Like cleansed air after a spring rain. She was like Leah. A piece of goodness with an unexplainable inner light. Though a part of him wanted to hurry up and end the uncomfortable parts of the conversation, he couldn't bring himself to stop her from talking. He wanted to hear her words, her voice, her optimism about how a daily walk would fix him and his dad's relationship. It wouldn't, but he wanted to hear her belief that it would.

"That's a random statement," he said.

"Hear me out," she said, her smile returning. "My dad's last year of high school he met this guy, a mentor, who changed his life."

"Okay, still random, though." He suspected she was about to explain how her dad went from a bad guy to a good guy, but he was sure her father couldn't compare to his dad—not even on his worst day.

"The guy," she said, "believed my dad's troubles were because he needed a way to focus his skills."

"What kind of skills?"

Her smile broadened as if she knew she captured him.

"Let's just say his skills had to do with manipulating people for their personal information." Her head tilted the way Leah's does when she's acting coy. "He then would use the information to get into their houses and steal."

He uncrossed his arms and leaned in. "Your dad was a burglar?"

She leaned in too, their faces so close he could smell pretzel on her breath. "Not merely a burglar," she whispered, "but a B&E mastermind by the age of seventeen."

"No way!" he said louder than he intended. His body was inclined as far forward as possible, the rest of the distance hindered only by the table. Random or not, he was captured by the introduction of this new piece of information.

"Yes," she said in a whispered voice that only added more intrigue. Then, slowly, she leaned back in her chair, leaving him to feel the hollow, empty, space between them.

Reluctantly he sat back in his chair, too.

"My dad was the mastermind behind this crafty older guy who lived upstairs in his building." She draped her arms across the table and tapped her fingers together, a gesture his friend Jaden's dad used to do when he was about to share a surprise. "My dad says the guy had a kind of mental control over him—it was only he and my grandmother and they were thoroughly poor, and the guy made promises to help them out with bills and groceries and such. But really, he was using my dad to break into people's houses and steal." She paused, searching his face as if making sure she captured his attention. She had. "See, my dad was the facts gatherer. He would accumulate personal information by striking up conversations with people–he's very charismatic that way—and by the time he finished getting to know a person or a family, he would have their daily work schedules whether they had kids or not, if they used babysitters, even their vacation times. Sometimes he would offer to pet sit or mow their lawns anything so he appeared helpful and friendly though he says he never stole while he was working. He would wait and become reliable, someone the people could count on, and then when the people were comfortable and sure of him, that's when he would break into their homes. Everything my dad stole, the jewelry, identifications, people's keepsakes, he would give to the older guy to sell for cash. Once it was sold, the old man would give my dad a cut of the money. My dad explains how he was the one doing the manipulating of the victims, but the old man was also manipulating him. His junior year of high school, the police caught my dad stealing from a senior citizens community where he did volunteer dog walking. After being arrested, my dad found out the guy covered his tracks by getting minors to do most of the illegal work. It turned out he had another kid running the drop offs after things were sold, that way the stolen items were never connected to him. My dad said the police were trying to catch the old man, not him. But the old man covered his tracks, well, and of course made sure my dad's and the other guys weren't. When my dad was arrested, which he says was the best thing for him, it was that undercover detective who became my father's mentor. The detective pleaded with the Judge and the lawyers to give my dad a choice: either jail or to turn his life around. He even said he would take sole responsibility for my father."

Benji let out his held breath. "Wooow. That's one crazy story. Movie style crazy."

"Nope, no movie. My dad says the moral of the story is about how the detective changed his life, not necessarily about how my father changed. His life changing was a good thing, and worth the credit, but the real story is about how someone was willing to see the best in him. My dad believes it only takes one person to see the good in you and to stand by you, and that alone is enough power to make a person believe in themselves and want to change." She smiled, pleased to have offered her inspirational story.

But Benji's face felt too heavy to muster a smile, it was again weighed down from remembering there was no good in his dad. No one will be coming along to help his father "transform." No one.

Besides, what could a sexual predator be transformed into that was worthwhile?

Tessa's story was enjoyable, even intriguing, he liked it, but it was *her* father's story. His father was not redeemable.

She continued, not fazed by his flat facial expression. "After school my dad would go to the detective's office, then after some time to his house. The detective would entertain my dad's mind by making up fake scenarios for my father to investigate. He said all my dad needed was to train his skills in a different way. Even the detective's wife helped my dad. She tutored him through the rest of high school and helped him get into college. My dad grew close with the detective's family, so did my grandmother. Their entire family welcomed them both. Including the detectives daughter, who was a loan person, or maybe the term is mortgage person I'm not sure, but she helped he and my grandmother move away from Detroit and to here. The detective and his family were the reason my dad decided to work for the U.N." She pulled and twisted at a stray piece of hair dangling next to her ear. "I keep saying detective but to us he is Uncle Scooby, though Paul Schneider is his real name. His wife died a few years ago and now he spends most of his retirement with his grandchildren, or on his boat fishing the Great Lakes. Every time we visit the states, he and my grandmother are the people we come to see. He's helped our family the most these last few…." She abruptly stopped talking, and a sudden glaze flickered over her eyes. She picked up her pretzel bite and dunked in into the now cold cup of cheese dip. It made a blob on the end like thick, yellow snot.

"Help with moving?" Benji was confused by the sudden dim light in her being.

"Yes, moving, that's right. This has been a big transition for us. Uncle Scooby helped more than anyone." As she nodded, a few pieces of glitter fell from her hanging strands of hair onto the table.

Her sudden countenance change made the air thick and uncomfortable. "I appreciate you sharing your dad's story," he cleared his throat, "but if you told me so I would think my parents are redeemable, or they will learn not to treat my sister and I like crap, that time is long gone. I don't foresee any future repentance on their part or any hero swooping in and transforming them." He shrugged and crossed his arms. "I mean, just last week I overheard my mom on the phone saying Leah is "homely looking," and maybe she should teach her to use makeup earlier than other girls." He knew he was thickening the uncomfortable air, and he didn't want to diminish Tessa's inspiring story, but there was rising in him a desperation to make her understand his parents were not, are not, redeemable. "And I know my mom was talking to her perpetual dieting partner, Mona. Mona is always on a diet, and for that reason so is my mom, which means Leah is too. Truthfully, I think my mom is just reflecting herself onto Leah simply because she doesn't like that she can't fit in her high school jeans. "Two more sizes she says," he rolled his eyes and looked over at Leah, her sweet face enjoying the playing kids and smiling to each of them as they passed. "How long does it take to get rid of two sizes worth of weight? My mom's got to be going on ten years of dieting by now." He huffed in renewed frustration. "Bottom line, she's ridiculous and fake and no one will tell her because it might break her sensitive psyche. Unlike the way she breaks my sister's." He regarded Tessa's face, wanting to see that she understood, that she might be on his side.

Her face gave away nothing. She took a bite of her pretzel then turned in her chair to angle toward the play area, looking over at Leah.

He began gathering his garbage as a rush of thoughts on how to make a cordial exit played out in his head. For a brief moment he considered saying, "Well it's been lovely hearing all about your fabulous dad—in comparison to my perverted father—but now it's time to get Leah home for bed."

But he said nothing. Instead, he watched Tessa wash down her bite with a long sip of her drink while she continued to watch over Leah.

"Did I say something wrong?" He pulled at his hoodie string. "I enjoyed your story. It's just not *my* story, is all."

She angled her body back to him. "No, no, I'm sorry. I faded into my own thoughts for a minute. I was thinking of something else, not about what you said. I was thinking about my sister." She grabbed her last pretzel bite, no cheese this time. "My mom says I wear my thoughts on the outside, I guess that's an example." As soon as she ate the bite there was another sudden silence between them.

A fresh, hot pretzel aroma domed the air with a strong waft. Behind Tessa, he could see the worker pulling a new batch of pretzels from the oven. Within seconds, a small line formed at their register.

Leah skipped up to the table, took a long swallow of her drink, and then with a smile and a wave she headed back out to the play area, her hair trailing behind her like flowing water.

Once she left, Tessa cleared her throat and said, "You know, I've been to places in the world where easily formed judgments have the ability to condemn a person to death. Most times, if the one judging would have known why a person does what they do they would judge quite differently."

From her last bite, there remained a little flake of salt stuck to her bottom lip. "You sound like a preacher," he said, wanting to reach and wipe the salt for her.

Tessa's face furrowed. She grabbed a napkin and wiped her mouth. Now the salt was gone, but her lips still held his attention. "I assume you do not mean that as a compliment?"

He didn't mean it as a compliment, but then again he didn't mean to say it at all. It slipped out while he was focused on her lips. He liked that she was talking again, but she was still making him defensive. As if he needed to justify hating his parents. "Are you trying to say I am unjustly judging my mother and father?"

"Sort of," she answered.

"So your bottom line is, I should not judge my mother while she tears my sister apart and that I should go on walks with my…," he fought the urge to say pervert. "…Dad."

"No, that's not what I mean at all. What I mean—"

"I'm confused." He cut her off. "When a criminal gets punished is that being judgmental? There was a guy on the news yesterday who kidnaped a girl, what about him? Should he be judged guilty?"

"I don't mean people shouldn't pay for their actions. I mean we should not hold it in our heart. It damages us." She shook her head as if to clear her thoughts. "Never mind. What I'm trying to say isn't coming out right. I only meant that your mom's heart might be what you could focus on. Underneath it all, I'm sure her motives are good. Maybe it's her delivery that's bad."

"And damaging," he added.

Tessa nodded in agreement. "That, I am sure, is true. Kids don't get to escape the damage a parent can do."

His phone vibrated in his pocket. He was with two of the four people who would contact him.

When he looked, his screen showed one email notification.

He opened the main mailbox and saw the title "Gotcha," in the subject line. It was what he programmed for the alert email, for when the hidden camera was tripped.

He had the rat. He definitely had him!

His mind snagged on a fact. Wasn't the rat at church? As fast as his hope rose it sank. It must be a mistake.

He called to Leah. "Leah, we gotta go."

"I've upset you, haven't I?" Tessa reached and placed her hand on his. It sent a jolt through his arm, warming it up to his shoulder. "I may be a world traveler but I have the hardest time relating to Americans. I'm sorry. I only wanted to share good things; a little bit of hope is all. That's what I'm used to doing. It's what my dad does well."

He wasn't sure it if was her hand softening his demeanor or the way she looked at him, her eyes pleading for him to believe in human redemption, but something cracked inside of him. A small fissure of longing.

"Why did you pick me?" he asked, knowing this girl, this literal stranger, was both amplifying and agitating parts of him he didn't want to feel. "The other day at Maria's. Why me?"

With their eyes locked, her innocence glaring against his hardened heart, he realized, in the long run, he was going to taint her—stain her with his crappy life like a smear of blood on a white cloth.

She smirked, and it seemed to reach up into her eyes. "I told you, I can spot strange." She gave his hand a gentle squeeze. "I've learned that those who like to gather in cliques and groups are not usually loyal, and those who stand outside of the groups tend to be very loyal. It's the same all over the world."

"Maybe those outside the circles are just rejects," he said, realizing now that he has tasted the feeling of not being alone he didn't want to go back.

"Rejects are the most loyal of all," she retorted, grabbing her garbage and placing it on the tray. He hurried to take the tray while she gathered her shopping bags from the extra chair, thinking, maybe rejects are the most loyal of all because they get hooked and don't want to let go. Though, he wasn't sure if that was loyalty or addiction.

Contessa went to retrieve Leah while he dumped their stuff in the garbage.

Benji
Twenty Two

Benji raced the fifteen-minute ride home, his adrenaline pumping so hard he felt it pulsing in his fingertips.

"I should have gone pee," Leah said five minutes into the ride.

"Can you make it?" Benji glanced at her in the rearview mirror, inspecting her face for how badly she needed to use the bathroom, hoping he wouldn't need to stop.

"I think so," she said, bopping her head in time to the music on the radio.

When they walked in the door, Benji wished he had taken his time and stopped to let her go to the bathroom, especially since there was no way to go get the memory card much less see what he caught. He hadn't saved time. Instead, he had added more temple throbbing minutes of waiting.

While Leah made a beeline for the bathroom, Benji sat down on the foyer bench to take a breath, his shoes off, and to reel in his thoughts.

At the mall, the three of them had waited outside for Contessa's dad to pull up. They made a quick introduction of Leah, who later said he looked like a surfer guy with is curly blond hair, and then Tessa was off again, pulling part of his being with her like a magnet. He could physically feel it sucking out of him as they drove away.

137

Tessa had seemed fine while they walked out of the mall, so he guessed he hadn't made her too mad with his ranting. She had thanked him for carrying her bags while Leah chirped, "I'm so happy you invited me, Benji. And I'm so happy to meet you, Tessa. When will we see you again? Do you go to the same school as my brother?"

In the living room, as if he never left, Rat was in his chair. The relaxed state of his demeanor made Benji wonder if something else might have tripped the camera. The Fake was across the room in the other chair, her legs tucked to the side in the chair and a steaming cup of what must be tea sat on the end table next to her. Her sharp nose held up reading glasses and in her hands was a book titled, "Healthy Dieting for Kids." The title made his neck muscles snap rigid. The book was the equivalent of a gavel smacking down judgment on Leah. As if Leah was made up of her number on a scale rather than a complete being, full of ideas and creativity and kindness.

"We're home," Benji announced through teeth as Leah bounced into the room with a bag from the jewelry store.

Leah went straight to Fake's side and pulled out the headbands he bought her. "This one I got because the color goes with my school colors. See," she slipped the blue and white headband onto her head, pulling all of her hair back from her face. "And this one Tessa said matched my personality," she smiled as she said it. That one's band was a mosaic of pink and orange rhinestones and faux glass pieces. It was indeed a match to Leah.

The Fake's lip quivered at the sight of it. Benji was quite sure she thought it was gaudy.

"And this one I think makes my face look skinny. Don't you think, mama?" Leah said. She slipped off the Blue one and put on the wider, leather headband.

Camille gave Leah one of her patented "that's nice dear," smiles and said, "I sure do like that one. It *is* a good choice for your face." Then she asked, "Who is Tessa? Is she a friend?"

Leah put her first two headbands back into the plastic bag. "Yeah, she's Benji's new friend. She's new here and she can really sing, Mama. I mean like a superstar can sing. And she is sooooo nice."

Their dad removed his eyes from the television to join his mother in looking at him.

Fake grimaced. "It's yes, not "yeah." And don't ramble, Button, it makes you seem pretentious." Looking at him over the top of her reading glasses she added, "And I was asking Benjamin."

"She's my friend. She's new here and she can really sing," he repeated.

The Fake snaked her feet out from the chair and placed them flat on the floor as if ready to stand. "It's not necessary for you to get smart, Benjamin," she snapped.

Leah's eyes jetted around the room, trying to avoid everyone's faces and sharp looks.

"Right. So unnecessary," Benji said.

Camille whipped off her glasses and tossed them onto the end table next to her steaming cup and stood up. "You know, I had such an enjoyable time with the ladies tonight and I come home and in one conversation you manage to ruin my whole day."

"*Yeah*. I ruined *your* day." Benji twisted on his heel and headed for the stairs. Behind him, he could hear Leah ramble without pause about her headbands and knew she was nervous from the tension.

From the top of the stairs, he heard Rat "oohing" about how pretty Leah looked in "that one." Who knows which one he was talking about but Benji was quite sure it was the opposite of the one the fake liked.

Before going upstairs Benji intended to work the conversation to see whether his father stayed home from church or not, but his mother's caked face and frozen words had gotten the best of him. Only after a long, hot shower and some heavy thinking about Tessa's dad's story did the Fake's words melt away.

With a few hours to go, Benji grabbed his tablet, climbed into bed, and finished his search of Mongolia. Travel images from the other night popped up again, along with maps and travel agencies all promising amazing tours of the most "undiscovered land in Asia."

He took a few more mental notes on Mongolia then Googled "United Nations employment." Looking over the list of offices, he guessed from their extensive travels that Tessa's father might be a Field Officer or Field Inspector. Which would also match what she said about his "skills," being refocused, though he doubted it would be listed as a required qualification.

"Should I turn the light off?" Leah asked from the door.

He reached over and turned on the lamp next to the bed. "Yep."

Leah was dressed in her usual pajamas: a gray button flannel top and matching pants that were covered in white paisley print and small English style flowers. She looked vintage Betty Crocker. Leah likes to wear his t-shirts to bed, she calls them "Roomy and comfortable." But Camille enjoys beating down Leah's choice. "It's not lady like to dress in boy clothes," she'll say. Or, "One day your husband will thank me for making you wear nightly, feminine attire." One time, after Leah slipped into a new pair of pajama's she got for Christmas, the Fake quoted the Bible. "Train up a child in the way he should go and when he is old, he will not depart from it." Benji had thought, if she were going to try to train her into some old fashioned fifties style wife, she could at least allow her to pick out colorful pajamas. Maybe something with a little orange or pink, or maybe gold. At least those are closer to Leah's personality rather than the grays and tans their mother requires.

"Did you enjoy yourself at the mall?" he asked as Leah tapped her pillow, fluffing it, and then climbed under her blanket.

"Yes, I really, really did. Tessa is a lot of fun. Do you like her?"

"Of course I like her."

"No silly, I mean, like her *girlfriend* like her?"

A little puff of spearmint hit his nose from her brushed teeth.

He knew what she meant, but the question caused a sudden parching in his throat. "We're only friends." He fluffed his pillow, too.

She snuggled down into her's, facing him. One hand tucked under the pillow and with the other she reached and laid it on his forearm. "I think she likes you." She yawned.

"What makes you say that?"

"I just do. Girls know these things."

He leaned down and kissed her on the cheek. She leaned in and hugged him tight.

"Night," she said.

"Night," he said as she turned away from him, cocooning into her covers, pulling them up as high as her ear.

From under the fuzzy material her voice, raspy and heavy with sleep, said, "Benji."

"Yes."

"What does preee...," she paused, releasing a big yawn. "The thing that mommy called me, what does it mean?"

He knew she meant, "Pretentious."

He lied, "She meant that you were acting shy. Now, go to sleep. It's late."

Silence said she was on her way.

Benji
Twenty Three

It was midnight when Benji stopped surfing about Mongolia, Indonesia, and U.N. Jobs and opened up the Blue Barbie file to scroll through its contents and split them into smaller subfolders: Texts. Emails. Address book. Social media. Passwords.

He still needed to retrieve the video card from the basement, but the last time he stuck his head out to listen down the hall, Rat was in the shower.

He already debated through different excuses to go down and bring it up to his room to view, but he axed the idea in case Leah woke while he watched.

No, watching in the bathroom would be safer; he settled. Especially after last year when, with his tablet in his lap in bed, he had pulled up a porn video and only a minute into the video Leah opened the door to his room. In his shock, he shoved the tablet off his lap and off the side of the bed onto the floor. It paused the video and landed face up on a zoomed in picture of a woman's breast.

While his sister asked from the door whether he could drive her to school for the pumpkin picking field trip, the two spotlight breasts continuously glared up at him like a condemning beacon.

That moment, his sister at the door and those spot-light breasts, had slammed the door on porn. At least he assumes so because he hasn't had the urge to surf ever since. Besides, the Rat uses porn all the time and there was no way he was going to be like him.

Benji powered down his tablet and set it on the charger. He would need a full charge to…

Oh god!

Benji began to pace, the moon making his lengthy shadow follow him on the wall like a stalking black panther.

In all of his planning and preparation, he never truly absorbed how he would need to verify that he caught the rat in the act.

How would he not gouge his own eyes out?

Tessa

After a fashion show of the clothes Tessa bought at the mall, and a scroll through all of the pictures she took, introducing Leah and Benji to her family through images, she, Marula and their mother sat at the island. Underneath Tessa's hand was a green, feather-printed kitchen towel and next to her was a freshly mixed bottle of henna. Marula was busy asking about Benji and Leah while painting delicate designs on Tessa's forearm.

"He looks like a teenage version of Jude Law," Marula said, making an intricate swirl that tickled the bone on Tessa's wrist.

"Oh, gosh, yes! I couldn't figure out who he reminded me of, but that's exactly it. He's a younger, shyer, version of Jude Law."

"Is he from Ann Arbor?" their mother asked. She leaned on the island, half her torso stretched across on the opposite side of Tessa and Marula. One of their grandmother's orange coffee cups sat next to her, the coffee inside making twirling, angry steam. Mikael would reheat the coffee at least one more time before she finished drinking it.

"I didn't ask him but I'm sure he is. If not, he's been here a long time. He is very nice. He even offered to carry my bags for me."

Mikael snickered. "And did you let him?"

"Actually, I did."

Marula continued a long tickling stroke with the brush, asking, "What? You let someone be chivalrous? I can't believe it."

"Me neither," said their mom.

"Well, we were in a deep conversation and I didn't want to make him feel any further...will you add a tail to that part," she said pointing to the wisp that Marula just finished, "uncomfortable."

Benji
Twenty Four

With the micro card tight in one hand and his tablet gripped in the other, Benji headed back upstairs to the bathroom.

Sitting on the ledge of the bathtub, thankful for its coolness, he set his tablet on his shaking knees and wrung his hands together, trying to get the tingling feeling to go away.

He fed the card into the slot on the back and then turn down both the volume and the brightness so it was only a dull glow on the screen. He wasn't sure if a darker screen would help his sick sensation, but he knew he didn't want to hear anything.

Hesitating, his hand quaked over the play button. He tried to push his mind to touch the icon, but a sense of something shredding him from the inside out ached in the middle of his chest. It hurt worse than when he confirmed it was his father that was the lollipop-for-alcohol guy. It was a sense that he was going to a place he might not be able to come back from. As if he was about to release a monster. The sort of monster that lived under your bed when you're a little kid. The one that makes you pull covers up close to your face as if the covers are your protector. Here he was, face-to-face with his bed monster, and it turns out he was real all along. Benji wasn't sure if he wanted to release the monster, much less face him. A sudden feeling of being trapped inside a glass cage jolted his heart rate to an out-of-control level. He could not get his breathing to slow down or his knees to stop shaking.

He forced the memory of his dad in Leah's room to surface; the Rat's white thighs bare and hairy, the look of shock on his face when Benji charged at him. He pulled up the memory of when he thought his father was a superhero because he'd run around the yard with Leah lifted high over his head like she was flying. Leah's giggles were like bursts of effervescent sounds the entire time. He remembered when Rat was at his sixth-grade teacher conferences and said to the teacher, "Benji is brighter and smarter than I ever was at his age."

"For Leah. I can do this for Leah," Benji hissed through gritted teeth.

Steeling his resolve, he touched the play button. The screen had gone dark but now it lit up again, ready to show its contents. It started out grainy, like an old VHS tape rather than modern high-tech equipment. A minute in, the grain disappeared and he could see a glow emanating from the left side of the image. He assumed it was the TV. There was movement, and the angle the camera caught was lower waist and elbow height, but the image that finally settled fully across the screen was half of a back and part of his dad's arm; his elbow, in fact. It was as if they had moved into the camera's range but too close.

The back of the T-shirt was the only evidence that it was his father. It was his red shirt from their trip to Mackinaw Island two summers ago, the one with bleach stained streaks just below the waist.

Stains that happened after Rat leaned against the kitchen counter, not knowing moments before the Fake had sprayed it with bleach. He had growled that it was his favorite T-shirt and that she should learn to hang a sign or something. To which she retorted that a bleached counter was not something you hang a sign on like a wet bench and that it was an "old rag of the shirt anyway."

For a moment, while Benji watched his father's elbow pivot back and forth and wondered if his dad was flying solo. He closed his eyes, afraid of the scar it would gouge inside of him to both see and hear his father, then he turned up the volume. Three seconds worth of sound was all it took. He hurriedly turned it back down, fighting the pull of a gag that formed in the back of his throat. His dad was definitely not alone.

"Sick bastard," Benji spit.

For the remaining three minutes of the video, Benji rotated between counting tiles on the floor and quick glances at the image of his dad's back and elbow. His breathing finally slowed. His heart rate no longer throbbed inside his head. But only seconds of calm went by before another crushing realization set in: he had sat perched, back stiff, resolved and steeled on the cold hard bathtub ledge, suffering through what he thought would be the most traumatizing image he would ever encounter, only to realize he hadn't even caught the rat.

A tear dropped onto the tablet screen when the video ended, leaving him with a blank screen and a complete feeling of defeat. With the back of his hand, he wiped the salty taste from his lips, not remembering at what point he started crying.

Sliding down off the edge of the bathtub to the floor, Benji shoved his tablet across the cold tile toward the sink. It hit the cabinet with a thud. His face sunk into his hands and he let the tears come in waves.

He wasn't sure what time it was when he lifted his head, stood to his feet, grabbed his tablet from the floor and left the bathroom. He was all cried out and now had the worst headache.

Since he soaked his shirt with tears and his sleeve with snot, he took it off and tossed it in the laundry then grabbed a new one before heading back to the basement. Along with some Aspirin and a glass of milk.

Benji stood in the basement, freely able to be caught, and erased the data off the card. When it finished and was blank again, he slipped the card back into the electrical socket, adjusted the camera lens to a wider angle, hit the lights and went back upstairs. He didn't go to his room, instead, he went to the couch, pulled the blanket off the back, curled up on his side and stayed there until noises from upstairs and peeks of sunlight through the blinds woke him.

Benji
Twenty Five

Thankful it was only a half day at school, Benji slid off the couch and headed for the bathroom. Camille, in a bathrobe her hair up in a towel and a cup of coffee in her hand, spoke into her Bluetooth as she passed him. "Oh Julie, I completely understand if you need to take a day, no problem. Be with your family. Family first, I always say." Her syrupy tone alone made him want to smack the coffee out of her hand.

In the mirror, he pressed on his full, aching sinuses and opened and closed his mouth, stretching his jaw. Crying was supposed to be a good thing. "A good cry cleanses the soul," he heard once at church. He disagreed. Especially now. Last night's video endeavor had been grueling. The waves of emotions had raged against his psyche like a battering ram. But it seemed the crying took just as much of a toll as the watching. His eyelids were swollen, his mouth was so dry he must have slept with it open, and his head hurt more than his stomach.

In the shower mirror, he inspected the red webbing of veins in the whites of his eyes while he shaved and made plans to come home after school and sleep. It took the entire hot water tank before his sinuses loosened, and still it was another five blows into a tissue before he could breathe again.

He wasn't ready when his phone vibrated against the bathroom wall. Peeking from behind the shower curtain, he realized he had laid it on the back of the toilet and its hard case corner was touching the wall. "Bzzzzz, bzzzzz, bzzzzz," the phone announced a second set of three vibrations. The very vibration sequence he set last night for Tessa while waiting for his dad to head to bed.

Benji hurried and grabbed his towel from the hook. Sitting on the toilet lid he read:

Tessa: Any plans today? Do you have to work?

Benji: School. Then work at 5.

Tessa: Want to do some "us" plans after school?

Benji: Sure

Tessa: GREAT! Evil conspiracy plans to be announced at school! See you at the front door for scheming.

"Us," plans he said to the bathroom walls. Life suddenly felt like a practical joke.

If there was a God watching out up there, molding and weaving His will into people's lives, He sure had odd timing. Though, Benji would have to admit, Tessa was a nice spark of happiness right smack dab in the middle of his hell life.

Revenge Chronicle: Snot and Sneezing
Revenge Risk: Easy
Revenge Date: January 13ᵗʰ, 2012
Chronicle Entry Date: January 21ˢᵗ, 2012

Chronicle, it was childish yet fruitful, but a great way to start the new year.*Can you hear my evil cackle?* Though, now that I'm thinking about it I could have done this scheme as a science experiment. *I just heard the Frankenstein movie quote, "It's alive!" in my head.*

So it went like this: My teacher was sick, very sick. Snot filled head, congested cough, and, yet, she still came to school. Lucky for my class full of kids, and lucky for me she managed to leave her trash can full of her tissues. So nasty!!! But on my way out of last hour—lingering longer so I was the last kid in the room—I gathered a few of her tissues in a plastic bag. (I used the plastic bag as my hand so I didn't have to touch them). How I managed not to gag is beyond me. Oh, and, I didn't particularly relish the idea of wiping the snot-filled tissue all over my parents toothbrushes, but the thought of this stupid stunt working gave me strength so I managed.

Presto! As if they were magic germs my mom and dad were both sick within two days. Though, it hit my mom harder than my dad and I wish it would have been the other way around. They stayed quarantined in their bedroom for four days, leaving it just me and Leah. And we had a blast! We ate delivery pizza, made ice cream sundaes, watched movies, even went down to the hill to sled all four days. We still did our normal household responsibilities, but it was nice to get a break from the fault finding twosome of Bob and Camille.

only 150 more days till summer vacation!!!!

Benji
Twenty Six

"Do you hear that?" Tessa rubbed her abdomen in small circles. They were standing inside the door of the front entry way of Benji's house. He tried not to gawk with awe as the afternoon sun shimmered off the black ribbons that hung throughout her hair and down over her shoulders. The ribbon mixed among her curls and waves like dark highlights.

Her father dropped her off, and Benji had been waiting, watching out the window in order to get to the door before she rang the bell. Now that she was inside, she didn't seem in a hurry to get back outside. Unlike him.

He shook his head "no," at her question.

Tessa cocked her head to the side. Her hand paused on her stomach. "You don't take hints, do you? That's my stomach complaining of hunger."

"Oh," he said.

"Is Leah here? Does she want to go with us?"

He started to say she was still at school, but the tight pitch of his mom's voice echoed from down the hall. "Oh, hiiiiii," she crowed, using the same high, falsetto tone she uses with her church friends. Walking toward them she glanced back and forth between him and Tessa. "And who might this be?" she asked, her eye contact direct on him, burning a silent hole through his head for not willingly introducing her to the guest at the door.

Benji took a second to inhale through his nose before speaking. When he finally did, it still sounded as irritated as he felt. "This is Contessa. Contessa, this is my mom, Mrs. Lockwood. We are heading out to eat."

"How wonderful. You must be feeling better then." She looked at Tessa, sizing her up with a full body scan. "He gets these terrible stomach aches. Barely a day passes without one. Poor guy." She looked to Benji. "Are you going to Maria's? If so, will you please bring me a slice of pie?"

His mind was a rush of thoughts, and he could sense his face heat up, but all he said was, "pie?"

"Yes, pie, silly. Blueberry, if they have some. Hold on a sec." She turned and headed for the kitchen, her gray stretch pants ringing like a bell against her ankles as she walked. With her mustard colored ruched shirt, today she looked more like a summer squash than eggplant.

He surveyed Tessa, trying to read her face, but she looked the same as usual: curious and innocent.

"Hurry, let's go." He moved to open the door, putting his hand on her waist to move her along.

"Don't be rude Benjamin." Camille was back too fast and had heard him. He could tell by her pulsing jaw bone, she was crushing her teeth. Her makeup had caked in her frown lines throughout the day, amplifying her age another ten years. "I want to give you some money for my pie." She handed him a twenty dollar bill.

"Great. Thanks." He crumpled up the bill and shoved it in his pocket. "I'll leave your change on the table. I'll be back late."

Clasping her hands together, she tilted her head to the side, innocent and respectable looking. "Oh, no, that's for you to use. My treat, of course."

At that moment, Benji realized she not only changes her words and tones, but she's also a master at altering her body language as well. She could win Oscars with her acting skills. She's whole body fake.

He blew a huff through his nose and opened the door, grabbing Tessa's hand and pulling her along. "Bye," he said as flat as he could. He didn't want Tessa to fall for the garbage his mom was shoveling.

They arrived at his car before he realized he hadn't let go of her hand.

Contessa was interesting and captivating to watch and listen to. "Women are like tedious toddlers who won't shut up," Alex, one of Big Timmie's shop guys, said one day while slamming down the work phone, pissed off that his girlfriend called to yell at him while he was at work. He'd gone on for another five minutes about it until Timmie told him to, "put a cork in it." Based on the shop guys, overhearing guys at school, and Rat, Benji made an assumption that it would be a difficult task to carry on extended conversations with a girl. Contessa was the opposite of that assumption. Maybe it was only her. Maybe other girls were boring and droning when they talk. But even the way Tessa ordered her food was charming. She smiled at the server, added gregarious "pleases'," and, "thank you's," to her order, asked how the server's day had been, and showed a genuine appreciation for being waited on. When the server brought her drink, she paused her story about how a lot of other countries think America is a wasteful place.

"Thank you so very much," she addressed the server with direct eye contact and a grateful smile.

The server, who was maybe sixteen-years-old, spoke fast and had black hair and a short braid that sat on the collar of her purple button down shirt. Her wide smile crinkled the thick black eyeliner that dragged out to the edge of the creases of her eyelids, speaking volumes for her appreciation of Tessa's kindly manners.

When the server left, Tessa continued. "Other countries like the idea of America and its freedom of expression. But at the same time they also think American, Americans, are spoiled and arrogant acting. Though, each place has their particular likes and dislikes about the States. For instance, the kids in Australia are fascinated by American pop and rap music, it's the same for the kids in South Korea. But I don't know much about American music myself, so I never have anything to share." She squeezed the wedge of lemon into her water and stirred it with her straw.

"Didn't you have access to the internet?" He sipped his soda. "Can't you share that way?

"Most of the places we lived, I mean for any long period, were usually remote so if there was internet it was often too slow. Though, sometimes that's because the computers are outdated and not necessarily an internet problem. It's usually not worth waiting on, not unless you need something important, for instance with school work. Music, in particular, can take forever, so I hardly bother. My dad has a special phone with internet access for work, but, for us, sometimes there are weeks in between where there isn't any internet at all." She shrugged. "But we're used to it, it's normal for us, so I spend a lot of my time drawing the scenery or writing poems. Sometimes my sister and I makeup songs and walk around singing to the locals. Singing is the best icebreaker in every country."

He remembered her singing into the fake microphone in the store. "I've never thought of singing as an icebreaker but that's because I can't sing. Even if I could, I doubt I'd have the guts to do so to a stranger."

"Singing is a universal sound, regardless of language," she said. "You don't need guts to share that. Singing is like giving a person a gift, and it makes it easier, more comfortable, for them to invite you into their world when you give them a gift."

Her explanation made him want to ask her to sing again. He didn't. "Must be nice to have a life of diverse memories? I want to move away from here one day, but I've never thought of being able to move to places like the ones you've been. Colorado is the farthest I've come up with."

"It hasn't all been roses and happy times but being with my family makes it all okay. My parents say, "Family should be something you want to be around if they weren't your family," which means if they weren't my family would I want to be around them. You know, to be friends with them?" She pushed her sleeves up to her elbows, exposing a long henna design that wrapped down her forearm and ended at her inner wrist. "But my family is easy to love, and I think seeing how big the world is gives us a different perspective on life."

"How so?"

"I'm not sure I could explain it well, but whenever my sister and I come to the U.S. we both see glaring differences between us and other kids our age. I think maybe it's because of our experiences," she said. "One time, when we were in Indonesia, my sister and I were at the fruit stand getting things for travel, and while we were paying a car sped by. It was not a big car, only a small compact one, but it missed hitting us by inches." Tessa's face turned solemn, and she began to stir her water with the straw. "It missed us but it hit the boy standing next to us. Before we could begin to process what happened, his little body had already tumbled around like a broken toy and landed face down on the road. It didn't happen in slow motion the way people say, at least not for me. It happened so fast that I froze." He felt the urge to count the circles she made with her straw but stopped himself. "I was aware of the arguing in my mind but it seemed impossible. I mean, the boy just looked asleep, right there in the dirt, as if he decided he was tired and wanted to lay down next to the fruit stand. Except for the small trickle of blood from his ear and one leg bent unnaturally, it didn't strike me that's what death would look like. It was as if my brain couldn't sort out that he was dead. My dad has seen a lot of deaths, but he has always protected us from those parts of his job." She sighed. "For a year my sister would wake up at night in a sweat, screaming. Me too. It's been a few years and sometimes I still hear the mother of the boy screaming in my dreams. And there is always this image that replays in my mind, one of her holding the boy, rocking back and forth, making this strange crying sound. It was kind of guttural...her sound." Tessa regarded her drink. Her expression turned to realization as if finally noticing that she had been frantically stirring while she talked. "People shouldn't have to make those kinds of sounds."

Her eyes lifted to Benji. She let go of the straw and leaned back into the booth and sighed. "Sorry, I'm doing all of the talking. You talk now. Tell me all about living here and all the memories of growing up in one place. I bet you know where every treehouse is in this town."

He rubbed his hands together under the table. "I don't have many stories," he said. "I like your talking. Keep going."

"No tree houses?" she questioned, tilting her head like a bird.

"No, not for a long time. I tend to stick to myself."

"I noticed."

"Do you mind?"

"Nope." She shook her head. "Not at all. I'm sure I mentioned how I'm not very good at relating to

American kids. They confuse me. You don't, though. But you will tell me if I'm boring you, won't you?"

He wanted to tell her that he doesn't relate to American kids either, but instead he said, "I don't think you could be boring if you tried." His heart surprised him by pounding hard against his ribs. As if a blend of excitement and nerves had shocked it back to life.

"That is kind of you, but my sister would say otherwise." She let out a huff of air. It was partly a snicker and partly a sigh.

"How old is your sister?"

"She is a year younger. A sophomore. But if you saw her you wouldn't know she's my sister. I think our DNA was split in half from our parents. She looks like our dad, and I look like our mom. Her name is spelled M-a-r-u-l-a but pronounced Muh-roo-la. She's named after a tree in Botswana."

"You both have interesting names. You don't often hear of people named Contessa, either."

"True, but mine is after my great grandmother, and Marula's is after a tree. Kind of makes my name story boring." She chuckled. "My mom helped deliver her friend's baby boy under a Marula tree in Africa—he's nineteen now and going to college in England to be a doctor—but the story goes, her friend was too far into labor and didn't make it the rest of the way to the mid-nurse. She gave birth to Ebe, that's his name, on a blanket from the car under a Marula tree. My mom already loved the type of tree, but afterward she called the tree a

162

symbol of hope and survival."

"Did you see a lot of lions in Africa?"

Tessa gazed at him as if he insulted her. "It's been a while since we were there, and yes, I've seen a lion or two, but you do know not all of Africa is like a safari, right? It's quite diverse."

He shook his head. Not that he did or didn't know, he simply never thought about it before.

"The north, the central and the southern parts, like South Africa, are all very different," she said. "It is a big continent with lots of different countries. Morocco is nothing like Somalia or Kenya, no more than Italy is like Germany except they are on the same continent."

He felt bad, as if he insulted her favorite place, though, he wasn't sure exactly how.

"Am I on your American's are bad hit list now?" He shrugged and tried to smile against the tightness in his face.

"Yep, I'm a total hater now," she smirked. "No silly, I am American. Born right here in Michigan. When I say I don't relate, I mean I don't generally have much in common. I'm not used to it here. The United States is largely "I" oriented; all about themselves as individuals. The places I've lived are more "we" thinking. If that makes sense? Oh, and did I use the "hater" word correctly?"

"What?"

"The word "hater." I have a list of words my sister bet me I couldn't use in sentences within a week. If I use the word wrong, I lose."

"What's on the list? Maybe I can help you use the words up."

She inclined her head toward him, "I don't know if that makes it fair."

"Your sister wouldn't have to know."

"I can't lie to her," she said with a laugh as if it was the silliest thing she ever heard.

"Don't lie then. Just leave it out and clarify if whether it was against the rules at a later time." He grinned and shrugged his shoulders. "You know, after you win."

She laughed a good, loud, hard "tee-hee, tee-hee" kind of laugh, which sparked a snicker deep inside of his chest. When he released it, it sounded more like a frog croak than a laugh.

She pulled a napkin from the dispenser on the table, then pulled the same tiny silver pen from inside her shirt and started writing a list of words.

Swag

Hashtag

Hater

Nom Nom

Shawty

Digits

Diss

Deets

Snowpocalypse

As if his croak of a laugh hadn't been bad enough, with each word there was a swelling of another croak. As he read Snowpocalypse, he ruptured into laughter.

Tessa joined him; her snickering through funny gasps, him croaking like a frog.

When he caught his breath, he asked, "Where did you get this list?"

"Smack!" Two big hands slammed down onto their table. At the same time, a guy said, "Boo."

Benji started and choked on his laugh.

"Heeeey," Tessa said in a bent, dragged out tone, her eyebrows drawing together as she glared at the person.

It was Car Wash. He leaned onto his arms and hands on the table, his huge hands splaying out like leather baseball gloves.

"You scared us," she said, her tone flat, official though still formally polite.

"You're new here, aren't you?" he asked, not taking his eyes off Tessa.

Tessa scanned Car Wash for a few heartbeats, keeping steady eye contact with him. Benji got the impression she was reading him. "Yes, I'm Contessa. And you are?"

He lifted one hand and rubbed his chin before putting it back on the table. "I am Leo."

Contessa extended her hand, "Nice to meet you, Leo."

He glowered at her hand like he didn't understand. She pushed it at him all the more. Finally, he relented and shook her hand, which he did with a puff of air from his nostrils. Even while making introductions he behaves like a bull, Benji thought.

"So, Tessa—" he began.

"Contessa," she corrected.

He stared at her. She stared right back. "Contessa," he started again. "You guys seem to be having a fun time over here, but if you're done eating we...," he gestured toward the front doors with a head nod.

Benji turned to see what he was looking at. Blue Barbie and another girl sat amongst three other guys in the long booth in the center of the eatery. He'd been so focused on Tessa he never heard them come in. Normally he's a radar, ready to go to alert if necessary.

Car Wash continued, "...me and my friends are wondering why you're still sitting here?"

"I'm sorry," she said. "I don't understand?" Her drawn together eyebrows now lifted to furrow her forehead. It was a confused expression.

Benji blinked a long, hard blink. A sensation like someone was about to spit at him rose up. He leaned back into the booth and looked down—at nothing.

Car Wash snickered, glanced over at his friends and then back at Tessa. "I mean *you* should come join us." He emphasized the word singularly. "My friend Mike over there is wondering all about you."

Right then, Blue Barbie slinked her way up to Car Wash and stood tight to his side. In his peripheral, Benji saw her raise her hand and put it on his shoulder. He was sure she'd done so to give a subtle girl signal to Tessa. The signal warned, "Careful, this one is my claimed territory."

Benji was aware of his heartbeat inside his ears. He stole a peek at Tessa. Something in his stomach bit down. It was heartbreak taking its bite, eating his hope alive, and it would happen all while Car Wash watched. Acid washed the back of his throat. There would be no revenge to fix this feeling.

Understanding now, Tessa's eyes and face slackened and she said, "Oh."

Still squeezing his hands together under the table, Benji dug his feet into the floor. Making sure to be braced for the jarring impact of rejection.

Tessa leaned back and crossed her arms. "I see. Well, please tell him I'm sorry but I'm about to enjoy my dinner with Benji."

"With who?" He lifted a hand and pointed at Benji. "This guy?" Blue Barbie made a "tsk," sound through her teeth. "Right," Car Wash croaked and chuckled as if it was the most absurd thing he heard all day.

"I'm sorry, maybe I am misunderstanding you," Tessa glared at him with a seriousness that touched her whole face. "Was it your intent to insult who I choose to dine with in order to ask me to join you?" Without waiting for his answer, she looked at Benji. "Forgive him, Benji. Leo here must be tired from carrying all his heavy arrogance around." Then she scowled at Car Wash. Blue Barbie inhaled, shocked, and dropped her hand from his shoulder. Like an animal hit with a tranquilizer gun, Car Wash's eyes glazed over. He licked his lips as if he wanted to bite except he couldn't manage to get his mouth to open. Tessa leaned into the table, making sure she held Car Wash's full eye contact. "So, now that you've pulled out your man parts and compared, I'd say yours is much bigger. Thanks for the show and tell."

Benji managed to keep his lips together, but he felt the bottom half of his jaw slacken from shock. Car Wash stood back to his full height, which maybe it was the angle, but Benji realized they were about the same height. Benji might even have an inch on him. Car Wash shook his head in disbelief and popped his knuckles, causing Benji's fight or flight to kick into higher gear. He was ready. For what he didn't know, but he braced none the less.

To Benji's surprise, Car Wash smiled, did a slight bow, and then took a few steps back before grasping the hand of Blue Barbie and leaving. Actually walking away and heading back to their table.

"That was impressive," Benji said, simultaneously feeling elated and jealous, and like the smallest man on earth. Wishing he could dig his balls away from where they had wrenched close to his body, he sat back and probed the face of the fearless girl across from him. Tessa had broken the unwritten rules and Car Wash had respected her for it.

Benji
Twenty Seven

Tessa extended her arm across the table, reaching for his hand. "Benji," she said.

He blinked her back into the main focus of his attention, rather than the murmuring going on behind him.

"Are you okay?" she wiggled her fingers. "Give me your hand."

He lifted his hand and placed it in hers; he felt it throb from wringing it with his other one under the table.

Her hand was surprisingly cold, but the cool helped draw him out of his thoughts and back to her.

"You're not okay," she said. But it was more of a statement than a question.

"Just tell me about Africa," he said, yanking his hand away then scrubbing his fingers through his hair and over his face.

"New Zealand is my favorite place in the world," Tessa said, a slow, cautious tone lining her voice. "It rains a lot but when it stops there is no place like it, and the people are the friendliest and most welcoming in the world."

"Why me?" he blurted.

Meeting her eyes, he saw they were gentle and soft, and in the cafe lights he saw hues of yellow rather than the greens that shown in sunlight. "I need to ask," he said rubbing his chin, feeling the stubble from skipping a shave this morning. "Why did you choose me?"

"I told you. I like the people who are different." She said it as if it was a hard fact. But it was a fact he didn't understand. She must have some intention, some string attached that would eventually reveal itself.

She bowed her head and looked at him through the tops of her eyes. It reminded him of the way a teacher looks when they want to make sure they have your attention. "You don't have any other friends do you?"

He sighed. "No." Might as well face it now. That way she can head off with Car Wash. Rip off the Band-Aid quickly, he thought.

"I figured it out the moment I found you counting your ketchup circles. And I knew for sure after the first day of school. Plus, you never talk about anyone else."

"Then why are you here? With me. Right now."

"Look, if you want to insult me this would be the way," she said, but her crooked grin showed she wasn't insulted. "By watching others I've learned to choose friends wisely and I could see who you were the first moment I spotted you. I wasn't sure if you needed or even wanted a friend, but I needed one. My family will be staying here longer than we've ever stayed in the States and I know how important having someone can be."

"But I'm a no one." He choked out the words. "And you're so comfortable being…," he waited, searching for the word, only to say, "Different."

"Now you've moved to complimenting me." She grinned with her whole face; even her ears and nose got in on the action. "I'm different in some ways, mostly because my perspective is that it's a very big world, but in other ways I'm not so different. I am made up of the places I come from, which happens to be everywhere, and most who live here are made up of where they're from, which is probably here. Even you. I've seen enough social groups to understand they form the same everywhere. And for me, I've figured out that groups like that guy's," she flipped her eyes toward the group at the table, "they aren't how I want to spend my life journey. I don't hold anything against them; they do what they need to do to fit in, to hide their pain and insecurities like everyone else." She shrugged. "I don't like to hide mine, is all."

"Nothing about you seems insecure." Benji heard light laughing and shuffling behind him and wanted to look, but he didn't dare turn around. He pulled his hoodie up over his head, rubbed the top of it against his hair, then slouched down into the booth, forcing his long legs to relax and spread out under the table.

"Oh, I have my insecurities. You stay on the lookout. They always pop up and embarrass me when I least expect it." She narrowed her eyes as if she were focusing in on something. "Though, I think maybe the difference you see is that I don't mind mine. I sort of accept them, even make fun of them, and I believe most people try to hide or over compensate for theirs. That's something my mom embodies: embracing your faults but staying focused on your good parts."

Looking into her eyes, seeing their inspiring sparkle, and the way she wanted to infuse him with a type of redeeming hope, he pushed his hoodie back off his head. "I had friends. Before, I mean. Some moved away, and others faded away."

She made an expression that was one part "duh" and the other part eager. "And you never wanted more?"

"I'm not sure what happened. I guess I've grown used to being alone." He wanted to spit out the real words, the true words crowding his mouth: *Because high school is jacked, and my family is made up of a pervert and a fake, and I don't think anyone would want an inside view of my crazy.* But he didn't.

"When I say I have a thing for strange, in you, what I saw was that even if you were alone you haven't changed your main identity to fit in. The pressure to do so is everywhere, but you hadn't. That's how I see people. If you ended up strange, and we shared nothing in common, it meant that no matter what you'd be you. The real you. I aspire to be the same."

"You give me too much credit. I often wonder what I could do to fit in better, even got an account online with a made-up identity to try to…" he trailed off, realizing he was saying too much.

"But you haven't. Even if you wanted to you didn't, and that's the part I see." Her smile was gentle, affirming.

He felt a swell inside. One that wanted to tell her all his dark secrets. One that wanted to confess, to show her how wrong she was. Instead, he turned to looked for the group. They had left the cafe. Only a lady with her two kids and a guy in a baseball cap bent over scarfing his dressing-drenched salad as if it were his last meal, were left.

As he turned back, the server pulled up a shiny metal food cart—saving him from having to say anything more—and began placing plates on the table. One large Hawaiian style pizza pie in the middle, a basket of breadsticks with garlic butter dipping sauce, and two small plates of fries. A true, "Welcome to America," meal.

He waited for Tessa to take the first slice before taking one for himself. The cheese stuck together in a rather commercial worthy way as he slid the giant slice onto his plate. He wanted to use his fingers to break it apart, but he didn't want to appear as if he was without manners so he grabbed the butter knife that looked twenty years old and cut through the stuck cheese; glad, for once, he had listened to his mom's years of demands for "manners at the table."

He folded the pizza slice New York style and took a smaller bite than he normally would. Tessa took a knife and fork and cut her pizza into small fork-able pieces. She noticed him watching right as she was about to eat a piece dangling from the tongs of her fork. His face must have spoken something he hadn't realized it was saying.

"In Europe they eat pizza with a knife and fork," she said, taking a bite and then tilting her head back as if relaxing. Her eyes closed. A low, "mmmm," hummed from her throat. Benji watched her chew. Never had he seen someone eat something with such appreciation. He now understood the point of women and food being paired together as sexy.

"I have to remember to bring my sister a slice." She forked and bit another piece. "Pizza is our favorite. No one does pizza this way. Not even Italy."

"Really? They should be great at pizza, you know, Italian and all."

"They do make good pizza, artisan pizzas, but no one does pizza like this." She regarded the pizza pie as if admiring a work of art in a museum. Her neck stretched so her nose could receive the fullness of the aroma rising from the table.

"Maria, the owner, is a Brooklyn native and she brought New York style pizza making with her. So it's true, no one else does pizza like this. At least not in our town."

"I already like this Maria," Tessa said, snapping her mouth underneath at a piece of dangling cheese on the fork, trying to catch it with her lips. Her lack of fear for looking ridiculous made him smile.

"Ever had Chicago style pizza?" he asked, thinking of a place downtown by U of M campus where he took Leah for lunch on her birthday last year.

"I've been to Chicago a few times, but always as a stopover on the way to somewhere else so we've never had the time to try their pizza. The crust is thicker, right?"

"Yeah, with the sauce on top of the cheese." He picked up a fry. "We could go sometime."

"To Chicago?"

"No, I mean here. There's a place downtown that makes Chicago style pizza. I can take you there, you know, for "nom nom." He pointed to the napkin of words she was supposed to use in a sentence.

"Oh." She giggled and gave him a thumbs up. "That would be great, you know, to go get some nom nom's." She took a drink of her water, wiped her mouth and then added, "Could we bring my sister? She loves pizza as much as I do."

"Sure. And maybe Leah."

"Oh, yes, bring Leah! Marula will love her." She stabbed another piece of pizza with her fork. A hunk of pineapple toppled back off onto her plate before she could get it to her mouth. "Slippery sucker," she said picking up the stray pineapple with her fingers and popping it into her mouth.

Benji
Twenty Eight

Benji wondered if maybe it was just him, but the air in Maria's seemed lighter after his table of nemeses left. Even the servers seemed to smile a brighter and walk a bit lighter.

"And who is this with my quiet boy who loves my apple pie?" Maria, the owner asked, coming to the table to say hello.

Tessa shook Maria's hand and made her introduction like a diplomat. Then she gushed with compliments about Maria's "fantastic tasting food!" She even asked about the seasonings on the fries and complimented the authentic Italian decor. All of it making Maria's aged, moist eyes look as if she is about to cry with joy. The wrinkles around Maria's eyes and a tuft of white in her black hair, right above her forehead as if a big drop of bleach accidentally landed there, were the only things that showed her age.

After a few minutes of swapping information about what part of New York Maria was from—and how, coincidently, Tessa's Great Aunt, who they used to visit in Brooklyn but passed away from cancer two years ago, lived in the same neighborhood—Maria excused herself to go back to the kitchen, kissing Tessa's cheek beforehand and saying, "These kids of mine would burn down the place if they didn't have me to teach them."

176

"How does your sister like living here, instead of all over the world?" Benji asked after Maria left, committed to sparking the conversation again. Either he was a complete moron, mesmerized by the first girl who would pay any attention to him or all those other guys were idiots for not knowing someone like Tessa.

But the change in Tessa's face surprised him. Her eyebrows hung deeper than before and her mouth turned down. A section of her cheek sucked in and he wondered if she was biting it on the inside. After a few uncomfortable seconds, she said, "Marula is having a rough time."

He was instantly confused, unsure whether he should pry further or leave it alone. Torn, he chose what he thought would be a safe question. "Did she like living in all of those places? I mean, as much as you?"

"Yes, for the most part, she does." Her eyes darkened, their color turning from tones of yellow to sallow. "Or, she used to. Now she's not sure of anything."

"I'm sorry," he said, still confused by her expression and tone.

She set her fork down on her plate and sat back against the seat. He knew he caused the sudden distant look that took over her eyes, but he had no idea how. A quick, uncomfortable feeling filled the space between them. She pulled her hair up high behind her head and ruffled it. It fell back down in a long cascade of waves and curls over her shoulders and into her lap. She took what he thought was a piece of material for a necklace, untied it from

177

around her neck and then pulled it up over her hair and off her face like a headband. She re-tied a simple knot on the side over her ears and dropped her hands into her lap with a sigh.

Now he could discover every inch of her face: The dimple in her chin, the way her hairline made a small widows peak on her forehead, even her pointy ears were exposed. Her earring holes, all five of them, didn't have normal earrings in them, instead there were little strings that looked like twine pulled through each one, and each was tied into a tiny bow that hung on the bottom. He had never seen anything like them. They were intricate, and something Leah would have loved to learn how to do.

"We came here to stay for a while for my sister," she said reconnecting with his eyes. "So she can heal."

He hurried and chewed the bite in his mouth. Setting his slice down on his plate, he grabbed a napkin and wondered what she meant by "heal."

Still weighing how to move the conversation forward, he said, "You don't have to tell me anything you don't want, but I'd like you to." There it was, out, polite but pleading. He had showed her he cared.

"Oh, I know that already." She forced a smile but then her mouth dropped slack as if the smile were too heavy. "It's not that. I don't want my sister to feel betrayed, is all. She's not doing well right now and I can't add to that."

He was confused. "Who would I tell?"

"It's not a secret thing, it's a respect thing," she said. "I didn't mean you'd tell someone, I meant whether I should tell someone."

Once again, her goodness was glaring. She didn't want to betray her sister because she respected her sister, not because she was worried about someone gossiping. He swallowed the lump of guilty conscious in his throat. "Oh," was all he managed.

"See," she began. "There is this idea of my sister that I remember, and sometimes it's hard because that doesn't exist anymore. There are pieces of who my sister was, but they don't show up often anymore." She crossed her arms, bringing them to rest on her abdomen, one set on top of the other in a type of self-hug. "When they do, it makes me miss her all the more."

"She sounds…," he paused, having no real idea of what he wanted to say.

Tessa filled in the space. "She's broken, Benji. Very broken."

Her eyes filled to a glassy shine. But she blinked fast, fighting the tears.

The pizza was getting cold right before them. Now it and the fries didn't seem as appealing as it had a few moments ago.

Tessa let go of herself, stiffened her posture, and then bent like a tipped straw closer into the table.

Benji copied her, leaning into the table between them.

Quietly she said, "My dad's best friend and longtime colleague was having sex with…," she swallowed, "molesting my sister. A relationship type of sex." She squeezed her eyes together as if to

179

further pull back their tears. "We found out a few months ago."

She sat upright in the booth, shoulders back, chin up, and her eyes dry. "There. I said it." She dredged in a breath then sighed. "Now I've betrayed her."

"I didn't mean to make you betray her." He heard the shake in his throat, but it wasn't from fear it was because they weren't supposed to have this in common. Not her. Not *her* sister. Not *his* sister.

Tessa's life had seemed so perfect. Perfect, loving family. A perfect world traveler who happens to like strange kids for friends. Utterly, jealously, perfect.

She got out of her side of the booth and slid into his side. He scooted over to give her more room. She angled to face him, drawing one knee up to prop on the booth. "No, no. That's not how I meant it, I promise. Remember that "relate" thing, it's just how I talk, and I forget that my inner thinking tends to display itself. I didn't mean the betrayal part toward you; I was speaking out loud to myself, about *me* betraying her." She leaned her elbow on the table and rested her head on her hand. With her head tilted like that, she appeared younger, more like Leah when she's worried about something. "My family hurts for my sister, and my sister is very confused right now. Victor, the guy, he was my dad's field partner, my dad trusted him with his life. We all trusted him."

The waitress approached the table. "Do you guys need anything? Is the pizza okay?"

"Oh, yes," Tessa said. "Thank you. I don't need anything." She looked to Benji. He shook his head no.

The server swept over the table with her eyes. Confusion was written all over her expression.

"We'll take it all home, don't worry," he said. An attempt to be nice but also to make her go away.

She did.

Tessa continued. "Everything that has happened has aged her. She was a normal girl a few years ago, strong minded in her beliefs, and a ball of sunshine whenever she walked into a room. She and Leah have that same quality." Her eyes dropped to stare at his pizza plate, or maybe it was through the plate. He assumed to a distant memory of her sister. "We were as close as sisters can be."

"What do you mean she has aged?" he asked, wanting to take her free hand into his. Instead, he grabbed his drink and took a sip.

Turning her body square with the table, she took a fry. They were hip to hip now, her looking down at the fry she held, him still looking at her. Him wishing she would turn back so he could read her eyes.

She pulled a small piece off of the fry and dropped it into a napkin. "She's sort of…addicted to Victor," she said, pulling another piece off the fry. It was getting smaller piece by piece. "He manipulated her with affection, made her feel like a grown woman, showered her with a love that isn't supposed to be felt until you're older. He also snuck her bits of alcohol and sometimes drugs to get her to have sex with him. He put it in her drinks at first, to soften her up so to speak, and she didn't know." She yanked the last of the fry in half then shrugged and dropped the last pieces onto the napkin. "It's all hard to explain, and we're still trying to understand the mechanics of the time frame, but over a short time it hooked her. He hooked her. She thinks she loves him."

Benji's eyes rounded; he felt their largeness and the strong wrinkle that formed in his forehead. He was stupefied. Tessa regarded him with another head slant, inspecting him. It made him hurry to try to fix his face. But it didn't work. "Hard to believe, right?" she asked, showing that she'd read him before he could display a softer expression.

He thought of his dad and all the girls. It *wasn't* so hard to believe. "It's not that," he said. "It's that you, your family, all seemed so perfect."

Her eyes bore into his and he knew that he said something wrong. Quickly, her face phased through a tangle of expressions: a partial frown, then squinting eyes and that sucked in cheek again, and then finally she set into a straight, flat face, no smile.

"Sorry, sorry," he stuttered. "I only meant that my family is crappy and you speak so highly of yours. Not that you aren't perfect. I mean, you look like the dream family, that's all."

"It's okay," she said, softening her features back to their normal, gentle appearance. "In terms of family, we are the best of all things. That's what makes it selfish and difficult for me. Victor shattered us." She sighed and picked up another fry.

"I want us back. I don't mean to make it about me, but I miss the old Marula."

"I'm sorry," he said again.

"I haven't talked to anyone about this, you're the first. Thanks for that." She demolished the second fry the way she had the first one.

"I don't know what to say," he said.

"I don't think there is anything anyone could say, so don't feel pressured. Your listening is a gift." Her half smile seemed more reactive than a genuine feeling as if she meant it but couldn't get past the painful thing she was talking about.

She moved out from his side of the booth and went back to her side. If he thought air and space could suck him in and over to her, he would let it. He would surrender and let it, as long as he could be closer to her. Never in his life had he experienced such a pull to a person. It was exciting and terrifying all at the same time.

The server showed up as Tessa sat back down. She must have been waiting because the timing was too perfect. "If you want, I can heat that back up for you? A quick pop in the oven, and voila, hot pizza again."

Tessa lifted her eyes to the server. "You know...if I could have you heat a slice that would be wonderful." She looked at him. "Benji?"

"Sure," he said. "A slice for me too, please. Can we have two boxes for the rest?"

"Absolutely," the server said grabbing the pizza platter and taking it with her. "Two hot slices coming up."

Tessa thanked her.

Benji scanned the cafe and realized there was only one person left—the salad guy though he was now onto a small pizza overflowing with sausage. He checked his watch. They had been there over an hour and he needed to get to work soon.

"Don't forget your mother's pie," Tessa said.

"Okay," he said. He wanted to forget about the Fake, but he wasn't about to show that to Tessa.

After the heaviness of information and the interruption of the server, he still wanted to talk but didn't know how to go about doing so. Tessa saved him from the burden. "You know, I guess I thought moving here would help my sister, but she seems to be warring even more."

"Warring?" he asked.

"Yes. Over who she is. She still loves him. It's hard for her to see him as an evil person the way we do. She misses him. She misses his attention. It's as if he cast a spell over her and she can't break loose. She knows what's right in her mind, logically, but the heart doesn't listen to logic and reason. It's a struggle every day because she has nowhere to go to escape from her pain. Nothing here is familiar, much less comforting."

"Can I ask how old Victor is?"

"He's forty-seven and looks a lot like Brad Pitt, except his hair is so dark brown it's almost black. Not that his looks matter in the grand scheme of things, he was still wrong." She fidgeted with the straw in her drink again. He realized she seemed to need something to touch while she talked. She had shredded the paper from her straw when she first sat down, and now she had shredded two fries and was picking at the edge of her straw with her fingernail. "You know what's hard? I could see it, or I guess my guts could discern it rather than a physical observation. I get my blindness for people's faults from my dad; he always sees the best in people. I guess that trait got in the way for both of us. My mom was the one who followed her instincts." She shook her head in disbelief. "I wish I had followed mine. We could have stopped it earlier."

"Don't blame yourself," he said, surprised at how much it tore him apart to realize she felt it was her fault. Though, he could relate. He felt it was his fault for his dad, too. It was why he wanted to catch him. Why his guilt drove him to plan the best revenge of all. He simply must make up for his guilt. *I have to...for Leah.*

"I know up here," she pointed to her head, "but like my sister, I can't help it in here." She lay her hand over her heart. "It's hard to realize that you don't know what evil looks like. It's not someone or something walking around exposing their evil, saying, "hey look at my evil right here on my sleeve." That would be too easy."

"Yeah, evil can appear pretty middle-class normal from the outside." His mind flashed to the video of his dad's arm dropping and his hand cupping the top of someone's head. His stomach cinched. It was bad timing since the server placed two hot plates of pizza down in front of them.

"I divided the pizza in half," she said putting two to-go boxes down on the table as well. "Hope that's okay?"

"That's wonderful." Tessa smiled as if nothing deep had been going on. "We also need a slice of blueberry pie to go."

"I'll get that ready. Do you want it heated up, too?"

Tessa looked at Benji.

"No thank you," he said.

The server nodded then left again. Tessa's face instantly returned to sad. "I've come to the conclusion that evil in its simplest form is really just selfishness," Tessa said lifting her pizza from the plate, no fork or knife this time. It drooped.

"Like this," he said, showing her how to fold the pizza slice in half. "That way the inner parts don't drop out."

She smiled and folded her slice over on itself. There it was. The bright teeth, the cheeks and the chin dimple. Benji's shoulders relaxed and he noticed his whole being loosen and calm. It was powerful, that smile.

"What was I saying?" She asked then took a bite so big her cheeks puffed out.

"About evil," he said, following her lead and taking an open-mouthed large bite himself.

"Mmmmm." She made the sound because she was chewing. After she swallowed, she said, "Oh yes, right. Evil is selfish. What I've come to realize is that evil is selfish because it's when someone wants what they want regardless of how it will affect the world or anyone around them. The other people are an afterthought, not a forethought."

He made a "humph," sound and said, "Makes sense to me." She had given a perfect description of

186

Rat Bastard. In fact, it was a great example of his mother too.

Benji
Twenty Nine

Friday afternoon there seemed no place for Benji to put his thoughts, they were consumed by Tessa: eating with Tessa…and talking with Tessa…and seeing Tessa smile…and when would he see Tessa again. He had spread his school books out on his desk, put on his headphones, and cued up "white noise" in order to wrangle his thoughts in and get what little homework he had finished. But the books only stared back at him. The words on the pages of his Government book looked like a jumble of black lines and repetitive images that wouldn't register familiarity in his brain.

"Blah, blah, blah," he said, slamming his book closed. He grabbed his phone and flopped down on his bed, wishing, for once, this wasn't a teacher's work day and that he had school instead of a day off.

Leah had school, and the Fake had to work, but Rat took the day off. While he and Tessa were at Maria's yesterday, the dryer burned out, and Rat needed to go to Lansing to get a new one. "I told you to clean out the vent after every load. You never listen," Benji heard him say to his mom when he came in the door last night. To which she'd replied, "Oh yes, it's me who caused this because we both know I was born to be your maid."

Tapping his finger rhythmically on the back of his phone, Benji studied Tessa's picture from the mall, willing the image to make him feel like he had at Maria's. The contrast between how he felt when he was with Tessa and how it felt when he was home was more striking than ever. The tension, the secrets, the sick and twisted blur of manic up and downs, it made the air in the house hardly breathable now. It was as if he was trying to take deep breaths but through a straw—there simply wasn't enough space within the negatives for breathable oxygen. Even getting ready for bed last night, his chest had felt tight and heavy. The only small, bursting relief was seeing Leah sound asleep and safe. He had climbed into bed, gently pulled her warm body closer into a hug and kissed her forehead. "I hope you were right about Tessa," he whispered into the darkness. Leah, the constant heavy sleeper didn't even stir, "Because I like her too."

"Benji! I need help!" Bob yelled from downstairs. It was already three thirty. He had been laying on his bed *still* thinking about Tessa.

As Rat tried to bear the weight of the dolly to get the dryer up the stairs to the second floor, he snapped, "Don't turn that way, damn it!" Benji pulled from above on the stairs while his father pushed from underneath, trying to lift the bottom of the dryer with a strap connected to the dolly.

"Why didn't you just get them to deliver it?" Benji snapped back. "This is ridiculous!"

Sweat began to bead on Rat's forehead from the strain of trying to lift the thing. Maybe he would have a heart attack. That would solve everything.

"You want to listen to your mother about waiting a week for this thing to get delivered? Pull to the left. *Your left*, not mine! You're going to hit…" he strained the words out, "the wall."

Too late. The dryer nicked the wall as Benji's left arm gave out under the strain.

"Damn it! I said your left!" Rat yelled.

Overtaking Benji's strength, a surge of angered adrenaline rushed through his muscles and he yanked the dryer and the dolly straight up the last three stairs, ignoring his father's yell as he raked the stairway wall with a half inch deep gouge.

Glaring at Rat from the top of the stairs, he waited for him to catch his breath and join him on the top stoop.

With a threatening scowl on his face, Benji wheeled the dryer down the hall to the laundry room: a single room next to the bathroom with enough space that it could be another bedroom.

Five minutes later Rat said, "Hand me the venting tube," while Benji watched him maneuver his way behind the dryer and try to squeeze himself and his protruding stomach between the wall and the machine.

"I could get back there, you know," Benji said, feeling a pop in his jaw socket. He had been crushing is teeth while standing by and watching Rat install the dryer.

Rat didn't answer, he merely, continuously mumbled about how stupid it was to have laundry areas on the top floor instead of the bottom. "Damn new construction, putting laundry on the top floor." "Why the hell doesn't that woman listen to me?" "Ouch! Shit! Turn, stupid screw."

"Can I go now?" Benji asked, raising his voice over the mumble of complaints.

Rat still didn't answer, so Benji headed down the hall to his room and plopped down on the bed, listening, in case his father called out. Everything about his father drove him insane. The way he switches between a passive voice and full vocal explosion in point five seconds. The way he walks as if he was a pious political leader adored by many. Even the way he smells like Old Spice mixed with peppermint gum drives him crazy.

Benji hardly remembers his early days anymore. The days when his father was someone to look up to, someone to admire and follow. He guesses if he thought hard enough, he could conjure up a memory or so of the two of them playing catch with a baseball in the front yard of the old house. "Excellent aim, kid," Rat had proclaimed. "Maybe you could join a team." Benji had played baseball for four years afterward, but lost interest before high school started.

He grabbed his phone and pulled up the picture of Leah and Tessa at the mall, contemplating at exactly what point he lost interest in baseball. He remembers pieces, small points of reference, such as being in the dugout and waiting for his turn to bat or polishing and perfecting his catch and fast release over and over during practice. He had been good at baseball, playing first base and shortstop for three seasons. But that was all before. Before finding out who and what Rat was. And during, when he caught him trying to climb into Leah's bed. It's those moments that are bigger now. Bigger than baseball, bigger than neighborhood barbecues, bigger than his six-grade Washington D.C. field trip and how much fun he had with his class. It's as if Rat's issues somehow flooded over the rest of the memories the way a giant wave wipes out a sand castle on the beach.

Turning his phone so the image of Tessa spun and became larger, he dragged his fingers apart. The image magnified, enlarging every part of Tessa's face. He could study her all day and still never find any detail of her boring. From her curls to the lines on her neck, every part of her made him want to trace it with his finger.

"Gotcha!" flashed on the phone screen over Tessa's enlarged face; his alert for Busting Balls.

"Crap," Benji shot up on the bed, listening for his father. Silence greeted him. Bob must have gone downstairs in the basement and tripped the camera.

Along with his pulse pounding in his ears he heard a door slam downstairs. "Benji!" Leah's voice called.

"Leah, why is it necessary to yell?" Camille snipped.

"Up here!" he yelled back, purposefully amplifying his voice louder than normal.

Moments later Leah came skipping into the room, her purple school folder in her hand. "Look," she thrust the folder Benji's direction.

He took it and patted the bed. She sat down.

He kissed the top of her head first and then opened the folder. Paper clipped to the stack of papers inside was a note: "Dear Mrs. and Mr. Lockwood," it began. "Leah is doing very well and is a joy to have in my class." Next to the hand written words written in red ink was a large A+.

"This is amazing! Great job!" He stood then snatched her up off the bed into a huge hug, wiggling her little body back and forth, her feet dangled side to side as he did. She giggled and threw her arms around his neck.

"I knew you'd be proud," she said nuzzling into the side of his face.

"I am soooo proud." He set her feet on the bed, so she stood almost eye to eye with him. "I'm always proud."

At that moment, looking into Leah's dancing eyes, he decided to forget about a Blue Barbie plan. He would free him and Leah and then he would close out this season of his life, along with anymore revenges.

Benji
Thirty

The voice on Benji's cell phone cracked and broke off after each sentence to take a gasp of crying breath.

"How many pictures are there?" he asked Tessa while looking at a magnet on the side of the refrigerator. Under the words, Toledo Zoo, there was a puffy polar bear next to a waterfall. A tiny replica of the polar bear exhibit at the zoo. He pulled it off and flipped it between his fingers.

"Quite a few but there's also two videos. Benji, they took a picture of her vomiting! With her own phone! And while she was bent over the toilet some guy was grinning into the camera and had his hands on her butt. His tongue was hanging out. Who does that? Why would they do that?" She gurgled the last part of her words in near hyperventilation and tears. "I had to go get her from off the lawn. Who does that?" she repeated. "Who dumps a human being on the lawn? In the cold!" Her voice heightened to a screech and then broke off into some sort of gasping, snot filled choke. He held the phone away from his ear when she blew her nose. She sounded like a baby elephant.

His guts felt like they would cave in on themselves when she switched to a softer cry. "Why would they do that to her? She's already broken, Benji. She's already hurting."

"I know. I'm sorry. I'm so sorry." His heart seemed to beat to the timing of her fast breathing. Speeding up and slowing down with her gasp and sobs. Everything in him wanted to jump through the phone and hold her. To turn back the clock so she wouldn't have to see the horror that people could be. He wanted to see her half smile and her hazel eyes look at him with that light of hope that seemed to dazzle underneath her expressions. She believed in people's redemption. She believed in the goodness of people, and he still wanted her too. The way Leah does. He wanted them both to keep that part of themselves. But, of course, the world would come along and steal it from Tessa, from her sister, and from Leah. He slammed his hand down on the counter, an involuntary reaction to his thoughts.

Benji stood in the kitchen but had awakened with a start by his phone ringing and Tessa's name across the screen. He half thought maybe she butt-dialed him, but it was five-thirty A.M., and unless she rolled onto her phone while sleeping, he realized there must be an emergency.

"I have to go wake my parents. They need to know," she said. He could hear her teeth chattering.

"Where are you?" he asked.

"In my gram's gazebo."

He closed his eyes and dredged in a breath. She was outside in the cold, shivering, crying and frustrated. All he wanted to do was get in his car and bring her a blanket.

"Maybe you should let her sleep it off, you know, and tell them later. After they wake up," he offered.

"I can't do that. They would want to know now, not tomorrow."

Once again, the contrast between her relationship with her parents and the lack of relationship with his was glaring. He bit his lip and thought things through.

"Okay. Where is Marula right now?"

He heard a sniffle and then quick, breathy inhales. On the final exhale, she sounded a bit more level. "She's in the front bathroom. I gave her a bowl and she curled up on the floor, on my gram's carpet."

"Can you put a blanket on her? Is she on her back or her side?"

"Yes to the blanket, and she's on her side." She started to cry again. "I've never seen her like this before. She wasn't even sure who I was."

He knew Marula had to be extremely drunk to not recognize her sister. "Go get a blanket and put it over her, and then go…," he swallowed and then made himself say the words, "go wake your parents."

"Okay," she said. "I'll call you later."

"Okay." He waited for her to hang up first. When she did, he stared at his phone, wishing he could teleport through it to her grandmother's house. Instead, he watched as the home screen went black.

Benji
Thirty One

Benji sat in the kitchen, his head on his arms on the table, face down, trying to review his camera plan for his dad. Except he couldn't think about the plan. Every time he thought of a camera his mind switched to Tessa saying there was a video of Marula, to the sound of Tessa shivering in the cold, and to Tessa wanting to tell her parents as if her parents would make things all better.

An hour later Tessa text him with an update.

Tessa: sitting with my sister while she sleeps. she looks peaceful. parents are sad. they are talking to Uncle Scooby.

Benji: k

Tessa: i have a favor to ask

Benji: k

Tessa: tell me a joke

He fixed his gaze on the phone as if the phone knew he was clueless for any jokes and it would somehow magically tell him one.

He googled, "jokes."

A moment later...

Benji: how do you make an egg roll?

Tessa: you push it :)

Benji: way to mess up my punch line

Benji: what does a vegan zombie eat

Tessa: i give up

Benji: Graaaaains

Tessa: Benji

Benji: yes

Tessa: thank you

He wanted to ask, "For what?" but he knew the answer, and he was grateful. Everything in him wanted to be there for her, but he had no idea how. But if a joke was what he could provide, doggone it, he was going to provide one.

He got an idea.

Benji: i have to get my car fixed, want to come with?

Tessa: YES, i would like to come with. what time?

Benji: around noon. i can pick you up

Tessa: okay

Tessa: Benji

Benji: yes

Tessa: thank you again

Benji: send me your grandms address. you are welcome. wish i could do more.

Tessa: already more than enough :)

It sure didn't feel like it, he thought as he crept back into his room, climbed into bed and pulled Leah closer. She snuggled into his chest. He kissed her forehead and fell back into a restless sleep.

Benji
Thirty Two

The ride to Tessa's was a fast dash on the highway. Two quick turns altered the landscape from suburbia to country as if there were an invisible line that said, "When you cross this you will need a farmer's hat and suspenders, and maybe a horse or two."

Benji had been to the area before, once, when Leah wanted her birthday party at a horse stable. It's a nice area—mainly horse ranches, a few off-the-path corporate offices he remembered belonging to the Domino Pizza Corporation, and a very posh golf course.

Pulling up to her Grandmother's house, Benji saw Tessa and her father were already on their way out to greet him. The level of emotions he felt seeing her was just short of hospitalization for anxiety. How was he going to be helpful to her? How was he going to control his breathing around her? And why did her dad have to come outside with her? He pushed his hood back off his head, raked his fingers through his hair, and then stepped out of the car.

Tessa shuffled her feet across the gravel in the new boots she bought at the mall. The thick tread "could handle anything," the store clerk had said. Her cheeks flamed with a rosiness that he assumed was because of crying, and there was a faraway look in her eyes. She was dressed in a multi-colored cape coat that tied at the waist and a long asymmetrical brown skirt that was shorter in the front, to her shins, and long enough in the back to cover her boots. The cream sweater tights underneath would keep her warm since they would be walking outside from the auto shop to the coffee shop.

Even from a distance, he could see Tessa's father's eyes were shadowed dark underneath. His shoulders slumped forward as they walked, his arm surrounded Tessa in a way that seemed as if he was using her to hold him up. Twice now he met her father, and both times Todd had made direct eye contact and used Benji's name multiple times, as if to clarify that he was indeed talking to him, and therefore he should focus and listen. He had seemed like the sort of guy who was on a perpetual mission in life: confident and driven, and happy about being so. This time, he wasn't any of those things. Now, he appeared older, tireder, as though he had aged overnight.

Was this what happens when good parents care about their children? It makes them walk with broken, weighty steps as if their heart is filled with so much pain it's heavier to carry.

"Benji," her father said, extending his hand.

"Hello, sir." Benji shook his hand.

"Tessa tells me you're going to get your car fixed." Her father scanned the car, "It's a fine looking car. Whereabouts are you going?"

"Thank you, sir. I'm taking it to Michigan Auto over in Ypsilanti. There's a coffee shop nearby, we can wait there until they give me an estimate."

"Benji," he said. Benji didn't remember his voice sounding as raspy the first two times they met. "Please, call me Todd."

He would be uncomfortable calling him by his first name, but he said, "Okay," then added, "Is there a particular time you would like Tessa home?"

"Benji, thank you for asking but anytime is fine with us. Good coffee and a friend are the things I think my sweet girl needs." He kissed the top of her head.

Tessa leaned into him with a hug. "I'll call in a little bit and let you know where I am. Tell mom and Rula I'll bring them chai tea."

"Okay, honey." He made a small, tired smile that matched the way Tessa smiles. "You two have a good time. And Benji, drive safe, that's treasure you are driving around."

Tessa's eyes met Benji's. They were glassy and sleepy looking, making their green tones pop brighter than the day before. He realized she hadn't yet spoken. "Hey," he offered.

She smiled. A dim, heavy smile, the same as her father.

"We should go," he said, motioning toward the car. "I have a one-thirty appointment and it takes about a half an hour to get there from here."

Tessa's father gave her another squeeze before letting her go and said, "Alright. Call us later."

They got in the car and left to "Todd," waving over his shoulder as he walked back to the house.

Benji
Thirty Three

When they turned from her Grandmother's onto the paved road, Tessa pulled her phone from her purse. "I took some of the pictures from my sister's phone, and I want to show you," she said. Her hair was down again, and there were more strands of tan twine weaved throughout sporadic tiny braids. She held the phone in one hand and with the other she tugged at a single curl that hung over her shoulder.

He was relieved she spoke first. With her lead, he could follow, since more times than ever the last few days he simply had no idea what to say. What do you say to someone who's hurting? Do you jump into what's bothering them? Or do you leave it alone and pretend nothing is going on and that today is a normal day like any other? He had fretted on the drive over, about how to start things off, even memorizing a few jokes just in case.

"Are you sure you want to show me? Will she be okay with that?"

Tears pooled in her eyes, glassing them all the more. How could someone look so beautiful when they cried?

"Since you're trying to protect my sister that tells me all the more that I want to show you." Her voice cracked, taking a chip from his heart as it did. "But

I wanted to show you because you may know who the people are in the pictures."

They pulled down a long entrance and around to the back of an old dilapidated building off of Michigan Avenue. The outside of the building was deceptive and spoke of shoddy work and carelessness, but that was far from the truth. Inside, where the smell of oil and exhaust greet you, they're like car ninjas with modern car repair weapons.

"Benji!" Reese, the son of the owner and the usual front desk guy, greeted Benji. "I saw you on the books for today. How's Big Timmie treating you? My mom can't stop talking about how much better she feels with the security he installed."

Big Timmie had personally gone out to evaluate what their house needed for security. They live in a posh part of Ann Arbor, but after years of, as Timmie calls it "false comfortability," their house was broken into. Their daughter, Reese's sister, was home sick from school when it happened. She managed to call the police and hide in the closet until they came, but it left her traumatized. Reese's sister was one of the few people in school who would make a point to say hello to him if she saw him in the halls.

Reese looked from him to Tessa and his smile brightened. "Wait, forget about you. Who might this be brightening our shop with her beauty?" He gave a flick of his head to get his hair out of his eyes and a fast lick of his lips. Reese reminds Benji of a young gangster. If he slicked back his hair, he would make a perfect Al Pacino from the movie Scarface.

Benji put his hand on Tessa's low back. "This is my friend Contessa. Contessa, this is Reese. The only wolf in sheep's clothing who admits they are a wolf."

Reese laughed. "Don't listen to him. He just wishes he had hustle with the ladies, like me."

Tessa smiled. "Very nice to meet you, Wolf."

Reese laughed again and put his fist out for Benji to tap knuckles with him. But long, thin fingers don't make the most masculine fist; compared to Reese's tanned, hairy knuckles, Benji's hand looked more like a girl's when they tapped them together.

"I like her already," said Reese, giving him a wink. Then he leaned forward over the counter closer to Tessa. "When you get tired of this guy's stimulating conversations about security cameras and how to wire your car to turn on a lamp, come find me. I'll bring the excitement into your life." He winked at Tessa and gave Benji a soft punch in the arm.

"We'll be at Mug Room, can you text me?" Benji said.

"Sure, man. She's next on the lift and I'll let you know what we find." Reese said as Benji handed over his car key.

"Would you like some coffee?" Benji asked.

Reese pulled his head back, conveying curiosity. "Ms. Contessa, you must be a good one because he's using his manners." He chuckled and put out his fist for him again. "Sure man. A double shot red-eye would be great. Thanks."

Benji knuckled bumped him and they turned to leave.

Benji
Thirty Four

To get to The Mug Room Coffee House, they walked back down the long entrance to Michigan Avenue and past a few shady looking houses that nestled between the auto yard and the newly built strip mall. The Mug Room was the first store to open when the strip was built last year, and it was a hop on the bus route from the university and on the way home for those coming to and from work in Detroit. Its location and coffee already made it the new favorite place for local college students, moms in yoga pants, employees in power suits, and anyone else who wanted to relax or have coffee and talk.

The space inside The Mug Room was split into two levels. From the entry, there are six steps up to the glass-encased food counter and coffee making area, where long windows on the back side boast drenching buckets of sunlight and a panoramic view of the Huron River. Square high-top tables and chairs splatter throughout the top floor, which is painted in Mediterranean reds and yellows. The top floor setup seems to elicit a sense of focus and an exchange of ideas—evidence by the many laptops, earbud wearing students, and fast paced conversational hand gestures dotting the tables of the upstairs.

Four steps down from the entrance is the downstairs. "The pits," they're called, is an area with sunk down circular blue and green couches, with round tables in the middle and inset vases that hold wisps of baby's breath mingled with bamboo sticks. There are twelve pits in all: six on one side and six on the other all accessible by a catwalk running down the center—the furthermost couches illuminated by ambient light and less natural light. Unlike the top floor, the pit area speaks of quiet conversation and book reading.

"This place is amazing!" Tessa said, setting her coffee and cinnamon roll on the table in the first pit on the right. She flipped off her boots, untied her cape tie, and pulled her knees and feet onto the couch with her and under her cape. Before her arms disappeared into the arm slits, she untucked her hair from beneath the collar. Her curls fell like a cascade down around the cape. She looked like she was being swallowed by a giant, colorful wool bag. Her whole tucked-away-safe image made him want to reach out and take her face in his hands—and kiss her.

"I'm glad you like it." He heard a slight stutter in his voice. He sat down next to her but while she made herself comfortable he fidgeted with his jacket zipper and tried to figure out how close he should sit.

Glancing at the others in the pits—the last two couches at the end had people in them—he settled that an arm's length was a good distance. "So, how was your sister doing this morning?"

"She was laying on the couch in my mom's arms with a bottle of aspirin and a bottle of water." She leaned her chin on her covered knees and fixed her eyes on her coffee cup sitting on the table. "The moment she woke she began crying. She knew, Benji. She understood."

"Knew what?"

"What she has done…that she has started a cycle all over again. She might not remember much from last night, but she knows she's woken a monster of regret." Tessa turned her head to him, her cheek now on her knees. Her eyes were tired, and he hadn't noticed before but she appeared paler than normal. He longed to touch her face. If only to swipe the long curl that hung across her cheek out of the way.

As if reading his thoughts, she reached and tucked the strand behind her ear. "We'll watch her closely for a while and try to help her focus on the joys of life, but the sense of escaping from the pain will probably call to her. It's hard to face realities when reality is a confusing mix of pain and regret. We, especially my parents, never thought of having to worry about things like parties and teens with alcohol. It simply wasn't a thought for them—us. Making sure she found new friends and began again has been our main focus. My parents aren't saying so, but I know they feel defeated."

"Was last night an escape sort of thing for her, the party I mean? Or was she pressured?"

"Probably some of both. I think it was the party, the people, the idea of fun. It's all easier here. Phones, computers, the parties, of course, those sorts of things are an access we aren't used to having; the alcohol, too. In some countries, finding alcohol can be easier, legal even, but people tend to raise each other's kids as if they are their own so they keep an eye out for one another and that makes it harder to get into trouble. When you're a parent and a whole village or street is watching out for your children, you feel pretty safe." Her eyes shadowed dark. "We thought Victor was doing the same thing. That he was looking out for Marula, too. But he wasn't. Instead, he was convincing her she was an adult who could do adult things."

"Like drinking?"

"Exactly like drinking." Her eyes became wet and dull.

"How did your sister end up at the party?"

He saw small movements under her cape, then her arm popped through the slit holding her phone. "She told me this girl…" she opened the phone and tapped her photos icon. The screen filled with the image of a group of girls on top of a table, beer bottles in all angles close to their mouths as if they were lollipops. "This one, the blonde that was at Maria's, she said was the one who invited her."

He took the phone for closer inspection. But he already knew. The blonde she pointed to was none other than Blue Barbie, smack dab in the middle of an entourage.

Marula had been invited to the Friday night party he'd decided not to revenge.

Benji
Thirty Five

"Her name is, Claire Morgenstern," Benji said, trying to wrap his brain around the information he was receiving.

Tessa flipped through more photos, all different cliché high school drunk pictures, complete with beer bottles, duck lip expressions and peace signs. He watched as her forehead furrowed deeper and deeper. She stopped swiping the screen and focused in on the one with Marula vomiting and the guy's hands on her butt. "Isn't this the guy from Maria's, too?" She looked at him for confirmation.

Sure enough, it was Car Wash with his beefy hands on her butt and his tongue hanging out.

"Yes. That's Leo." He almost growled his answer. Marula's head was in the toilet, her blonde hair hanging over the toilet seat, some in and some out, and some stuck to the vomit on the seat. You couldn't see her face, but you could see she had barely made it to the toilet because there was also vomit down on the floor next to her. Car Wash didn't seem to care about the puke, only the ass in his hands. He was proud, smug, and not helping.

Benji's mind raced with branching scenarios and possibilities: How would things have played out if he had come up with something for Blue Barbie, or for Friday's party? Would Marula have been at the party to witness whatever his plan would have

210

unleash? He'd been distracted by Tessa, and he settled that his fathers' plan would be his last revenge, but now… what if he had come up with something for Blue Barbie's party? Would he have been able to prevent Marula from going? Maybe he could have come up with something to end the party. Maybe then, Marula wouldn't have gotten so drunk and been dumped on the front lawn of her Grandmother's house.

While staring at the image, the possibilities blurred into a mess, replaced with a hate for Car Wash and how his revenge did nothing to change him. A hate for Blue Barbie not helping Marula—a girl he never met and hardly knew anything about.

A sudden bitter taste washed his mouth, and he needed to take a drink of his coffee. Why didn't things ever change? Why did he feel even more powerless than before? Before Tessa life was black and white, the bad guys against the good guys and the bad guys deserved whatever he planned for them. It was all justified. Like Big Timmie catching the bad guys in action with his security systems. He thought of himself as one of the secret good guys. A revenge hero who made the bad guys pay a price for their crappy ways. Now though, looking at the image of Car Wash treating Marula like a piece of tail, it mixed up his thoughts. Now the thoughts sounded confusing, like a babbling brook instead of a steady, focused stream cutting through rock. The worst thought: Tessa's sister being at the party would have grouped her as one of the bad guys. In his eyes, she would have been guilty by association with the cronies. And he wouldn't have known she

211

was there. That a *good* person was there. A "broken" girl, as Tessa described.

He tried to move away from the thought, to step outside of it, handle it like you would a puzzle box that needed to be looked at in different directions. He wanted to hold onto Blue Barbie as a bad person, to think about how she deserves what karma would give back to her through him, but now it wasn't so black and white. Marula wasn't a bad person, only a hurting, confused girl, who had found her momentary escape through a party.

A sniffle broke his musing. The recessed light above their heads made the tear on Tessa's cheek sparkle.

All of his thoughts parted, clearing, allowing one single streaming thought: Tessa.

He scooted closer to her and put his arm around her, drawing her over so she could lean her head on his shoulder. Another sniffle told him she was trying to cry as quiet as possible.

He rested his chin on her head, in her hair. She still smelled like fall.

"So," he said. "I heard the weather man say we might get an early snow next week."

"I'm glad I bought Michigan clothes," she said, wiping her cheek with the back of her hand.

"It might be an *apocalypse* type of snow." He stressed the word "apocalypse," for her.

"Sounds scary. Will they close the school?"

Before he realized what he was doing, he reached and tipped her chin for her to look at him. Her eyes drawing him in the way a cloudless sky begs for you to admire it. They were rimmed pink from crying, the whites speckled with tiny red veins.

She didn't move away from his hand so he kept it on her chin.

"I was trying to make a joke but apparently I have bad timing."

Her face scrunched, curiously and cutely.

"I was trying to help you with a word from your list."

She stared at him with a blank expression. It was a long enough look for him to lose himself in the waves of green and brown in her eyes. He hadn't realized how long her eyelashes were until that moment. They rimmed her eyes like natural brown eyeliner.

He whispered, "Snow and apocalypse."

Her face widened in understanding. "Ohhhhhh!" she exclaimed. "A Snowpocalypse."

She unfurled from inside her cape and laughed a deep, raspy laugh. An out of sort kind of laugh that made the people in the farthest pit turn and glance over at them.

It must have been a type of emotional release because the laugh was in conjunction with new tears.

She fanned her face with her hand and reached for a napkin on the table. "Marula will be proud of me," she said with a final sighing laugh. Dabbing her eyes dry.

"Well, that's good but I personally think you're a lost cause. Needing help with your list and all," he said with a chuckle.

A fake gasp erupted from her, and she placed her hand on her chest. "Complete. Lost. Cause. Where would I be without my hero, Benji, the Dictionary of urban slang?"

He matched her gasp with his own exaggerated, shocked look, pulling his head back and fanning his face. "Well, I'm glad you appreciate the fact that I had to up my word game when I met you. Your world traveler intimidation tactic worked. I'm fast becoming a trained slang master."

"So glad I could help break you down into submission to my world domination of the male species."

"Lofty goal."

"I aim big," she quipped, her cheek lifting on one side, making the half smile he longed to see since he picked her up. It was uniquely crooked and imperfectly perfect. Every single edge of her face was like that, from the tiny fleck of a mole under her left eye, to what must have been a chicken pox scar on the corner of her jaw line. Benji had the same type of scar on his shoulder. It had been the first pox to show up and he had thought it was a mosquito bite. He'd scratched it throughout the night, only to wake covered in more itchy, oozing sores. Was the one on her jaw line Tessa's beginning pox?

"So that's the secret you are hiding. I have found you out. It's male domination. I knew there was more to you than a gorgeous smile."

His words had come out before he realized they were coming. Now, all he could do was feel the weight of her stare and the pause that hung in the air. It was as long as a few blinks, but it seemed like minutes passing.

The voices of the others came into hearing range. They had been there already, like background music you don't notice is playing until one of the songs gets stuck in your head. Only now, he was acutely aware of their sound.

After his heartbeats had counted like a slow clock, she said, "You've found me out. I feel much better now that my secret is out in the open. Male domination is the answer." Her head angled forward, drawing closer to his. Her breath tickled his lips when she whispered, "But, you're a lost cause."

He couldn't help the laugh that escaped. It was from deep in his stomach. A nervous, joyous, mad-with-fascination laugh. It only lasted a minute or so, but it was long enough to vent a release. Like a leak from a balloon, his conscience being the air inside. He welcomed the ease that settled in its place.

Is this what having a friend does? Is this how people were supposed to feel? As if their hearts are enjoyed by another person.

"I thought everyone was redeemable in your eyes," he said, his cheeks beginning to feel sore from smiling.

She cocked her head like a bird. "How did you know that?"

"Know what?"

"That I think everyone is redeemable."

"From the story of your dad."

"Ah, yes." She shrugged and grabbed her cinnamon roll from the table. "But that's a part of my plan to dominate the men of the world. I go about making people believe everyone is redeemable, it softens them up, and then I swoop in…," she made a flying motion with her hand to represent a bird diving in, "and take over their mind with a smile and a word list."

"And the word list accomplishes what, exactly?"

"A new, all-girl urban language with which to communicate without the males understanding what we are saying." She took a bite of her roll, and just like with the pizza a sound of enjoyment came from her throat. "Mmm."

"Seems like a flimsy plan to me. Be prepared for war over words like Snowpocalypse and nom nom," he chuckled, watching her fight the sticky around her lips by licking and wiping them. Freaking food was indeed sexy.

"I'll secretly teach you the words so at least *we* can communicate with each other," she said, setting her roll back on its plate.

"Now I like your plan," he said.

"Ha. It's better than your twisty plans."

His insides froze. He was sure his surprise showed on his face before he could stop it. "I have twisty plans. What twisty plans?" An odd jitter fluttered down through his legs, and he had to keep from bouncing them up and down.

"Plans to dominate through spy cameras."

"What?"

"Hello, in there." She waved her hands in front of his face. "You work at a security store that sells spy cameras. Big Timmie's is merely a front for your evil plan to dominate the world through spy glasses and tie clips. Work with me here."

Swift relief flooded through him, and he laughed. But it was an empty, tense laugh. "Oh, that. Haha. Yes, that's the plan, and Big Timmie is the architect." His reply sounded stupid, but he was dumbfounded with nervous thoughts. On one hand, he was aware that he wanted to tell her his plans, and on the other he was petrified of thinking about them in her presence.

She reached and brushed her fingers over his ear and through the side of his hair. "You sure are a jumpy person," she smirked and lay her hand on his.

Before he was aware of what he was doing…

The kiss was clumsy and wet and amazing. Her lips reminded him of a moist marshmallow. Against instinct, he pulled away but only because he felt he might be torturing her with his lack of skills. Her head remained in his hand, heavy and relaxed. Her hair was thicker than he'd imagined.

"That okay?" he asked.

She smiled, her eyes were soft and enchanting. "Yes. That's okay."

But the boldness he held moments ago drained out of him as quick as a sink plug being pulled. Her words of affirmation bounced off of a stony place inside his mind. "You sure?"

She lifted her head out of his hand and took his other hand in hers. "Benji, I am sure. I promise. I would have punched you if not."

"Okay."

She smiled. "Was that your first?"

He looked away, but she lifted her hand to his cheek turning his face back. Ruffling her fingers through his hair, she held him with her eyes.

He tried a smile, but it felt heavy, "No way. Didn't you see the line of girls waiting to experience these lip skills?"

He set his forehead on hers. She smiled and it reached into her eyes.

"I'll have to put out their eyes now."

He chuckled and kissed her nose.

His cell phone alerted him to a text from Reese. If pulling apart wasn't already difficult, it was almost unbearable this time.

Tessa

"Oh my goodness! He did!" Marula squealed. "How was it?"

"It was nice, very nice. New'ish but nice," Tessa said. "I was his first kiss." She smiled and flopped back on her bed. "I like that I was his first kiss. It's sweet."

"You make it sound like you have a ton of experience," Marula laughed. "Kissing three guys does not make an expert."

Tessa rolled onto her side and faced Marula, who was in the other twin bed across from her. They were separated by a small bedside table and floor lamp. Marula's face still looked peaked, as if she needed to throw up a few more times, but at least there was a brightness returning to her eyes.

"I only claim two kisses. You know Ahaman doesn't count."

Marula smiled, her head was snuggled into her pillow, the green and pink quilt on her bed pulled up to her neck. She looked like she did when they were ten years old and they would whisper to each other in the cabin in Kenya, trying not to wake everyone with their chitter and excitement to be on the elephant reserve again. "His black eye where you right hooked him counts."

"Well, that's what he gets for trying to kiss me without permission."

219

Marula chuckled. "Fair point. Okay, two guys doesn't make an expert."

Tessa rolled to her back and stared at the ceiling. "Benji's lips are so soft. I think he must use Chap Stick on them all the time. And he was so nervous I could feel him quivering." She reached and touched her fingertips to her lips.

"I miss kisses," Marula said.

Tessa went to Marula's bed pulled back the quilt and climbed in with her sister. Forehead to forehead, she whispered, "I know you do. I'm sorry I reminded you."

"I'm sorry I reminded *you.* I shouldn't have." Marula kissed Tessa's nose and then replaced their foreheads together. Snuggling the quilt up to their chins she said, "Now, tell me all about the coffee shop and the soft Chap Stick lips you kissed."

Benji
Thirty Six

Benji woke to Leah singing in her room. Something dance worthy because he could also hear her feet bopping back and forth on the wood floor. Sundays are normally a quiet day. A day where he sleeps while the family goes to church. But today, not only could he hear Leah, but there was also a commotion coming from the kitchen. Double checking the time, it was after nine, he swiped the covers back and felt the soreness of his muscles as he stood up. He had been assaulted by another fitful night of sleep. "I think I get into fist fights while I sleep," he imagined himself explaining to a doctor. But though his body was sore, his mind was concluded and peaceful, which felt good.

On the drive to drop off Tessa, clarity had hit him: it was for the better that he had not come up with a revenge for Blue Barbie. While he would be left wondering if he could have saved Marula from the party altogether, he was happy that least Blue Barbie will be confronted for having a party in the first place. According to Tessa, her father planned to contact Blue Barbie's parents about the party, the alcohol, and the pictures on Marula's phone.

"Do you know if Claire's parents are the sort of parents who know their daughter would throw a party like that?" Tessa had asked during the drive.

Benji had wanted to tell her they were out of town for the weekend, but he couldn't since he only knew that from eavesdropping on Car Wash's conversation at Maria's Cafe. "*The very same day you walked into my life*," he thought.

"Why are you guy's home?" he asked Leah, standing in her bedroom doorway. A huge yawn overtook him and he wiped sleep boogers from his eyes with his sleeve.

"Mom's got a cold," she said, still twirling and holding onto a plastic stick connected to a long ribbon.

"Practicing ribbon dancing?"

The ribbon tail swirled above her head before settling down around her in a circle. "Yep. I mean, yes."

In the bathroom, he heard his phone vibrate from on top of his metal desk while he brushed his teeth and washed his face. Over the night, a sizable zit had formed in the middle of his forehead. "Great. Just great" he said to his reflection.

His phone vibrated against the desk again as he searched through the cabinets for something to tame his new forehead friend. He only found Peroxide. He dabbed it on the bump then ruffled his hair with his fingers, trying to pull some of his bangs down to cover it. Hoping peroxide works quickly, he headed to retrieve his phone.

Tessa's texts peered up at him from his phone screen, immediately making his sore muscles relax.

Tessa: morning! still sleeping?

Benji: nope, about to eat breakfast. did you sleep well?

Tessa: yes, i slept very well. face time later?

Benji: sounds good

Tessa: yay! it'll be my first time on a camera chat.

In the kitchen, his mom was beating eggs in a large bowl. On the counter next to her was a package of turkey bacon, already opened, along with four pans on the stove waiting for the breakfast contents.

"Heard you're not feeling well," he asked his mom.

Camille turned to him, still whisking. "Yeah, not sure if I have a cold or it's allergies from the warm weather burst last week. The coming snow will knock it out if it is allergies."

"Can I help with something?"

Her eyebrows drew together into a sharp point. "What's got you in a good mood?"

"Nothing." He grabbed four plates from the cabinet and began setting them on the table.

"Well, that's helping right there." She motioned with her head toward the table. "Are you hungry? It's rare we eat breakfast together so I'm making banana pancakes, bacon, eggs and some fruit."

"Nutritious," he said opening the silverware drawer.

"Yes, it is," she agreed, with less piety and more genuineness in her tone than he was used to.

Setting the glasses on the table, Benji wondered what type of breakfast they ate at Tessa's house. Do they all sit down together? Do they eat randomly? One with a bowl of cereal, another with a full cooked breakfast. He pictured her grandmother making a spread that included fresh blueberry muffins. He could hear Tessa make her happy sound, the same sound she did when she ate pizza and cinnamon rolls. That, "mmm," sound. As if it were the best thing ever and deserved a satisfied noise for an ovation.

"What's the smile for?" Camille asked.

Revenge Chronicle: Porno or Family Time
Revenge Risk Rating: Easy AND Hilarious
Revenge Date: March 23ʳᵈ, 2012
Chronicle Entry Date: March 23ʳᵈ, 2012

Chronicle, what a bonehead my father is. "How about a movie night?" he asked Camille, Leah and me—to which I was quick to say that I had to do homework. Which made my mom snap her teeth at me. "Of course you have something to do. I bet you don't even have homework." Chronicle I think I heard a growl when she said it. *Maybe she's really a werewolf.*

I'll admit it to you, she was right, I don't have homework.

"Benji, would you get I-Robot from the den before you begin your homework," my dad asked settling down in his "bane," chair. Then he told Leah, "Go ahead and take your bath and put your pajamas on before we start. I'll get the movie and the popcorn all ready."

On my way to the den an impromptu idea clicked. *Insert a trademark evil cackle right here* I waited for Leah to get in the bath and then did like I was told and went to get the I-Robot movie. But I also tip-toed to their room, to the secret (not so secret) place inside their armoire where they keep their "Techniques to Keep a Marriage Happy," porn. It's one of the three porn movies I found while digging in my dad's drawer for a black pair of socks—I needed them to match the black pants I

225

had to wear for the church Christmas Eve service. On the DVD cover is a plain, homely looking man and woman in a hot tub, the woman sitting on the edge with no bathing suit and the man...well, that doesn't matter. Anyway, I grabbed that one and swapped out the DVDs. Now the porn was in the I-Robot case and I-Robot was in the porn case.

The rest went as anyone can imagine...and I'm smiling as I think of it! It only took a moment for my mom and dad to realize it was the wrong movie and for my mom to begin screaming at my dad. "That's completely irresponsible of you! You idiot, how could you mix up the movies!"

I shall take my bow now....

Benji
Thirty Seven

After breakfast, Benji volunteered to clean up the kitchen while his mom went to take a nap. Her allergy medicine kicked in right as they finished eating. Bob made his way to his chair and spent the day parked in front of the television. Last Benji saw before heading upstairs he was watching something on the history channel about airplane dogfights.

Comfortable in bed, he dialed Tessa on FaceTime. Her earlier texts said her family drove up north to Frankenmuth for the day, but she decided to stay home and paint her Grandmother's bathroom for her.

"My mom wanted to do it for her as a surprise, but my grandmother has a radar for lies and we were found out," Tessa explained while he watched her on his tablet screen climb the small ladder and reach above the large bathroom mirror. "My dad spent all week taking off the wallpaper. He called it "ancient paper.""

"How is Marula today?"

Her paint splattered t-shirt rose when she reached for a spot up high, exposing her trim abdomen. Her belly button was flat with a sun-shaped tattoo around it: the protruding rays were different heights and filled in with a filigree design that resembled tribal art. It was a fine line delicate tattoo. He wanted to ask her about it but wasn't sure he should.

She brought her arm down, rested the paint brush on the top of the ladder, and looked into her phone camera, which from the angle seemed positioned on a shelf of sorts. "She's tired. My grandmother ran her a bath with lavender and made her a good breakfast, but she was very quiet."

"Lavender?"

She pulled her hair over her shoulder and began braiding it. "My Grandmother has a greenhouse and she grows lavender. Do you like lavender?"

He watched as her hands crisscrossed her hair into a thick braid. "I'm not sure I would recognize the smell."

"Hmm. I'll have to bring you some."

"You'd bring me flowers? How kind of you."

"Embrace your feminine side," she grinned and pulled a black tie off her wrist and attached it to the end of the braid.

"More world domination through flowers and girl language?"

"Oh yes. The plans I've made to make the world smell good and communicate better are stellar." Half her mouth lifted, ready for a smile, but then her face veiled serious. She looked right into the camera lens. "Can I ask you a question?"

"Sure." He leaned back against his headboard, balancing the tablet on his legs, putting his arms behind his head.

"Now don't worry about my motive with what I'm about to ask, I am only curious."

"Should I be scared?"

"Ha! Of me? Not at all." She winked into the lens.

"Is it going to be about my lack of kissing skills?" He covered his eyes with one hand.

"Oh stop. You are not a bad kisser. Take your hand down." He did. "You didn't hit my teeth, bite my lip, or push too hard; you were fine. Though, I could feel you shaking." She smiled. "Maybe next time the nerves will be over."

"At least you want a next time." He felt a wave of relief and then a sudden excitement. The prospect of another kiss made him light headed.

"What's the question?"

"Well, I was wondering, I mean, I like you and think you are clever and nice—"

"You're making me scared with this prefacing," he interrupted.

"Sorry, I am not sure how to ask." She reached for the paint brush and dipped it in the can. "What happened to your friends? I mean, you're great so I'm wondering."

"That's a good question." He shifted the pillows behind him and moved to lie on his side, propping the tablet up with Leah's blanket. It was as if her face was right there lying next to him. "But the answer is, I am not sure. It sort of happened, as if I fell into it the way you fall into a hole by accident. One moment I was walking along and the next I was walking along alone."

She went back to painting, "I'm listening," she said, dabbing at a spot in the ceiling corner.

"I had a couple of friends when we lived in our old neighborhood. Mostly the kids I played yard soccer with, but I did have two close friends I hung out with all the time."

A small "mmm, kay" sound came from the camera. "Are you still friends?"

"No. Anthony moved to Brazil with his family, something for his dad's work if I remember right. The other guy, his name was Jaden, we were friends since Kindergarten and we spent a lot of time together, especially on the weekends. We played baseball and a lot of basketball at the Rec. Center, or we went to the skate park to try to taunt the girls who hung out there. Sometimes went knocking on doors in the neighborhood to see if someone would pay us to wash their car or mow their lawn, or in the winter shovel their driveways, anything to make a little extra pocket money. Though, our best times were Friday nights. That's when I'd stay the night at his house, and we'd play video games all night. His mom kept a stock of Pizza Rolls on hand just for us."

"He sounds like a nice friend," she said, dragging the paint brush in a straight line down the side of the mirror. It was fast and without flaw, and he wondered if she knew how to draw as well as sing.

"He was nice," he said. "But at the start of eighth grade his parents transferred him to another school, and because of my dad's promotion we moved out of the neighborhood and into a new school district, too. Though, looking back, I don't think we would have been friends much longer."

"Why do you say that?"

"Because the year earlier, in seventh grade, he joined the lacrosse team and was already spending more time with those friends rather than with me. I think he's some hotshot on his high school team now, at least that's what I read in the school paper. There was an entire article about him leading the team to a victory the last two years. Even in the seventh grade the lacrosse guys were cocky so I couldn't see it getting better over time. I guess when Jaden moved on I never bothered with other people."

"I may sound mean but…"

"Mean. Can you be mean? Not possible?" He smiled and winked at her when she looked into the camera. "Should I brace for impact?" he asked. It was a joke but now his insides were unsettled. Had he said too much? Would she leave him now? Now that she knows how much of a loaner he really is.

"Are the people in high school not the sorts of people you like?" she asked.

"Is *that* your "mean" question?"

"Yes."

"Did you change how you planned to say it or something because that's not mean at all?" His insides relaxed.

She sat down on the edge of the sink cabinet. "It is what I wanted to ask. Are they not good enough people?" Her head tilted to the side like a sparrow, and he wondered how she could ever think she was capable of being mean.

"I may have to inspect your question, you know, check my perspective or something, but no, it's not that they aren't good enough, it's that I am not good enough for them." He swallowed down a sigh. "They don't like me."

"How can they not like you? Maybe if they get to know you, they would."

"Are you passively asking do I put myself out there to get to know people?"

"Do you? I've only known you a few days, but I know you're super nice, aren't a crowd follower, loyal to your sister, respectful to teachers. I can't figure it out."

"Wow, you make me sound…well, not like me."

"It *is* like you. I see how caring you are."

His eyes shifted to Bob Marley instead of the camera. "Caring is not a good trait for a guy in high school. Tough and popular would be the necessary traits for high school success."

"Benji, look at me," she said. He did. "You're successful because you've stayed yourself. Don't be fooled into thinking that high school is the finality of life. The world is much bigger than high school; I promise."

"I'm beginning to think that might be true…" he finally released the trapped sigh, feeling like an anomaly, "after meeting you." Her sudden smile took over her entire face. "And I'm beginning to think I may be missing out on the big, life picture. You've lived life, uncommonly lived, and I've…well, I've been alone for a while now, and I've grown comfortable being alone. For the most part, anyway. Then you came along. Usually, when I look around there isn't much to choose from in terms of friends, at least not who would be worthwhile. I don't know, maybe that's judgmental

232

of me and maybe they're out there wandering the school halls the same as I am, but by the time you are a junior in high school the friend groups are pretty much formed and they're generally solid and not too inviting. It might not be like that everywhere, but it's the way things go here."

Tessa's smile faded and was replaced with a deep look of compassion. Her mouth was soft and straight. Her chin dimple faded into its landscape. Even her eyes were shadowed from the bathroom overhead lighting.

He continued. "Sometimes I think I don't have friends because I'm ordinary. I mean, from what I've seen in our generation, you have to be extraordinary at something. Usually athletic, excessively good looking, and an extrovert. Or even extraordinarily bad, like the kids who go to the principal's office and then brag about it as soon as they get back to class. I'm none of those things. I'm a no one. I mean, if I stood in the hall at school and screamed at the top of my lungs everyone would just stare at each other and say, "Who is that screaming?" They wouldn't ask why I'm screaming, just who. Maybe the cronies would recognize me as a kid they occasionally shove around, but really, most would not even know I exist."

Studying Tessa's face, he wondered if what he thought was compassion was, in fact, pity. His jaw tensed at the thought of her feeling sorry for him.

"That's why you asked me at Maria's? About why I picked you. And why that Leo guy said what he said."

He nodded.

"Is he one of the…what did you call them?"

"Cronies."

"Is he? Do they harass you?"

He tore his eyes away again. He couldn't take it if her expression were pity. And now he wasn't sure if he wanted compassion, either.

His stomach did a sudden lurch at the realization that he shared so much. Why hadn't he simply lied? Played the "I'm busy being a better man than those idiots," card.

He hadn't answered her question yet, and now he had to force himself to answer. "Maybe I'm a lost cause," he said. "Run for the hills while you can." The urge to turn off his tablet was so overwhelming his hand began to shake. He balled it in a fist next to him.

"No one is a lost cause; everyone is redeemable," she offered. "Besides, I'm not running anywhere. I just got here."

He wanted to check her face, to see her expression. Was it filled with truth or pity? "That's because you haven't had time for comparison," he said to Bob Marley again.

"Are you kidding me? Didn't you, seconds ago, say I've lived, and now you doubt my discernment of character? Ha. My skills at picking strange are mastered by years of study and development. And you, Benji, are my kind of strange and lovely."

Still afraid of the expression he would find, he forced himself to look at the screen. "Lovely and strange. Those are two opposing words, are they not? Kind of makes me think I am a lab experiment."

Her chin drew down, and she regarded him through narrowed eyes. "Yes, you indeed are my petri dish of tall, blonde and lovely, with a side of strange."

He couldn't help his smile. She just said he was lovely as if it was the truth. He looked at her braid, the small strands of string still weaved throughout her hair. He thought of her clothes that bag and wrap and don't fit anyone else's style around town. Was that what strange meant to her, to be yourself rather than try to fit in?

"I truly hope this "strange" word you keep using is a good thing." He relaxed his tight fist. His hand tingled from the released pressure.

She giggled. "Yes, it's a good thing. At least to me it is."

"No running for the hills then?"

"Nope. You're stuck now. I've cast a kissing spell on you."

He felt his cheeks rise from smiling. She definitely had cast a spell on him. Now, if only he could cast one on her.

"Do you think I'm asking too much from the world?"

"Meaning?"

"Meaning, for high school to be less rejecting." And my family filled with one less pervert, he thought.

"Maybe that isn't the right question. What if the question is, how can I, you, be the change in the school for it to be less rejecting."

"What in the world? A Gandhi quote, for real," he laughed. Though, he wondered if she had a point. What if he could make a change?

She giggled and clapped her hands together. "Yes! That's it! Be the change. That's perfect!" She snorted at the end of her giggle, and it made him laugh more.

"I don't think that is what I was saying, but it sounds reasonable so I'll take it," he said and she clapped again. "Though, I think with all your world travel your perspective is a bit skewed."

"Oh, sure, as opposed to your dark and twisty perspective about the world."

"And how do you know my perspective?" he raised an eyebrow at her, unsure if he felt exposed or comforted.

"It's obvious. You like to count everything as if you need some type of order in the world—don't think I didn't see you count the cups at the coffee place, and I bet you love to kill people in gory video games. Oh, and you work at a place that practices spying on people."

He retorted. "You forgot the no friends' thing."

"Nope, that's different. I think you don't have friends because you're dark and twisty and strange." She spread her arms apart, paint brush still in one hand, and looked up to the ceiling. "The fresh air of strange and skewed perspectives. I love it!"

And he laughed. It was the best laugh he had in years.

Benji
Thirty Eight

For as long as Benji could remember falling asleep had been the hardest thing to do if he hadn't worked excessive hours. If he were not exhausted, his brain would churn with thoughts and plots and ideas. But not this night. Tonight, he would fall asleep with good thoughts. Thoughts of Tessa's arms in the air and how elated she seemed with his "strange." Thoughts of confronting his dad and telling him to leave and threaten the cops on him—maybe that would be enough to make him leave and never return. Thoughts of how Leah was excited to see Tessa on his tablet and talk to her about how beautiful Tessa sang, and how there must be another mall date in their future. They both sang the eighties' song Tainted Love together, Tessa holding her paint brush like a microphone and Leah with her arms out straight holding the tablet in front of her like a karaoke screen. "Sometimes I feel I've got to run away...I've got to get away from the pain you drive into the heart of me...The love we share seems to go nowhere...And I've lost my light for I toss and turn - I can't sleep at night...." That was when Tessa told them their family has impromptu dance parties to eighties' music. "Someone hits play, and we gravitate out of our places and all come together and bop around. My dad is a horrible dancer, so we have a great time making fun of him.

But my mom is fantastic! You must come to our house for a dance party, Leah. You would have so much fun." Tessa's invite caused Leah to light up so bright that Benji thought his room somehow trapped the sun.

When the floating space between awake and sleep captured him with its rhythm, he realized two things. He would definitely forget about any future revenge schemes, but the most amazing thing—he fell into a deep sleep without thinking about, "Busting My Dad's Balls."

Benji
Thirty Nine

Benji never looked forward to a day of school in his life, much less a Monday. Aside from getting his grades high so he could get the heck out of Dodge after he graduated, school was nothing but a stepping stone to him. But there he stood, ten minutes early in *their* meeting spot.

The halls waited quietly for the onslaught of bus kids to spill inside and fill the empty space. Normally the quiet was soothing, but right then it was eerie without all of the human sounds bouncing off the walls. Even the long lines of gray lockers and shined linoleum seemed nightmarish rather than academic. In the nook of a classroom, a couple was kissing though they seemed to be mauling each other rather than in the throes of passion. It was almost barbaric and far too early in the morning to be that worked up. Benji needed to look away to not gag at their sloppiness.

Slam!

A pound against the glass of the door gave him a start, but the face smashed against the glass settled him instantly. Tessa's eyes were crossed and her nose smashed upward showing a clear line of view to the inner side of her nostrils. The sun made an angelic, golden halo around her hair.

He placed his hand on the cool glass opposite her squished face as if touching her. She pulled away and opened the door, her face smiled, but it was tired.

"Hey there, Picasso," he said.

She reached and took his hand. As he slipped his fingers into hers, she leaned in and kissed his cheek. "Hey, yourself."

"Are you okay?" he asked, keeping a hold of her hand. Though, he kept his grip soft in case she changed her mind and wanted to let go.

"It was a rough morning. My mom and Gram left early to go to an Amish town down in Ohio and Marula was sick in the middle of the night so I stayed up with her. I'm going to need a nap later."

"You have any classes where you can take a cat nap?"

She narrowed her eyes at him. "Are you promoting bad student behavior?"

"Well, if you put it that way…" he covered his eyes with his free hand.

"That's right, hide your eyes you anarchist." She bumped him with her shoulder. "I might sneak a nap at lunch but I'll wait until I get home to sleep. I like my teachers and my classes."

"That's a good thing, I think."

"Of course it's a good thing, oh strange one. I've been homeschooled, or traveling, or enrolled in tiny village schools for most of my life so opportunities to learn differently is my thing."

He stopped walking and faced her. "Wow, there's so much to know about you… villages, homeschooling, what else can I learn?"

She surprised him by reaching up and cupping his cheek in her hand. "I'm just a box of mysteries, aren't I?"

"I like mysteries," he said, picturing Pandora under his bed and realizing he liked the mystery box named Tessa better. His hand reached up to touch the ends of her hair. "That was a pretty swag comment," he added, with a wink.

"That word has been used so it's not on the list anymore." Half her mouth smiled, but she still looked tired.

He started walking and she followed. "Oh no, I missed my opportunity. Who stole it?"

"Marula," she mumbled with a weariness in her tone.

Benji
Forty

At lunch, there wasn't any need to line fries up on the ground. For two reasons: one, Tessa ate them all, and two, because she lay her head down on his shoulder and dozed off, and he didn't want to move around and wake her; even though her sleeping weight twisted his coat neck uncomfortably to the side.

In the peripheral of his eyesight, he saw Leo and the Cronies pointing and saying something about him and Tessa. In response, he laid his head back against the tree and closed his eyes. He didn't want to think of them, or conjure in his mind what they might be saying. He only wanted to take in Tessa's scent—less apple orchard today and more pine tree—and her soft and steady sleep breathing.

His phone alert went off at the same time as the lunch bell.

Tessa stretched her arms and legs. "That was a decent nap," she said. "Now to get through the rest of the day."

Her eyes were droopy with sleep. He noticed the color appeared brighter than this morning, and they showed more greens in the warm sunlight. He never realized how multifaceted hazel eyes were until he met Tessa. Now, he constantly longed to look at them and study their color variations.

After tossing their trash, he checked his phone.

He couldn't believe it...

The time of the day was right. He made sure the batteries were fully charged. He knew the angle of the camera was good, so it had to be...

He had to have caught the Rat this time.

Benji
Forty One

It took all Benji had to stay in school and not leave to go home; it was seeing Tessa after school that did it. He wasn't about to miss out on saying goodbye to her only to go home and endure watching his father get his rocks off with some desperate girl.

But now, perched at his desk before anyone got home the video began, queued by Rat walking into the frame and his khaki pants dropping down. At first it was only the back of two hairy legs, but somehow they managed to angle exactly right when the girl showed up.

He couldn't believe it. He got it this time. The right angle, the right lighting. The thing most evident was his dad's ugly, hairy thigh, and, thankfully, the scar from a burn he got when he was a teenager. That scar was going to be his proof. For a moment, he thought he would have to scrap another attempt, but the scar was his life saver. There would be no denying it now. As for the hoeing girl, he couldn't see much of her face because her hair hung enough to cover most of it, but there was a glimpse of the girl's ear and a small patch of cheek skin peeking from between hair strands. The patch of skin was flushed with red blotches. She seemed to be working quickly. The rat ended with a quiver, and the girl slinked down out of frame while he pulled up his pants. Leave it to his dad to be a quick shooter. In all, it took about three minutes.

Benji hurried and blurred out anything that wasn't necessary. Especially the one flash of private skin he had no urge to have embedded into his psyche. He edited the rest of the video into crisp focus to clearly show the scar. It was good enough to see the delicate details of the girl's earring and a small freckle on the outside edge of her ear lobe. Satisfied with the results, though he wished he could have a better view of the hoes face, he hit send. It went to the entire group of contacts he stole from Blue Barbie's phone. Then he logged into her blog with her password and leaned back in his chair, relaxing, and imagining the fierce sharing of the video that was about to commence. In a matter of time, everyone would be asking about it.

If he was a friend, he would have patted himself on the back and said, "Great job Benji."

Tessa

"Marula, wake up!" Tessa shook her sister's shoulders, but her head rolled heavy on the pillow. A white foam trickled from the corner of her mouth onto a splat of vomit already soaking through the pillow case.

"Mom!" Tessa screamed shaking her sister harder, panic rising so fast in her chest that the next yelling breath trapped in her chest cavity. "Da…" She tried again, "Dad!"

The smell of vomit and urine battered against her senses, but she bit her jaw tight and held back her gag reflex. She dropped her head to Marula's chest and waited for a rise of a breath. It rose but only with a wheeze.

"What's the matt—" her mom turned on the light. Mikael crossed the room in four rushed strides and was next to Tessa in a blink. She immediately rolled Marula up onto her side. "Todd!" she screamed, wiping the foam that began to trickle from Marula's mouth with her pajama sleeve.

"What is it?" Tessa's father entered the room. His presence, like a beat on a life monitor, sent an instant blip of hope through Tessa's heart.

Surveying the scene, his eyes calculating all the variable parts in an instant, he said, "I'll call nine-one-one…make sure she stays on her side. Tessa, get some warm water in a cup and wash rag and make sure the water is very warm. Mikael, Is she breathing? What does her pulse feel like? Fast or slow?"

"I can't tell," Mikael said. "It feels faint. Oh God! Todd, do something!"

After a checking for a pulse in Marula's neck, he motioned for Tessa to go do what he asked. She forced herself to pull away from her sister and run down the hall to the bathroom, almost slamming into her grandmother who rubbed her eyes as she came out from her room to see what all the noise was about.

Tessa ran the sink water, compelling herself to take a moment longer to "make sure it's warm;" thinking how strange time plays with humans. It's as if it has all the power to puppet them in the direction it desired. One minute in good conversation was not the same as one minute trapped in terror.

The steam rose from the running water while she listened to her father speak clearly and calm to what must have been the nine-one-one Operator: "Yes, she is breathing. No, I do not know the cause but I suspect alcohol poisoning. Sixteen. Yes, she is allergic to penicillin…Mikael, add another pillow under her neck, so her throat stays open…Mom, please get a pile of towels."

Tessa handed the cup of water to her father. He covered the phone, "Now go get some ice in a small bowl, about five cubes is good…go quickly…yes, ma'am I'll stay on the phone. Mikael, I'm going to try a trick I've used in the field—"

His voice trailed as Tessa tore off down the hall and rounded the corner to the kitchen. Her heart beating as hard as it did the day her father and mother sat her down to explain that Victor and Marula had a relationship and that they would all be heading to live in Michigan for a while. "Time to heal our baby," they'd both said.

But with the acidity smell of vomit and the trickle of foam planted in the forefront of Tessa's mind, as if branded there like and old flash on a camera, the kind from the eighteen hundreds that made a loud popping sound as the bulb burned and broke, Tessa felt the crushing weight of the words "heal our baby." They'd come to help Marula heal her heart and mind, to remove her from the trappings of a selfish man, and, instead, she was dying right before their eyes.

Tessa ran back to the room with a bowl of ice cubes in her hand. Her mother sat on the bed pressing a wash rag soaked in the water from the cup onto Marula's face. Her grandmother was on the opposite side rolling towels and propping them along Marula's spine and legs so she couldn't roll onto her back.

"Take off her socks and take a cube and rub it gently up and down the bottom of her foot," Todd told Tessa. "Just enough to make her body pay attention to what's going on down on her foot. Here," he pulled the corner of the sheet and placed it in Tessa's hand, "use this for your fingers."

Tessa moved to the tiny, crowded, twin size bed. As she sat, bowl in hand, her heel banged into something. Between her legs, she lifted the bed skirt off the floor and picked up what she had hit. A bottle of Vodka. Empty.

248

All eyes drew to the bottle as if it were a magnet that attracted retinas. Her father's eyes filled with glassy pools and her mother inhaled sharply. From her side, she heard her grandmother begin to murmur quietly under her breath.

Tessa took off Marula's left sock, and with her fingers draped in the corner of the sheet she took a cube and began to rub it back and forth on her sister's foot. Watching the water trickle as the cube melted fast, Tessa began to pray. "Heavenly Father, this human right here with us is our love, our sister, our daughter, our granddaughter…Her life is a gift and a treasure to the world, please, please, Father, save her. No matter what it takes, save her. I love—" Tessa began to sob.

Benji
Forty Two

It was pouring outside. Tessa stood on the front stoop, all but a few lone strands of her hair tucked into a knitted slouch beanie. Both the hat and her green jacket were shiny with rain water.

A blue Ford Taurus, with a gray-haired woman waving, pulled out of the driveway. "What are you doing here?" Benji asked, reaching out to take her sleeved and pull her into the house.

His parents had left for work and Leah had already caught her bus, but he didn't need to leave for another ten minutes. It used to be twenty, but that was before he met Tessa.

"My grandmother brought me," she said, her voice shaking. Her shoulders rolled forward as if carrying a heavy load on her back, and her head arched low and down.

"Come in. You need to warm up." He guided her into the house and to a kitchen chair.

Drops of water fell from the ends of her hair onto the table. Her eyes looked hollow as if she was looking through the space she was into a distant place.

"Marula," she choked out her sister's name. "Hospital."

"You need coffee or some tea. Let me get you something." He rose from the chair with intentions of warming her up, but she caught his forearm and held tight.

"No. Marula is in the hospital." Her voice was sharper, less shaky this time, and he wondered if she had sounded shaky from the cold or because of something else.

"Is she sick? Did something happen?"

She tucked a long wet strand of hair behind her ear. "Yes, something happened."

"Something bad?" He sat down and held her hand, but feeling its cold he began to rub it with his.

For a few heartbeats, she watched his hands move briskly against hers, and then she inhaled as if to reset her strength and spoke. "She sounded funny. I heard her sounding funny and went to wake her, but she wouldn't wake up. My gram was going to make waffles for us this morning. I found an empty bottle tucked under her bed. And the ambulance came. Maybe my gram's waffles would have woken her. They always do. No one makes waffles like Gram."

Her disjointed rambling made a thousand thoughts shoot through him. He reached and drew her close. Her wet hat seeped through his shirt; its cold instantly shocking his skin. The smell of fall was stronger with her hair wet, but it was also tainted with a rancid smell he couldn't place. "Tessa, where, exactly, is Marula?" He asked as clear as possible, making sure to use their names the way her father does, hoping it would kickstart her into clear thinking.

"She's at the hospital. My mom and dad are with her. Uncle Scooby is coming, but I needed to get out of there. They're going to admit her and send a psychiatrist to see her. But I couldn't see her like that any longer. That's not my sister in there. It's someone else. It's not my sister."

Wanting direct eye contact with her, he tipped her head. Her pupils quivered, focusing on him. "I'm going to take you back. I think maybe you're in shock. Trust me, you need to be there."

"Her mouth was black," Tessa said, distance refilling her eyes again.

"Stay here. I need to get my coat," he said, taking her hand and placing it on the table. "Stay here," he repeated, hoping she wouldn't tip over or pass out as long as she could feel something firm and steady.

She let him slip away long enough to tear through the house and up to his room to grab his coat. His computer was still split screened between reading the comments and shares from the video and a documentary he had been watching about Mongolia. He turned it off, grabbed his phone, and flew back down the stairs in threes.

In the kitchen, he tapped his back pocket to make sure he had his wallet then reached for Tessa's hands.

Slowly, he led her out the door.

Benji
Forty Three

During the ride to the hospital, Tessa explained how she had woken to Marula coughing and choking and found her pillow soaked in vomit. And that she found an empty bottle of Vodka under the bed.

"What did you mean when you said her mouth was black?" Benji asked, lacing his fingers through hers and then pulling them up to the vent to warm them.

"I'm sorry, I can't think clearly. It was the charcoal they gave her after pumping her stomach. It's supposed to neutralize poisons, but she looked like a demon possessed person you see in movies. Black lips, red blood-shot eyes, and so weary. It was horrible."

By the time they reached the hospital Tessa's hands were warm and her cheeks weren't as flushed, but when Benji pulled into the parking lot and parked he turned and saw her eyes were renewed with tears.

"Come on, I'll walk you in."

"Will you stay?"

"If that's what you want."

She nodded.

He leaned across the console, tipped her head, and kissed her forehead.

Even though a wide isle and the chairs of the hospital waiting room separated them, Benji could see Tessa's eyes were veined and weary.

It was painful watching her and not be able to touch her. Every time he thought of her hand in his, his palms warmed. It was as if his hands remembered her as much as his heart. She leaned against her father's chest, one of his arms encircling her and his other encircling her mother, who looked like an older version of Tessa. Tessa told him she looked more like her mom than her dad, but it had been an understatement. Aside from smile lines around her mother's eyes, and the after-forty age creases around her nose and mouth, they looked amazingly similar. There was no mistaking they were related. Even her mother's hair held strands of twine dangling randomly through her curls.

When they first came in, Benji had kept quiet and tried to hang back as he walked Tessa back into the waiting room. He worried he would be unwelcome under such circumstances but as soon as they walked through the door Tessa's grandmother came to take her into her arms, at the same time as introducing herself to Benji with a handshake around Tessa's back. Her father remained seated but gave him a head nod, which Benji assumed was an approval for him to stay. Her mother also gave him a head nod and a quiet, "Hello."

After waiting an hour, a man dressed in scrubs came in to speak with the family. Everyone rose in unison as he entered the small waiting area, tired but eager expressions on their faces. Benji decided that was his cue to go to the hall.

He was only out in the hall long enough to watch an elderly man slide money into a snack machine and complain that the package of M&M's was too small, before Tessa came through the heavy double doors. He immediately reached to cup her neck and face in his hands, kiss her forehead, and then pull her in tight to his chest. Unlike earlier, her face was warm though her usual smell of fall was still tainted by what he now realized was an echo of vomit. The odor triggered his thoughts to the basement and the video. He had finally been successful, and now it seemed completely irrelevant in light of what Tessa was going through. Leah would be free, and he was happy about that, it's what mattered the most, but now the idea of his dad paying for his evil seemed almost pointless. All along he had wanted to protect Leah, but he also wanted the Rat and the Fake to pay a price for their ways. As if exacting a price would repay him and his sister for their misery. But now, none of that part mattered. Blue Barbie no longer mattered. The Leo's of the world didn't matter. Girls' lollipoping his father didn't matter. Only Leah mattered. And now Tessa and Marula.

Tessa's voice was flat but light as if she used far too much energy crying and hardly had any left to speak. "Thank you for bringing me back…for being here."

"I'm so sorry. I wish I could do more. I wish I could change time for her, and for you. For all of you." His eyes misted with tears.

Tessa looked up and saw them. "Thank you for caring. Thank you so much. You can't possibly know how much it means to me. To us." She gripped tight to his waist. He felt her warm breath on his chest as she cried.

Benji
Forty Four

"How are you doing?" Benji asked. He had been at work for an hour and was anxious to receive a text from Tessa. They text back and forth a few times throughout the day; him to send a few jokes for her and her to return "thank you's" and smiley icons. She had stayed home from school, which left Benji facing the emptiness of lunch and the hole that her absence made when he went in and out of the main school doors.

But she didn't text. Instead, she called.

"I'm doing okay. Tired but okay. My gram brought me home to make cookies for Marula. It's all she's been asking for."

He smirked at the idea of Tessa flitting around the kitchen, bare feet, yoga pants, hair braided over her shoulder with some sort of twine or feathers interlaced.

"Cookies sound like a winner for quick healing," he said. She responded with a huffy sound that must have been a sigh. "Maybe you can make cookies and sleep for a while. Or sleep for a while and make cookies after."

"I don't think I can sleep, my mind won't be quiet."

The weary tone in her voice made his chest ache. "Any more news?"

"Unfortunately, yes."

257

"Hang on a minute, a customer is coming in." Benji set his phone down next to the computer but didn't hang up. The customer was a player for the Detroit Tigers who Big Timmie set up with complete security last year at his house in Novi. But the player's daughter broke one of the cameras last week.

"Hey. Big Timmie in the back?" the player asked, handing over his credit card for the new camera. They could have shipped it, but he liked to shoot the breeze with Timmie. Watching them interact was like watching two bears give each other knuckle taps and chest hugs.

He picked up the intercom phone and told Big Timmie there was a guest who wanted to see him. "Drew," he answered when Timmie asked who, then promptly said to send him back.

He glanced at the clock. Two more hours of work and then maybe he could stop to see Tessa on his way home.

He picked up his phone. "What time are you heading back to the hospital?"

"I'm not going back tonight. My Dad is taking her the cookies. I need to get a grasp on my emotions. Tomorrow would be better."

"Is she worse?"

"Not actually...well, yes, in a way," she paused and he heard a clanking of metal. Maybe a blender and bowl. "The doctors told us there were some pills mixed in with the alcohol in her stomach."

"Does that mean...," he stopped himself, unsure how to ask whether it was a suicide attempt.

"She says she didn't want to die, only that she wanted to make things go away for a while. She vaguely remembers that her head kept hurting so she took aspirin. We think she took more than she realized over the hours since some of the pills were more dissolved than others, but truly we don't know. I hate to think of her as not telling us the truth, but I never heard her get up and I think I would have heard her if she got up more than once."

"Maybe you were extra tired," he offered, wanting to help. But he could detect the fruitlessness of his words in her sigh.

"There's more," she said. "It's about why she wanted to make things go away."

"Go away? What does she want to go away? Memories of the party?" he asked remembering when he would ponder the taste of bullets. That was what he felt like, a sense of making things "go away." A way to make the stress stop. A way to end the pointlessness of his existence.

"Oh Benji, it's bad. Really, really bad. I don't know what to think, where to turn with my anger."

"It's okay to be angry. Don't you think it's natural?"

"No, you don't understand. Marula did something."

"Whatever she did it can't be that bad. It's terrible that she's made a mistake, but it must be fixable. From what you've said, she's a strong girl. She can be strong again. She has to. She has all the support of her family and that's what counts."

A sniffle and a mumble came through the phone at the same time the guys in the back got loud with "ah yeah's and alright."

"Sorry," he said. "The guys in the back were loud, I barely heard you. You said something about her phone."

"I wish I were there instead of here, this is hard to talk about over the phone," she said between sniffles. "I said that I went thru her phone last night and found a video from a group message, from the people she went to the party with on Friday. And there were a lot of texts from that girl that was in Maria's—I think you said her name is Claire. Apparently she's the one who sent out the horrible video."

"What video?" His voice quivered.

"A video of my sister…doing…oh god!" The yelp that came over the phone cut straight through him.

"Tessa, what do you mean a video of your sister?" His breathing turned to a pant. "A video of what?"

"Oh god, Benji, of Marula giving a guy oral sex!"

"What? That's impossible," he said, swallowing down the sudden regurgitation of his earlier soda. It burned the back of his throat like acid water.

"I wish it was impossible. She said she found out about a guy who would give her alcohol, but she had to do it first. She took a taxi to him…," she choked off the words. "It's horrible! The whole group thinks the video is funny. Every text message is joking about it."

His mind fought to piece things together as quick as possible. A tumble of information with holes cycled throughout his reasoning, and all the while he kept praying that somehow this was all a mistake. It can't be Marula with his dad. It just can't be. He had blurred the girl and there was no way to tell who she was. He even blurred the top of her head to make sure nothing of his dad's parts showed.

"But ho…how?" he stuttered over his wording, trying to remember if Tessa told him on Monday that Marula had stayed home from school. "Are you sure it's her in the video?" He scanned his memory for the images of the girls on the table holding their bottles like microphones. He had only recognized a few of the girls in the picture, and the picture of the girl vomiting didn't show a face, only hair over a toilet. He tried to tunnel all of the pictures into one sharp image in his mind, but there were too many. A wave of heat swept over his body as he realized that he never asked Tessa which one was Marula.

"Yes," Tessa said. "Marula confessed to me. But I knew it was her as soon as I saw the video because she was wearing my earrings. They were a gift from my friend in Indonesia."

While she described the earrings, Benji fought the full, churning weight of his stomach contents.

"That man gave her the bottle she drank yesterday," she explained. "Marula said she remembered a story from the girl…from Claire, from all the girls at the party, about this guy who gives them alcohol if they do that. She said she was sick with nerves but that she wanted the alcohol to make things feel better, less heavy. Then she received the video." Another sob echoed through the phone, followed by a thick sniffle. "I don't think anyone else knows it's her, at least not from what I can figure out. They only think it's some random girl. But she's ashamed and won't look at my dad or even speak to my mom, she will only talk to me." Benji jumped when the front door chimed, alerting him to a customer entering. "I threw away the earrings an hour ago. I don't ever want to look at them again. I don't know what else to do, she's hurting and I'm trying to make cookies and wishing they would take away her torment. How ridiculous is that?"

The most painful ache Benji ever felt swelled in his throat. He slumped back against the counter. It felt like someone poured hot water inside his head and was swirling it around.

A second customer entered the store and he fought to right his blurring, teary, vision.

This couldn't be happening. There was no way it could unfold like this. He needed to hang up the phone. He needed to get to his tablet. He needed to get out of the store. "Tessa, I have to go. Someone came in. I'm sorry. I will call you in a little bit. I'll fix this somehow, okay. I'll fix it." He clicked off as she asked what time he would call back.

He lifted his eyes to look at the customer walking up to him. The man's mouth began moving, but through the rushing sound in his ears, Benji only made out the word, "battery."

"Excuse me," he said and turned and smashed through the double doors to the workshop, running straight to the office and yelling to Michael that there is a customer up front who needs help.

Big Timmie and the baseball player jumped with the start when Benji blasted into the office and bee-lined to the box where he kept his school bag. He snatched it and headed for the bathroom, leaving Big Timmie yelling after him.

He slammed and locked the door behind him. Hugging his bag to his chest, he slid down the wall. He needed the floor, his legs weren't going to hold him much longer. He balled his hands into fists and rubbed them back and forth against his jeans, trying to calm their tremor. Somewhere in the back of his spinning thoughts he was aware that he was tapping the back of his head against the wall. A rhythmic tap as if he would knock things straight again.

He opened his backpack, pulled out his tablet and opened the cover. He watched as small icons, one by one, unfolded across his screen. The one he needed to see would be in the folder marked, "Busting Balls." He already knew what he was about to find, but he needed to anchor himself to it. He needed concrete verification. He needed to see for himself that the bomb of his tainted life was truly exploding.

He touched the file. It began playing the last video capture of his dad. It only took a half a minute before the girl moved into the frame. Immediately he honed in on her earrings and the small freckle on her earlobe. A grunt escaped his throat. The earring, a delicate filigree of silver braided together with a tiny green stone dangling from the end, was exactly as Tessa described. Tessa recognized the earrings because they were a gift from her friend Simmeron for her birthday last year. "The Jade stands for good fortune," Tessa said, and Marula had borrowed them from her for their first day of school. She hadn't given them back, yet.

At the proof, Benji let his body slide down the rest of the wall, crumpling in on himself until he was flat on the cold, nasty tile. It smelled like piss and Lysol, but he didn't lift his face up off of the nastiness. It was what he deserved. Down by his sides he made fists, rhythmically squeezing and releasing his fingers from inside his palms.

Marula had gone to Rat Bastard for alcohol. She'd gone to him to find her "escape."

A heavy pounding resonated on the door. "You okay, Benjamin?" Big Timmie asked.

He didn't answer. He feared if he did he would vomit all over the piss stained floor.

Timmie pounded again, "Benji, man, I need you to answer. Are you sick?"

He burst into tears. "Leave me alone."

"Tell me if you need an ambulance? Don't make me get the key only to come in and find you dead."

He wasn't sure if Timmie didn't make sense because he just didn't or because he was hearing him wrong through the sound of his pulse in his ears, but he managed to answer. "No ambulance."

"Okay, man. I'll be back to check on you in a few minutes. Pound the wall if you need help or something."

Through the small crack under the bathroom door, he saw shadows of feet moving away from the door.

On the floor, staring at a large crack in the grout of the black and gray tile, he tried to wrap his thoughts into a tight ball, but it was like wrestling an octopus. The tentacles outstretched so far that even if he could wrangle one thought another thought would burst out of his grip. He couldn't show the proof to his father now. How could he, if it meant showing that it was Marula in the video, too. In order to out his father, he would have to out Marula. Another tentacle escaped through a single dredged sob, right onto the pissy tile. He inhaled deep, willing the pee smell to poison him.

Then, like a knife slicing through the tentacles of thoughts, a sudden clarity hit him: Tessa didn't know he was responsible for the video. Neither did Marula.

Holding to the thought, he pushed himself up off the floor.

Benji
Forty Five

Benji drove in circles around the highways intersecting Ann Arbor before heading north. Two hours passed since he got up off the bathroom floor and told Big Timmie he was sick and needed to go home. He'd never gone home early before so Timmie was quick to pat him on the back and say, "Text me tomorrow so I know you didn't die."

For the first hour, Benji toyed with the idea of running his car into a pole or off a cliff. But the poles continued to whiz by mile after mile, as the night squeezed in around him and blackened the road and landscape.

With darkness swallowing him, he longed for a plan to manifest, one that would make things right for Marula and for Tessa. But nothing came, and the reality of helplessness pressed against his skull, squeezing a headache that ached down his back and shoulder blades.

He flipped on the radio but there was only a nasally preacher yelling with a hell, fire, and brimstone tone about the need to repent before the end comes, and a country station playing an old Kenny Rodger's marathon. He left it on the country station.

Nine o'clock came and went. Ten o'clock passed. It was eleven thirty when Benji finally put all the pieces together in his mind: One, he was a ridiculous joke when it came to masterminding. His plans had certainly worked enough times for him to believe he had some sort of control over things, like a mad scientist or, maybe, a mad psychiatrist. But there was no such thing as being in control. No one was ever humbled by his schemes. No one changed. No one was ever going to vindicate him or apologize, or even change their mind about him or about the world. Maybe everyone was right, he was not worth knowing much less friending.

He reached and turned the radio volume up to blasting, and he screamed. He screamed and screamed and screamed until his voice was exhausted. He screamed and screamed wishing the night air and the dark highway would choke him dead. But it didn't. Instead, he merely felt translucent. His insides now hung on the outside as if they belonged that way and not the other way around. He wondered if he stopped driving…if he ran into another human, would they be able to see right through him, through his evil and his anger. Would they see his unfair life? Surely they would know God made him wrong. They would know he was an oops on behalf of heaven. "Saint Paul, you grabbed the wrong one. That soul goes in a different life journey," God must have said.

His life was crap. His life was unfixable. His life— He stopped the thought, realizing something: his thoughts were all "me, me, me," and "I, I, I," just like Tessa said.

When his car sputtered, emptied of gas the way he was empty of screams, he pulled over on the side of the road, turned off the radio and leaned his car seat back. He grabbed his phone from his pocket, lay it on his chest, and closed his eyes and prayed to that phantom God that Tessa would not call or text him until morning.

As he fell asleep, he noticed the sign post on the side of the road where he ran out of gas. It said. "Welcome to Hell Michigan."

Benji
Forty Six

Big Timmie stepped out of his truck, Caesar following closely behind. In his dark hoodie, it looked like Benji was about to be attacked by a huge black bear—except for the red gas can in the bear's hand. Caesar greeted Benji with a sniff and a sit, and he gave him an ear scruff in return. "Hey, Caesar boy." His tail wagged, and he returned to his heel position next to Timmie.

"Hey, man," Timmie said, his deep voice echoing in the darkness.

It was five A.M.; Benji had woken an hour before by more video notices on his phone. They screamed at him like a morning alarm, triggering an avalanche of reality: He'd fallen asleep, his face burning from the salt of dried tears, and last night he'd driven all the way to Hell Michigan.

"You know you're gonna have to explain this right?" Big Timmie said, unscrewing the cap on the gas can.

Benji opened the gas cap for him and Timmie poured "I'm real sorry to wake you, but I couldn't call anyone else."

"Were you drinking?" Timmie asked.

Benji eyed him, thinking that after Marula and his dad he would never touch alcohol in his life. "No," he said with a snap that made Timmie turn his head and stare him down.

269

"Rough night?" Timmie asked his scowl holding firm.

"Rough life," Benji answered looking up at the Hell sign again. As soon as the gas can was emptied into the tank he knew Big Timmie would begin interrogating him, and there would be no running or lying his way out.

Benji's chin fell to his chest as the sinking realization hit him that all along he probably could have gone to him for help. If there was ever someone who he could trust, it was Timmie.

"Man, you need to spill because you look like you might throw up." Big Timmie put the cap on the empty can and leaned against the car, crossing his arms like an interrogating father. "You can tell me anything, you know that right? I got your back."

By the time Benji raised his head again, there were fresh tears welling in his eyes. One spilled onto his cheek as he said, "You won't want my back after I tell you."

Benji
Forty Seven

"Face it," was what Timmie advised after Benji downloaded everything, including about his father and Leah, the video of Marula, and Tessa.

"Don't make any more excuses and face it, step by step. Pay for whatever consequences fall." Timmie shifted in his seat. They'd moved to his truck to finish talking because his back was aching standing in the cold.

"But how do I do that? What if the consequences are losing Tessa forever, or not getting my sister away, or worse, jail?"

Timmie's chest heaved with a big breath. "The thing about consequences is they are up to fate, not us. I hope you see that you couldn't control what was happening in your life or your so-called schemes, but you also need to realize you can't control consequences either. From what you've told me there's been a lot of bad shit going on for you for a long time, and I'm pissed you didn't think you had anyone to go to for help, but now you have to gut-up and face things head on. I know inside you is a good heart, so learn do what your heart says not what you anger dictates. Be self*less* for once."

Benji wanted to argue, to justify himself and say he wasn't selfish and that he had a right to protect Leah, but he already tried. Timmie's response was a long but effective lecture, saying, "You can't claim you're not acting selfishly when, in fact, you're doing things to others in order for *you* to feel good. That's not doing it for them wholeheartedly that's doing for yourself and trying to convince yourself it's for others. There's no greater form of selfishness. If it had all only been for Leah, rather than fifty percent for Leah, then you would have found a different way. A way that didn't consist of tearing everyone apart."

"I'll be there for you but you have to stay open with me, okay?" Big Timmie offered, pulling at his beard thoughtfully.

Benji managed an "Okay," and ruffled his hair, which felt thick and gross from sleeping in his car.

For the next hour, together, they went over a plan on how to deal with things step by step, the last being his father and the video. The first, facing Tessa. "No matter the consequences," Timmie said.

Benji
Forty Eight

Benji sat in his car in the hospital parking lot, breathing and making humming noises through his nose. It was his version of an "om," and it usually worked, but as soon as he saw Tessa the courage he conjured scurried out of him.

Tessa's tied up cascading curls and bright blue cape were an instant heart sinking beacon as he walked up to the doors where she waited among the herd of people just inside the entrance of the in-patient building. Marula had been moved to in-patient earlier in the morning, and though he knew where it was Tessa insisted on meeting him.

When she flung her arms around him with a fierce hug, he gripped the envelope in his hand, trying to will it to help him keep his resolve.

Up on the fifth floor, he and Tessa were only allowed to sit in the family waiting area because non-family members weren't allowed in the room with Marula, which he was glad since he didn't think he could face her anyway. Tessa's mom was slouched down in a yellow waiting chair, asleep, with a book rested on her stomach and a small knitted blanket on her knees. Attached to the bottom of the blanket ran a length of yarn that went right up to Tessa's grandmother, who held a crochet needle and was tying, threading, and maneuvering the yarn into a longer and longer blanket. The image struck

273

him as symbolic as if they were connected to one another and Tessa's gram would always be there to comfort her if only with a blanket.

Her Gram put down the yarn work and made her way over to him. "Benji, is it?" She grasped his hands with hers. "I'm so grateful that you came to keep my Contessa company. Would you like something to drink? A pop, maybe some coffee. I brought a big carafe of coffee from home, it's the good stuff." She leaned into him and whispered, "Not that old hospital coffee they serve here."

He crumpled the envelope in his hand. "Thank you, ma'am, but no thanks. I had my fill this morning." Which was true, since he guzzled a pot while getting ready. He was sure all the caffeine wasn't helping the mental war or his stomach, but he needed the energy boost in order to keep going.

"Okay then. I'll let you two have some time together. If you need anything, please let me know. I'm a grandma who likes to mother everyone." She patted his shoulder and then turned back to her knitting and her chair.

"Want to go outside or stay here?" Tessa asked looking around the waiting room. There was a small group of people huddled around a television in the corner, listening to what looked like a Do It Yourself channel, but other than Tessa's family it was empty.

Benji glanced at Tessa's mother and grandmother and gripped the envelope tighter. "Would you be okay with going out to the courtyard? Maybe get some air?"

Tessa leaned into him and kissed his cheek. "I'll get my coat. It's in Rula's room with my dad."

"I'll meet you at the elevators."

"Perfect," she said.

As she left down the hall, his heart split in half. He thought he felt its cold venom flow into his stomach. Sick but managing a head nod to Tessa's grandmother, Benji headed for the elevators.

Waiting for her, he thought about how at Maria's Tessa said evil is selfish because it's what happens when someone wants what they want without thinking about how it will affect the people around them.

When Tessa met up with him, immediately threading her fingers into his, he remembered that day and how he had marked her definition of evil as another sign that his father was indeed evil, but now he understood, according to her plumb line he was evil too.

Benji
Forty Nine

Thankfully the courtyard was empty, and Tessa and Benji had the pick of cement benches and fall colored trees to sit underneath. It wasn't bad outside, just chilly enough to feel the cool breeze whisper against his ears. He pulled his hoodie up then tucked his hands into his pockets. He still hadn't let go of the envelope, though now it was crumpled wedge.

Tessa reached with a finger and pulled at his hoodie opening, peeking at him. He was staring at the ground, not wanting to look at her.

"Hey, in there," she said.

He forced himself to meet her eyes. She deserved at least that, though he felt his eyes quiver from the weight of chaotic thoughts. Each thought squeezed down on his mind like a vice, and all of them reminding him that was a coward and couldn't do this.

"Hey," he said back, coercing a small smile to break his weighted cheeks.

She reached her hand into his jacket pocket and wiggled it into his fisted palm to cover hers. Its warmth spread up his arm but also made his other hand clench. The envelope would be useless if he kept this up.

"I didn't hear from you after work. I was worried," she said.

"Worried? Why would you be worried about me?"

She leaned her head on his arm. "Well, the truth is, I hardly know you. It feels like I've known you forever, but last night I realized I don't. Not really. And I've walked into your life and dumped a whole bunch of burden on you, so it made me worry. I mean, I like strange but what if you don't like strange back." She shrugged. "I'm very sorry this is how you've been introduced to my family. This is not who we are."

"I know who you are, don't worry." He swallowed the backwash of acid that slid up from his guts. It forced him to turn his head and cough into his shoulder.

"You do?" He could hear her smile. He didn't even need to see her; it was in her voice. In her innocent voice. The one he was about to lose forever.

"Sure, your family is loyal, supportive, adventurous, and quite amazing." He took his hand from his pocket, smoothed the envelope out the best he could, and handed it to her. "And I am sorry for all the bad things that have happened…are happening. Sorrier than you can imagine."

She took the envelope and shook it, running her fingers over the small lump in the middle. "What's this?"

"That's for your father. Please make sure he gets it." He squeezed her hand in his pocket and then took it out and let it go.

She looked at her hand, and to the envelope, then scanned his face with her eyes. "I don't understand. Did I do something? Are we okay?"

Her question stung. How could she think she would ever do something to him? He was the evil one. The one who was cringing under the brightness that emanated from her soul. "No, you didn't do anything. I did. I don't deserve your time or your friendship."

Her forehead furrowed, drawing down her eyebrows and cinching her eyes into a probing squint. "Benji, are you using a word from the word list or something because I'm lost. And I'm hoping you are not trying to leave me or break up, or whatever they call it here in the States. That would hurt more than you know. Please, just tell me."

The idea that she felt they were together enough to "break up," snapped what was left of his resolve. Her apple smell wafted in the air, hitting him like a cold glass of water to the face. "Stop it!" he blared. "You can't be nice to me. You just can't. You'll see. Just take that to your dad." His attempt to form the words and make them come out and tell her, to take the step he was supposed to take, weren't managing to surface. His brain was busy trying to get him to stand up and run as fast as he could to his car. To leave it so that her father would tell her what he'd done, not him tell her.

She reached and touched his face. "Benji—"

He snapped his face away, cutting her off. "You. Are. Perfect. It's me. You can't be with me. I'm not good. I will taint you. I have already and you don't even know it."

"I don't understand why you can't see that you are kind and caring, and amazing. I'm sorry the world has told you otherwise, and other people's actions have made you believe less of yourself—"

"No," he whispered, the guilt eating him from the inside as if he swallowed rats. "You don't understand what I'm saying. I have to tell you—"

She placed her finger on his lips to stop him. He felt so sick he feared he might vomit right on her finger.

"You have to tell me it will all be okay," she said. "That's what you have to tell me. You have to tell me you will be here—"

"It was me damn it!" he snapped. Sudden tears scratched like sand against his eyelids, raking them with each blink. "I made the video that has Marula in it."

Tessa's face flattened. Her lips dropped into a flat line. Her eyebrows hung heavy over squinted eyes. She looked at him as if through a foggy lens, trying to focus on the image. "Wha…what do you mean?"

She pulled away from him. Her face phased through expressions of curiosity, denial, and then finally understanding.

"It was me. I released it. It was about my dad."

"I don't understand. How could you… Why would you?"

Now it was him who reached for her, but she yanked her arm away.

His skin ached at the rejection and longed for her to touch him again. Just her fingertips against his fingertips would be enough. Anything to promise

there would be more touch, more time, more…
Simply more. "I'm sorry." He hung his head, and
his eyes burned. "I'm so sorry. It was supposed to
be about my dad. I was trying to catch my dad."

"What does your dad have to do with my sister?"
He imagined her reaching for her hair, her henna
stained fingers shaking as she pinched and twisted
the ends.

"My dad…," he stopped, flashes of the video
playing in his head again: Marula's earring, her hair
color, the disgust of it all. He fought a gag but no
longer fought the tears; he let them flow. "It's such
a mess. I didn't mean to harm your sister." His head
shook "no" involuntarily, caused by the sheer
disbelief he felt inside. The horrors unfolding were
beyond comprehension and acceptance. Nothing in
his planning provided for this. "I was after my dad.
I didn't think something like this was possible. I
didn't mean for anyone else to get hurt that's why I
blurred the person." He lifted his head to face her.
To take what would come.

Her face was hard, stiff with anger. "Your father
is the man…," Her hands reached to cover her
mouth. Her voice returned to a whisper. She
repeated "Your father is the man and my sister…my
sister was with your father. But that can't be."

"My father gives teenagers alcohol in exchange
for…for…" he couldn't even say the words.

"Like a dealer or something?"

"Or something," he said. "He gives alcohol to
underage—"

She cut him off. "And you knew this?"

"Yes, but—"

"No!" she snapped, abruptly standing. "There is no "but." You knew!"

He wanted to stand, to run, but his feet were stuck to the ground, cemented in their position. Her voice choked, and his head gave out again, his chin hitting his chest. "I knew but I never thought." His eyes closed, heavy with tears. He opened them back in time to see one drip onto his knee like a bulging rain drop. "I was trying to get my sister free of him."

Her gasp echoed throughout the cement benches and the cobblestone walkway. "Your sister? I don't understand, was your father... Did your father *hurt* your sister?"

"Yes."

He could see her feet pace back and forth but was too afraid to look up at her. To see her face. And her hatred.

"My mind is trying to put this together. Help me here. Your father is a dealer of some sort—"

"Alcohol."

"Okay, a dealer of alcohol then, and you made a video for some reason, which happen to have my sister in it. Do I have it right so far?"

"Yes."

"And you decided releasing a video for the world was the best way to handle your dealer father."

He shuffled his feet, trying to ready them to stand. "I was trying to protect my sister."

He could hear her breath quickening. "What does Leah have to do with all of this? I don't understand."

A sudden surge of reasoning and rationalization coursed through his mind, and he stood up to meet her. "It's just that you never pointed out who your sister was in the pictures. I didn't know. Didn't you say you and she don't look alike? How would I have known?" He had an overwhelming urge to grab her and kiss her and beg her not to hate him.

"You cannot be serious! That's your excuse for hurting people!" She stopped a few steps away from him before whipping back around. "Your excuse for hurting my sister is that you didn't know which one she was in the pictures! So if you had, you wouldn't have splashed her all over the internet."

"No. I was trying to get my dad, not anyone else. I wouldn't have."

It was sudden, his body giving out. He barely realized he had crashed down until the pain shot from his knee caps upward.

Tessa's hands rose to her mouth again, her face turned a crimson. He thought she might get sick.

"My dad has been doing this a long time. Blue Barbie and others use him, and he uses them back. But Leah, she is innocent. I only wanted her away from him. I only wanted to catch him and make him go away."

"My sister is innocent too!" she screamed, tears streaming her face like lacey spider webs. "Why would you do this to anyone? How could you? And what in the world is a Blue Barbie?" Her tone was like ice picks against his conscious, stabbing him with their sharp points.

He looked up to her face from his knees. The dimple in her chin was like a darted hole from his angle. "Her house was the party. Claire is Blue Barbie."

"Do I even want to know why you refer to her as Blue Barbie?"

"It doesn't matter," he answered, desperate for a grand intervention. Was there no divine leading to help mankind? No God to help Leah. No God to help Marula. "None of it matters now." A whaling sob rose from his chest.

A sternness came over her voice. "Benji, what is in the envelope? What am I taking to my father?"

"Just take it to your father. There is a letter inside explaining everything." He rose to stand, feeling the ache in his knees and the shredding of his heart.

He took off full sprint to his car. The sound of Tessa calling after him grew fainter with each stride until he couldn't hear her sweet voice anymore. When he got to his car, he slammed against the door with his body and punched his fist against the roof until his knuckles swelled and burst open with blood.

Benji
Fifty

The house was quiet. It was noon. The clock above the kitchen sink ticked loudly in the silence, telling Benji it would still be another few hours before anyone else got home.

He ran his knuckles under cold water, inviting the pain as it burned and stung the gashes of skin. After wrapping his hand in a clean towel, he threw up into the garbage disposal.

Sitting at the kitchen table another hour passed while thoughts of Tessa flicked, one at a time, across his mind like an old, slow speed shutter movie. Flick: her at the coffee shop cocooned in her cape. Flick: her at school the first day, greeting him as if he was worth greeting. Flick: her with Leah at the mall decked out in feathers and colorful jewelry. Flick: her kiss. Her soft mouth on his and her light radiating into his being as she breathed out enough for him to feel her warmth on his lips.

He turned slightly, intending to gaze out the window, to think and ponder about how to fix everything, but Leah's calorie chart caught his eye. There was a new red "x," on the chart for yesterday's date. Inside the date box, written in Camille's tiny block handwriting, it said, "Second slice of pizza," and a frowning face.

"Are you kidding me!" Benji yelled as he bolted to the refrigerator, ripped off the calorie chart and shredded it into tiny pieces. It fell to the floor like snow.

It was sudden, like the strike of a match; his breath quickened, he tensed as a fire of anger snaked from his mind out to his entire body like a gasoline anointed blaze. He yanked open the refrigerator door and began pulling food off the shelf and slamming it to the floor. First a pack of lunch meat, then yogurt, then another yogurt and another, all splattering in a rainbow of gooey colors onto the green travertine tile. Then he threw a can of diet soda that burst open like a fountain, spraying half the wall and refrigerator, and his pants. Then a can of meal replacement shake, its label a bright red and white and covered with a giant American Heart Association stamp and a slim movie star. It hit the floor with an unsatisfying thud.

He noticed a pulsing heat in his ears, it fevered over his face making his forehead bead with sweat. Years of suppressed anger boiled over in an instant, running through his blood and muscles, cramping his legs as if he was braced for an earthquake to begin underneath him.

With another burst of fury, he spun and seized the Keurig coffee machine, sweeping it to the floor in one brisk motion. Its water and parts shattered into hunks of mechanical pieces and broken plastic on the hard floor.

Images of his father flashed before his mind as if something was falling into place. Puzzle pieces of a lifetime that formed a grotesque picture of perversion and passivity. His father in the morning, a coffee cup in hand and ignoring the fact that Leah was hunched over her "diet," food with an expression on her face like that of a dog forced to eat its own vomit. Bob never once did anything to stop the torture. Sweat trickled down Benji's face as he grabbed his father's coffee cups, one by one off the wall hooks, and pitched them like baseballs into the wall.

The last of the mugs ricocheted against the dented drywall making a shard fly at his face. He felt the nick from the ceramic when it sliced him under his left eye.

Spent, he slid his back down the wall until he was on the floor. Pulling his knees into himself, he surveyed the surreal pile of food, and cans, and shards. Its colors and sharp parts a mess that yelled so loud if it contained sound and language it would be deafening for the ears that dared to listen.

Shoving his hands into his hair, he grabbed a tuft and gripped tightly, making it want to hurt. Hating every part of himself and his life. Car Wash slammed into his thoughts. Blue Barbie's face in his at his desk. Rat and his perversions. The Fake and her face thick with makeup, never able to truly cover who she is.

Benji dropped his head and wept. He cried for Leah and her calorie chart, and for Tessa and Marula and their shattered lives, and he cried because of the lack of help from God.

He let the towel drop from his hand, shoved away from the wall and headed for the basement. After all, they were right there in the file cabinet, only twelve stairs down, and he could easily break the lock.

Two stairs.

Leah would be fine with only their mother…

Two more stairs.

He could leave a note behind, and Tessa's father could confront the Rat. Maybe that would make his mom divorce him. He could also leave a note for Leah, explaining everything…

Three stairs.

The image of Leah's face, peaceful, snuggled up and deep with sleep, safely next to him for so many years…

Three more stairs.

Could he keep going on if he only focused on Leah? Did he have the strength? Was there any way to forget about Tessa and the Car Wash's of the world and his jacked up parents, and focus solely on her? Was he still capable of controlling his anger and hate, of stuffing it down in order to keep going as he always had?

The wall socket camera stared back at him. Its double faces blaming him for thinking he could outwit everyone. "You fool," the sockets would have cackled if they could speak.

Bile churned in his guts, washing part way up is throat before descending back again.

No, there was no way to fix the disaster he caused…

He hadn't meant to cause it.

He looked from the wall to the file cabinet.

Life *cannot* be undone…

There was no reason to keep going.

He reached for the cabinet handle.

Benji
Fifty One

When he pulled the handle, the drawer didn't open. He already knew but assumed he should check before getting tools to pry it open. File locks were easy and this one wasn't commercial grade; it was simply a home cabinet with a small, metal twisting hinge. He could pry up the top lip and easily slide out the drawer. Though the gun boxes would be a different story.

His dad's work area was a smorgasbord of tools and he waded through them looking for the perfect flathead screwdriver and mallet hammer.

He plopped them down on the file cabinet with a clank then pulled off the socket camera and tucked it into his jean pocket.

He shoved the screwdriver into the crack between the drawer and the lock.

The basement door opened, immediately followed by footsteps on the stairs.

Twelve stairs! Twelve stairs! That's all there are and you only have to be on stair six to see into the area.

After yanking the screwdriver out, he dropped them beside the cabinet and turned in time to see his father; his glasses sitting on top of his head instead of his face; his belly covered by a starched and ironed button down suit shirt. Right behind him, eyes big as a doe caught in headlights was a young, red-haired girl, her hand in Rat's, him to leading her.

"Ben..ji…" he stuttered. But before he could say anymore the girl tore away and dashed back up the stairs.

By the time he heard the front door slam, Benji had reached his father and was yanking him down the remaining stairs.

The rest he observed as if life hit a fast forward button. Him straddling his father with his legs, his knees pinning his thick arms down so he couldn't get free. He felt the rat trying to twist and turn and lift his legs for leverage as he pummeled his face with his fists. The felt gash on his hand began to flow blood again and it mingled with the cut opening on Rat's eyebrow. With each blow, it opened millimeter by millimeter while the rat moaned and cried out. But all Benji heard was Leah's screams, Tessa's tears, and the girl who made slurping noises on the first video and how she had been a trash can for his father.

"She had to throw away the earrings!" Benji heard himself saying, but he sounded like he was underwater, gurgling with ragged breaths.

His arms tired. His fists shook with pain and adrenaline. His father stopped wiggling underneath him. Benji grabbed at his shirt and pulled his upper torso up to face him. Tears and spit and sweat splattered on Rat as he yelled, "I hate you! I hate you! I haaaaate you!" And then let him drop back to the hard floor with a thump.

Benji rolled off of him and onto his back, his anger raging and shaking him from his core outward.

When he heard his father moan and turn, he turned too, away from him, and curled into a ball and cried. "I hate you, God. I hate you even more."

Benji
Fifty Two

Benji remembered hearing once on an Oprah show, that molesters and predators find a way in their minds to make their victims a part of their excuse. Saying things like, "they (the predators) merely responded to their victim's bodies, or that the victim did not say no so they must have wanted it too." Even rapists justify their means with things like, "They were dressed like a slut so I treated her like one," or, "She didn't say no until after we began. She can't change her mind and then expect me to stop."

But he couldn't believe his ears were hearing his father blather to Camille about how "Each one of them came to *me*. They act like it isn't a big deal since they do it all the time now-a-days."

Benji, Camille, and Bob sat at the kitchen table, Bob holding an ice pack on his face, and Camille with her arms crossed tight across her body as if trying to close herself off from the horror.

Benji's fists balled, both hands trickling blood onto a towel on his lap. He truly had expected his father to get down on his knees and beg his mother to forgive him. Any sort of admission of guilt, such as, "I'm sorry, I just have a problem is all." But there was none.

When Benji finally got off the floor of the basement and went upstairs, he called his mother

291

and told her to take Leah to Cassy's before coming home. He flatly told her he beat the crap out of Bob and that Leah didn't need to see his hands or his father's face.

"Go ahead, call the police, I don't care," he yelled into the phone at his panicking mother. "All the better for everyone to have their shit exposed." Making sure to add, "Which will include the video evidence I have of your husband and his problem with teenage girls." That part had been enough of a threat for her to calm down and listen, and do what he asked.

At the table in the kitchen, the yogurt now drying like sludge on the floor next to them, the shards of the coffee cup like sprinkles on top of melting ice cream, the Fake's face ran with mascara the way Benji dreamed for so long. But instead of satisfying, it tore Benji apart. "I thought you were just watching porn down there," she cried. "How could you?" "Am I not enough for you?" "Maybe you're just sick," she cried, before dropping her face to her hands and sobbing.

While his mother tried to put things right in her mind, repeatedly asking, "But why, Bob?" a distance grew inside of Benji. He was physically sitting with his parents, his mind a rush of thoughts and puzzle pieces, yet another part of him floated on the ceiling and watched everything from a hazy distance. The floating him could see all the parts playing out: the past, the present, the future. It was as if someone aimed a beam of light at the four of them and he suddenly understood the dysfunctional cycle that trapped them all. For his entire life he felt lesser, as if born with a leveler that told him he was lower on a scale than the rest of humanity, which like a spiritual and mental DNA had come down from his parents. Why else would Camille use everything from thick makeup to constant dieting and her sinless, holy-roller image around people? She felt lesser, and that's why she was so hard on Leah; she is petrified Leah will grow up and be a no one, like her, like Rat, and like him.

Bob is the same; his out of shape body, his receding hairline and reading glasses tucked into his pocket. His self-worth merely that of blowjobs and accomplishments at work. He's a predator making excuses for his low self-value, all the while making every one of those girls the trash where he dumps his crushed masculinity. He's a victim causing more victims.

"What are you going to do with the video, Benji?" Bob asked.

There were several facts neither Bob or Camille knew: One, he gave Tessa's dad the only true recording and he already wiped his tablet clean and set it back to factory reset. Two, it's Marula in the video and Marula is Tessa's sister. And three, he released the tape over the internet and that the cops may already be informed by Tessa's father.

"I gave the video to Big Timmie for safe keeping but I haven't decided," Benji lied. Then with a forthrightness he wished he always owned, he added, "But I want you to move out. And I want you to move out tonight. If you don't, I will have Big Timmie go to the police."

"But where would I go?" Bob asked, and Camille made a crushing sobbing noise that made him want to reach out and touch her hand. For once, he understood her chaotic emotions and wanted to comfort her. "I don't care," Benji said. His teeth ached from grinding them. He hated how he couldn't get his thoughts in order, that the floating part of himself would not come together to help him control the spiral of decisions and information.

Benji squeezed his hands into fists and focused on the pain, willing it to make his consciousness come back together as one. He felt the flesh that was beginning to clot and stop bleeding unzip open again, and the blood begin to flow. Staring his father down, he pushed his mind to focus on Leah and held it there. "Get out of this house," he said as if the words were made of acid and would melt his father's resolve.

"I'm not leaving my house! I pay for this house, not you!" Rat bellowed, making a vein in his forehead bulge.

When Rat stood from the table and stormed out of the kitchen, knocking over the vase on the stand by the stairs, Big Timmie text, checking on him: "Everything going okay?"

"Come to my house. I need help," Benji text back after reaching over and placing his hand on his mother's, who started when the vase hit the floor.

Benji noticed her eyes were red and swollen, and her mascara was completely washed off from tears.

Benji
Fifty Three

Ten minutes later, when the doorbell rang, Benji was still sitting at the kitchen table, staring off into the distance and listening to his dad upstairs slamming doors and drawers. Benji hoped he was packing.

Camille's head snapped at the chime, and she frantically wiped at her face with her sleeve. As Benji got up, she began digging in her purse.

Benji opened the door, expecting Big Timmie's girth to be standing there, ready to back him up and scare off his father for good. Instead, there was a tall, distinguished man with close-set eyes and a clean-shaven face. His hair was a cap of white, and his skin was tan. He wore a collared shirt under a sweater and scarf and tan pants.

"Are you Benjamin Lockwood?" the man asked.

Instant shakes vibrated down from Benji's head to his hands, and his heart slammed against his rib cage. "Yes," he managed, realizing his hand left blood on the door handle. It looked like something straight out of a murder scene.

"I am Paul Schneider. I'm a friend of the Knightly family," he extended his hand to shake. "May I come in and speak with you? Or if you are comfortable, you can come out here."

Benji showed him his hands and that it wasn't a good idea to shake them. He scanned his mind for the familiarity of the man's name. Where had he heard it before?

Was the man's "come out here," a trick to get him outside? He leaned forward and searched the yard for cars or hidden police armed and ready to tackle him when he stepped out.

"Huh?" was all Benji managed.

"There is no one else here with me," the man said. "I am here as a favor to Mr. Knightly, Todd, and his family, including Tessa. Does it help if I say they call me Uncle Scooby? Though, I've always thought of myself more as Shaggy rather than Scooby." He offered a light smile to break the tension on his square face.

The recognition was instant. Uncle Scooby was the man in Tessa's story about her father. He is, was, the detective.

"I guess you may come in, but it's a bad time."

"Oh," the man said stepping forward and right into Benji's personal space. "I'm sure it's probably the perfect time."

Benji had no other choice but to move out of the man's way. Benji himself was tall, but this man stood at least six foot four and his body frame was that of a lean athlete. By the lines on his face, and Tessa's story, Benji deducted the man was probably in his sixties, but apart from the white hair he looked to be in his mid-forties. He was distinguished and formal, like a diplomat, and in no way did the man's presence conjure the name "Uncle Scooby." He was more like a gray haired Liam Neeson instead of a cartoon character.

"Umm, my mother is in the kitchen," Benji mumbled, unsure of what to expect but definitely making it obvious for the surprise guest to know others were home. Maybe it was to make sure Mr. Schneider wasn't there on a murder-for-hire mission.

"Good, I may need to speak with both of your parents as well."

Benji led Paul Schneider down the hall to the kitchen, acutely aware that the upstairs had gone completely quiet.

When they rounded the corner, Camille snapped closed a makeup compact and put it back in her purse. Benji realized that in a matter of minutes, she had managed to cover the red blotches on her cheeks and apply fresh eyeliner.

Benji shook his head in defeat. In light of the circumstances, Camille still needed to make herself over when someone came to the house.

A deep sigh had escaped Benji before he realized he was doing it. It caused both Mr. Schneider and his mother to examine him. He glanced back and forth between them before pulling out a chair and collapsing down. He suddenly felt exhausted, and he no longer cared whether or not he was going to be arrested. He flopped his arms on the table; the blood had begun to clot so now his hands looked red and black and swollen. He was half ready for Mr. Schneider to pull out handcuffs and place them on his wrists. After all, he's the one who distributed the video.

"Hello, ma'am, I am Paul, Paul Schneider. Are you Mrs. Lockwood?"

Camille flattened the wrinkles in her shirt with her hands and then touched her cheeks as if to perk them up before reaching out her hand. "Oh yes, um, I am Mrs. Lockwood. It's nice to meet you. What can I do for you? Can I get you a drink or something? I made fresh iced tea this morning." She was already turning to the cabinet for a glass when Paul answered. "Thank you, but no thank you." When she turned back, she wore a twitchy smile. Benji noticed she quickly clasp her hands together and he wondered if she was shaking, too. She had to figure it was odd timing for a strange man to come to their house.

"May I sit?" Mr. Schneider asked.

"Oh, yes, please," Camille pulled out her chair and sat down. The whole formality of it reminded Benji of a nineteen-sixties movie: His mother, the perfect wife and homemaker, and a salesman coming to sell vacuum cleaners. Had Paul worn a fedora hat and accepted the ice tea the scene would be complete.

Paul sat, placing his arms on the table as well, only he threaded his fingers together, his first fingers straight out and meeting one another. "Benjamin, are you okay?" he asked, surprising Benji.

He hadn't expected concern to come from Paul. Tears uncontrollably welled in his eyes. "No," he managed.

"I see. Well, I am here because I am a longtime friend with Todd Knightly, and Benjamin here has shared some personal information with his daughter,

298

Tessa. Do you know whom I am speaking about, Benjamin?"

Benji nodded. A tear fell in a long streak on his face.

"Mrs. Lockwood, do you know whom I am speaking about?"

"Of course, I have met this Tessa but only momentarily," she confessed. Her hand reached to fidget with her necklace. "May I ask again, what can we help you with?"

"Ma'am—" Paul began.

She stopped him. "Call me Camille, please."

"Camille, is it possible for me to speak with Benjamin alone?"

"I'm sorry, is there a particular reason you are here? Are you the police? Is Benjamin in some kind of trouble?"

Benji's head snapped up and he smacked a flat hand on the table, making a bloody palm print stamp the table top. Paul didn't flinch. "Me! You're kidding right!" How could she have instantly jumped to the conclusion that he was the one in trouble rather than the rat?

Paul waited, looking at Camille as if it were a valid question.

"Ex…cuse me, Benjamin," she croaked, her hand going to her chest, feigning shock, "You don't need to speak to me like that. Would you please pardon my son's attitude, Paul, it's been a hard day."

Benji felt sick as the tears flooded down his face. He needed to wipe the drip of snot from his nose, but he was stunned, paralyzed by the moment. His body begin to pull away from itself again; as if someone gently tugged his inner being backward and down a long hall that would keep him safely at a distance. Maybe this is what people mean when they say they experience out-of-body moments.

"Ma'am—"

"Camille," she corrected.

"*Ma'am*," he said again this time with a strong emphasis. "I am not here on an investigation, I am here as a friend of the Knightly family and I would like to speak to Benjamin alone."

Benji counted five pounding pulses of his headache before Camille pushed away from the table and, without a word, left the kitchen, her black bootleg pants swinging against her ankles.

The quiet finally shattered when Paul rose from the table and took a paper towel from the roll next to the kitchen sink, then opened a series of drawers until he found a hand towel. After running water and dampening it, he lay it gently across Benji's hands. Next to it, he put the paper towel. "That's for the tears," he said then sat back down, his arms out on the table, his fingers knitted together, all but the first ones, which again formed a steeple.

"Are you here to arrest me?" Benji asked.

"Let's clear that up first. No, I am not. I am here to help," Paul said.

Benji nodded. "Okay."

"I am here because I've been told some scary information and I'd like to hear it from you."

"Do you mean the video?"

"That…among other things, but the Lockwood's and I will make some decisions about the video later, for now I am here for your story. The Lockwood's are concerned for you."

"That can't be right," Benji said. "I did this to them, not the other way around. Marula, the video, her trying to find an escape from life, or possibly trying to kill herself, I did this. It's all my fault." His knees began to quake under the table so he squeezed them together.

Paul reached over and tucked the towel around Benji's hands. In a whisper, he said, "Let's clear another part up as well. Don't say anything further about Marula, ears may hear and I don't want "others" to have more information than I can deduce from them. Do you understand where I am heading by saying that?"

Benji nodded, but he didn't understand.

"Now, what I want to hear from you is about your father. If you would be more comfortable, we can speak outside, or in my car, or we can simply go for a walk in the neighborhood." He must have seen Benji stiffen because he added, "I promise you, I am not here as a police officer and I have no ulterior motive. You are safe. Okay?"

"A walk would be alright," Benji muttered, taking the paper towel and wiping his nose.

"Good, but let's get those hands cleaned up and wrapped first. Does your mother have a first aid kit or some bandages?"

"Yes, there's a first aid kit in the cabinet over there," he inclined his head to the wine rack and the doors underneath.

"I'll get it and you go to the sink and run cool water."

Benji
Fifty Four

The running water stung, but Benji's knuckles were already near numb so when Paul wrapped them with gauze and medical tape it hardly hurt.

Paul asked him polite questions while he cleaned, dried and wrapped his hands. "What grade are you in? How old is your sister? Have you lived in Michigan your entire life? What do you think of the skiing? Do you know that some of the best beaches in the world are right here on Lake Michigan?"

Benji tried to stay focused on the things Paul asked but still wondered if they were set up questions designed to soften him and get him to say things that could be used against him later. Deciding he didn't want to hide anymore, and as Timmie had said, "Face it all, no matter what," he answered everything Paul asked, even when he asked if he liked it at home with his family. "I'm here for my sister and that's all," Benji said.

With his knuckles wrapped, Benji pulled on his coat, a winter cap, slipped into his steel toe boots, and left the house with Paul...Uncle Scooby. His mother and father didn't make a sound or come downstairs.

As they walked down the driveway, Paul said, "I noticed your mother didn't come down to see us out the door?"

"Yeah, my dad is upstairs and I think he's hiding."

"From me?"

"Probably."

"Mmm, I see."

"And your mother, she didn't tend to your hands," Paul said as if speaking out loud to himself and not Benji.

Benji snorted, "But she sure had on her makeup pretty quick, huh?"

"What do you mean?"

"She cried it off before you came and then put more back on before you made it from the door to the kitchen."

"I see. Why was she crying?"

Benji felt as if he might rupture. As if his sternum and ribs had caged back a monster all this time and now the monster desperately needed to get out. He began spilling everything, beginning with, "Because, my dad has been getting his rocks off with girls."

They walked the length of the road, passing Mr. Planter's house, the playground, and the neighbors with the big dog sitting still behind the line of the underground wire pet fence. Paul kept his hands in his jacket pockets, nodding and saying, "I see," a half a dozen times. But he never interrupted or stopped Benji while he rambled on about trying to catch his dad, and about making sure Leah was safe, and the night he found his Dad crawling into her bed half naked. As he talked, a part of him wondered if this was how interrogations worked before the person is arrested: break the culprit down with niceness and understanding and they will eventually spill it all for you. "I didn't know it was Marula on the video. I would never have…" he choked the tears back this time, stopping them before they overwhelmed him again.

"I understand. As I said in the house, we will get to that part but first I have to discuss it further with Mr. And Mrs. Knightly. For now, I am here for you."

"But why for me?" Benji stopped walking and faced Paul. "Look, it's killing me inside, are you going to have me arrested for distributing the video?"

"No, I am not. Mr. Lockwood is not interested in seeing you locked up, nor is Mrs. Lockwood."

"And Tessa? Does she want me in jail?"

"No, of course not. Of the whole family, she is the most concerned. You have made an impression on my Goddaughter, you know. I've never seen her so…well, how would I say in your age language…starry eyed."

"Huh?"

"Not a good depiction?"

"No, it's not that, she should hate me is all."

"Hate is not a word the Knightly family will ever use, much less feel. Of that, I can assure you."

Paul began walking again. Benji followed, his feet kicking at the gravel and small pieces of broken concrete as they walked up and down the road.

"Benjamin, I understand you are cautious and nervous of me but I came because of what you shared about your father with Tessa. I am here to listen to your side, and to see what I can do to help you and your sister. I am not here with malice or ulterior motive or even to present anger, though, I will be honest, I am in pain about Marula. She is one of my treasures and what you've done to release her sins to the whole world is quite hard to have to witness." Paul paused, then placed a hand on Benji's shoulder. "So that you know, I am the only one who has seen your memory card. Mr. Knightly handed it over to me and has not watched. Nor will he. I alone will carry that part for them. The only thing I need to know is…is that truly the master copy? Are there no other videos out there? Ones that you may have texted or shared with close friends."

"It's the only copy." Benji's head sunk into his shoulders. "The one I released was the blurred one. Only I had the original and I wiped my computer tablet clean and put it back to factory reset after I had realized it was Marula."

"That's good. You are very clever with these devices, you know."

"I work for a—"

"Hey kid, you okay?" Big Timmie's truck pulled up next to them when they turned around at the end of the street. Caesar sat upright in the front seat, his seatbelt harness around his chest, watchfully observing the three of them.

When Big Timmie opened his door and stepped out, Benji noticed Caesar put his nose to the air as if inspecting the added new comer's scent.

"I'm okay," he said. "This is Tessa's Uncle, Mr. Schneider."

Big Timmie stuck out his hand. "I'm Tim Stouten. Everything okay here?"

Benji looked at Paul, "This is my boss. I called him for help. To help me get my dad out of the house. He knows everything."

Paul seemed to appraise Big Timmie with his eyes, reading his stance, his clothing, Caesar, and even the big emblem on the side of the truck that read, "Big's Custom Security."

Big Timmie did his own appraisal. It was like watching a lion and a cheetah size each other up. One with brawn and might and the other with speed and stealth, though nearly the same height.

"We've met," Paul said. "A fishing buddy of mine, Amir, had you overhaul the security on his house and his restaurant out in Silver Lake last summer."

"Ah, yes, I thought you looked familiar," Timmie increased his handshake and patted Paul on the upper arm. "Paul, the retired detective right? Sorry, I don't remember your last name. How is Amir? I saw him in the fall and stayed at his cottage on the lake. There's great fishing out there."

Benji wasn't sure what to do with himself while he watched Timmie and Paul swap fishing stories and remember how they met one another, followed by what, exactly, brought Paul here to Benji's house. It was as if Benji's life and Leah's life, and

306

Tessa's life, and Marula's life were all hanging right there out in the open, as if they all had been filleted by the world, by him, and these two were merely exchanging niceties over their open, wounded bodies.

"What do I do now?" Benji interrupted as Paul explained how he's a friend of the Knightly family and was here to speak with Benjamin.

"You mind if I'm in on this conversation?" Timmie asked. "I have to protect my kid, he's pretty important to me."

"If it's okay with Benjamin?" Paul looked to Benji for approval. "I honestly am here to help him and his sister, nothing else."

"Not investigating?" Timmie asked, squinting at Paul.

"Not formally, only as a family friend. They are worried about Benjamin. Everything said is between me and Benjamin, and you, if he agrees, is confidential."

"Care to say it into my voice recorder?" Big Timmie asked pulling out his phone.

Paul's eyes widened, and then he broke into a smile. It took a moment for Benji to realize it was admiration. "I can oblige your request, no problem."

Timmie hit record and put the phone to Paul's mouth.

Benji
Fifty Five

When the three of them walked into Big's Custom Security store and then back to the shop area the guys working all stared, studying them as if trying to piece how the trio belonged together: Benji looked like he'd been in a car accident, his face swollen, a small slice under his eye, his hands bandaged, his eyes red and bulging. Paul kept his head held up, confident, trailing the air of a diplomat behind him. And then Big Timmie, silent, chest out and with an expression that warned, "It's none of your business, get back to work."

Two hours went by while the three of them talked, only pausing long enough for Benji to call and check on Leah and to ask Cassy's mom to keep Leah for the night, for Timmie to make a fresh pot of coffee, and for Paul to speak with Todd and let him know he was with Benji and that Benji was safe.

But the more they talked, the more Benji's energy drained. The steady focus and resolve he normally depended on now seemed like it never truly existed. "I couldn't stop myself. My anger just boiled over," he said, explaining his tore up knuckles weren't only from punching the car but also because his father had come downstairs with a girl right as he was about to get the gun, and because of it he had lost it on his father's face.

"Benji, man, it's awful to say but I'm actually glad he came down and interrupted you," Timmie said while pulling thoughtfully at his beard. He sat behind his long metal desk while he and Paul sat in chairs facing him. "That interruption saved your life, dude. And you being there, right at that moment, probably saved that girl from becoming another victim."

Paul nodded in agreement.

Benji looked up from a black inky spot on the floor that shared his attention. "I guess, but I never saved any of the other countless girls. I never even thought of them that way, as victims I mean. Not until Marula."

At the mention of Marula being a victim, Paul shifted forward in his chair leaning his elbows on his knees. It seemed an unconscious, braced, visceral response to the reality of what had happened between Marula and the Rat.

"I was always focused on Leah, but it's also about the revenges," Benji admitted. "They made me feel…I don't know how to explain it."

"Empowered," Paul offered. "They made you feel empowered."

"Yeah, I think so." Benji nodded. "I couldn't take it anymore, a few years ago I mean. With school, with my dad, every day was swallowing me." He dropped his forehead in his hand, shaking it at the remembering of how crappy everything felt, then and especially now.

"That's when the revenges began?" Timmie asked.

"Yes, I don't remember what triggered the first idea, exactly, but I remember the first one. I remember how great it felt to get one over on someone. It was…," he looked at Paul, "yes, I think it was empowering." Timmie nodded. Paul sat still, observing, listening. "The more I did, the bigger ones I got away with, well, I eventually looked back and realized that somewhere over time I stopped thinking about…," he swallowed forcing himself to say the words, "killing myself. Then I became focused on saving Leah—I thought about it all the time. I really thought I could do something good for her. To change her life direction, I guess. I remember when I did this one to a kid at the car wash and he got caught and I didn't, that's when I knew I had to do something big to pay my dad back, and also to get Leah away from him, from both of my parents."

"You mean that kid that vandalized the car wash over on Michigan Ave. You did that to him?" Big Timmie said, his pale blue eyes round and wide. "I remember it being on the news,"

"Yes, I did," Benji rubbed his forehead. The stress made his head feel like it was full of water. He wasn't proud of himself at all. Instead, he felt like crap.

Paul again shifted back in his chair. His head cocked slightly to the side as if surveying something in his mind and trying to fit pieces of a riddle into place. Slowly at first, but then picking up speed he began tapping his fingers on the arm of the chair.

"It sounds bad, now," Benji confessed, "as I say it out loud, but when it was happening it felt good to finally put people in their place. I thought I could put my dad in his place, the way I did to the rest of them. And I wanted that place to be outside of our house, not living with us anymore."

"Benji," Paul abruptly said. "Did you ever write down the things about your family, specifically about your father? Such as in text messages to friends or maybe emails."

"No, I don't have people…friends, I mean."

Leaning forward, Paul put his elbows on his knees. His eyebrows drew in, his eyes looked both at Benji and through Benji, studying him. "In my experience anyone who does the type of thinking you have done when making these types of plans…when you thought through your, what did you call them, revenge schemes, that type of person always has an outlet for their thoughts. A place to keep memories of the events."

"Whoa, wait a minute, what do you mean "that type of person?"" Big Timmie leaned into his desk. "What are you implying, Paul?"

Benji glanced back and forth between them, curious as well about Paul's statement. Did he think he was a psychopath or something? He wasn't. He loved Leah too much, and right now he ached for her, and for Tessa and Marula. A Psychopath wouldn't feel the level of heartbreak he did.

Paul didn't respond to Timmie, his eyes stayed set on Benji. "Is there anything…anything at all you can think of where you have kept a record of your life, a place you put your thoughts about Leah and getting her away from your father? You said you wiped out your tablet, did you have something in there? A file of some sort where you expressed your thoughts and plans. Anything I could use to help figure something out for your father?"

Benji's head sloshed around with thoughts. He did have something. He remembered. But what if all his fears of jail time would be realized and Paul had tricked him all along. "Yes, there is something," Benji said, figuring it wouldn't matter in the long run? He deserved more punishment than he was getting right now anyway.

Timmie's back straightened. "Wait, before you say anything more, kid, what would you do with it, Paul? What are you thinking?"

"I'm thinking there might be another way to handle Mr. Lockwood without having to uncover my goddaughter and her involvement."

"Ah," Timmie said nodding his head up and down as if he understood a secret message being passed to him. "I see where you might be going."

"I don't," Benji said. The pain in his hands began to settle into a rhythmic throb that beat along with his heart.

"What do you have?" Paul asked.

Benji regarded Timmie, who nodded his head, "Go ahead, kid, I think you can trust this guy."

He swallowed the knot in his throat. "I have this box of stuff and it has a spiral notebook…a journal of sorts. I write about my revenge stuff in there."

"Only the revenge plans?"

"Yes."

"That won't do. I need something about your father."

Benji snorted. It was a reflex. A relief response that Paul wasn't interested in his revenges, the illegal parts of them at least. He rubbed his hands through his hair and then put back on his knit hat. "I might have something else."

"Spit it out, kid," Timmie said.

"I have these fake internet profiles where I am a Belgium girl and there are chats with some of the girls from my school." Timmie chuckled, and Paul smiled. "They talk about my dad in them, how they get alcohol from him like he's the local liquor store."

"You're a damn genius, kid." Timmie rubbed his beard, and he and Paul exchanged glances. "Not that you should have used it all for this bad junk you were holding inside, but you are still a genius."

Paul nodded in agreement.

"I'm not a genius, I'm an asshole," Benji said, staring at his hands, a sudden remembering of Tessa's face when he told her it was his fault for the video and that it was his dad with Marula.

"That too," Timmie said. "But we can help with the asshole part, right, Paul? Hell, I was an asshole most of my life."

"I printed them, but they're also still in my messages in my account," Benji said.

"Wait a minute," Timmie stood up. "Benji, I need to talk to Paul, alone, for a few minutes."

Paul leaned back in his chair, studying Timmie's face. Benji glanced between them, trying to deduce what was going on. Paul finally nodded to Timmie, a type of silent agreement Benji didn't understand.

"It's all good, kid. I only want to cover a few things with Paul before you hand over all this information to him."

Paul nodded again. "I can agree to that," he said, standing to meet height with Timmie and shake his hand.

Without a word, and needing more aspirin, Benji left the office, leaving behind a lion and a cheetah to talk about his future. Whether in prison or free, he had no idea.

Tessa

When the doorbell rang, all of Tessa's trapped anxiety bubbled up and came out as a loud burp. The sound of it made Marula laugh. The two of them had been sitting at the island for an hour talking about the new four inches of snow that fell for Christmas. It had been a long time since they saw a white Christmas this beautiful.

"It's time to start healing," their father said a week ago, prompted by Uncle Scooby who said it would be a good thing for the family to meet with Benji face to face. "He's hurting too," their mother had said, her face a still, stoic mask, even though Tessa could tell it was hard for her to forgive Benji. She knew her mother was justified in her anger, after all it was her baby's face that had been splashed across student's cell phones and internet chats.

From what they could tell no one ever found out it was Marula in the video, apart from those that had sat at the dinner table discussing their healing, and Benji.

This dinner though, tonight, would be the first time the family and Tessa would see Benji face to face and Tessa was a ball of nervous anxiety.

Over the months, Benji apologized several times on the phone and once to her entire family on speaker phone, but this would be different. It would

315

be a test of their ability to move on. And another test of their forgiveness.

"Everyone has a story," Tessa's grandmother had said eyeing Todd the night Uncle Scooby suggested a dinner together with Benji. At gram's reminder Tessa's father's face melted of its anger and became soft and innocent, as if he were a young boy again and remembering his own fear and pain; his own willingness to do anything to help and protect his mother.

Uncle Scooby had relayed to them about Camille's inattentiveness and self-absorbed manner, and about Bob after officially meeting him at the police station. "He acted like his life had been disturbed by this inconvenient moment," Uncle Scooby told them.

Uncle Scooby had helped hatch a plan, along with Todd and Mikael, to have Mr. Lockwood arrested and prosecuted. "It's best that we attempt to keep the video out of the entire thing. We'll use it as a threat, but only, and I mean only, if it's the last possible hope we have of prosecuting this guy will it surface." They all agreed.

Thankfully, Benji had an old box where he kept internet print outs of conversations about his father. In the end, the online chats were the pressure needed to get his father to plead guilty and the video wasn't needed.

Just this week the prosecutor told them Mr. Lockwood agreed to a plea deal and would receive five years of probation, his name on the sexual predators list, and won't be allowed around children eighteen years and younger, including Leah, unsupervised.

"Throw it away, burn it, I don't care. I took out the things I needed. The normal memories." Tessa overheard Benji tell Uncle Scooby on the phone about his box named, "Pandora." Uncle Scooby was using her dad's home office phone and had it on the speaker. She had stood outside the door listening quietly and aching over how much she wanted to hug Benji. Over how much she wished she could turn back the clock to before everything happened.

"You sure, Benji," Uncle Scooby chuckled at the "normal," comment.

"Yes, I don't want anything to do with it, with its secrets."

Tessa had listened to the tightness in Benji's voice and pictured him scrubbing his hands through his hair.

Scrubbing his hand through his hair was exactly his reaction when he came through the door behind their Uncle Scooby and saw Tessa and Marula laughing.

Tessa quickly cleared her throat, imagining how odd they must sound laughing right before such a serious moment in time.

Benji looked more beautiful than she remembered. His face was thinner, as if he hadn't been eating, and his eyes were shadowed underneath, but his hair was cut with a new fade on the bottom and the top stood up in just the right places. When he quietly said, "Hi," she immediately noticed his lips, pink and full, the same as they were they day she first saw him and dared to steal his fries. He looked tired but weightless at the same time, as if caught between gravity and the need to float away.

Marula stood first and Tessa followed though neither of them moved from the island. When Uncle Scooby pronounced, "let's eat!" while taking Benji's coat from him, their grandmother came from the dining room where she had been busy fidgeting with the table decor; a way to release her version of nervousness.

Todd and Mikael followed behind gram, both of them with their hands extended ready to shake. Tessa noticed her father didn't take his arm from around Mikael's waist as if keeping her braced and strong.

Seeing Benji reach his long arm, his hand quivering with nerves, and his sad demeanor, any bit of anger Tessa had left over melted away. She didn't want to yell at him—as she'd imagined several times in her mind— or lecture him about how he should have done things differently, or how he was terrible for causing Marula pain on top of her already piled-high pain. Instead, she wanted to hold him and to predict a bright future for him. She wanted to sit and talk about Leah and how she was doing, and if she understood or even knew what was going on. She wanted to kiss him…

Suddenly, Marula shot from the island and launched herself into Benji's chest, her arms enveloping his waist in a hug. Everyone stood motionless, as if trapped by a time spell, until Benji lifted his arms and surrounded Marula with them.

318

His head dipped, leaning on the top of hers, and he began to weep.

Seven months later…

"My mom found me a different psychiatrist. I like him. He seems good for Leah, too. He pretty much forbid my mom from putting calorie charts on the refrigerator," Benji said while he and Paul walked around his neighborhood. It was late spring, and the neighborhood houses all had their boats pulled onto the driveways, readying them for warm water season. Tulips were in full bloom, along with emerging dandelions, which had Mr. Planter on his hands in knees in his front yard digging them up, one by one. He waved and gave a friendly head nod as they passed his house.

"I can't walk by his house without picturing his bright, painted lawn, you know," Paul said with a chuckle.

"Yeah, me neither." Benji felt half his face pull up in a smile…a Tessa smile.

"Glad you like the new Doc. Sometimes it takes a while to find a good fit," Paul said returning Mr. Planter's wave.

"It was sort of strange to be able to outthink the guy you're paying to help you."

Paul chuckled. "I'm just glad you keep trying."

"Well, I owe it to Marula. And Tessa." Benji tilted his head back, surveying the dotted clouds and inhaled the fresh air. It was a perfect spring sky: bright blue with small cotton clouds.

"How are they, by the way?" Benji asked.

Paul had taken to visiting Benji once a month after he finished with his visit with Tessa's family. "To make sure you're on the straight and narrow," he'd say with a firm handshake and a manly pat on the back. Benji had grown to look forward to the visit. Paul shared stories from his days as a police officer, always ending the story by asking, "So, tell me the moral of the story." He also gave college advice and helped Benji sort through the constant overload in his head. But the visits also brought another thing Benji looked forward to, updates about Tessa.

"They're doing excellent." Paul glanced at Benji sideways. "I know you talk with Tessa sometimes, why do you always ask me how she's doing?"

"She tells me all about their horseback riding and the homeschool co-op group and how her gran's muffins are a hit with the other homeschool kids, but that's all."

"Ah, everything except what you want to hear, huh?"

Benji nodded. Every time he spoke to Tessa, he felt a sharp, shooting spot beneath his breastbone. He had grown to think of the pain as a reminder to keep on the "straight and narrow." But he also knew the sharp pain was there to remind him of his regret, to remind him Tessa will always be the one that got away. And that was his fault, too.

It wasn't until after Christmas that he had finally been able to make himself face the Knightly family. "Dinner with the family," Paul said on the phone the week before he came down.

The reconciliation dinner was almost five months ago. It was the day Marula encircled him with her forgiveness. All those revenges, all those years of plans, even the moment he caught his father, the sensation of justice that coursed through him, none of those things, none of those moments in time would ever compare to the very second a girl he never meant to hurt, or destroy, told him with a hug and a whisper, "I'm going to be okay. *We* are going to be okay, you and me. And I forgave you already so you don't need to ask."

"I have a secret to tell you," Benji said to Paul, picking a stray rock off the ground and tossing it back in forth in his hands. "I got into Michigan State. Not until the winter semester because I applied so late, but I got in."

"Oh, yeah! That's fantastic!"

Benji pitched the rock toward the woods at the end of the street. "Thanks. I managed a partial scholarship. The Junior Forensic Science Program scholarship, if you can believe that."

"Now that's irony if I ever heard," Paul let out a booming laugh and smacked Benji on the back. "I'm real proud of you." Paul shook his head as if he could hardly believe how life turned out. "Real proud."

Benji felt his cheeks redden when he smiled. No one had ever said they were proud of him, apart from Big Timmie, who was the one who found the scholarship and convinced him to apply. He even helped with the essay, claiming, "It's time to turn those scheming skills of yours into a super power for the good guys."

With Timmie, that day, Benji smiled and laughed over how Timmie called him, "the real Batman." Ever since then, smiling had become a bit easier. Each day that passed, the weight of all the years of anger lifted—only inch by inch but at least it kept lifting.

"How are you feeling about Leah being with your mom while you're away?"

"Bothered. Leah is having a hard time with the separation, she doesn't understand, and instead of helping Leah my mom flits around telling people she and my dad are divorcing, only she seems to spill it over and over for the sake of the, "Oh, I'm so sorry for you," and the "you poor thing," she gets from her church group. I don't really see regret on her part." Benji wrung his hands together. "I don't even think she tells the whole story or the real story. Just yesterday I heard her telling the neighbor my dad is a cheater and that the divorce is because she thinks it's best for, "the kids." But like you said, the only thing I can do for Leah now is make a good future and an example for her, and school is the way."

"Hmm." Paul nodded his head and said, "Real proud, Benji, real proud."

They came to a bench near the entrance to the nature trail and sat down.

"Well," Paul said, looking at the sky, seemingly observing its crisp blue. "Now that your father has taken the plea, and the paperwork is in order and finished, I've got a secret for you."

Benji met Paul's eyes, afraid of what he wanted to say. It still haunted him; his guilt, his fear of jail

323

and retribution from the world. It was as if the fear had taken up residence in the back of his mind and every now and again it would surface like a game of peek a boo, simply to remind him of his need to stay on the right track. "Oh yeah?" Benji felt his heart pick up pace.

"I destroyed the master copy."

Benji let out a breath. "*My* master copy?"

"Yep, back when Todd gave it to me. I destroyed it after I came to meet you for the first time, that night when I got home."

"But why?"

"At that time my god-daughter was a blurred face on the internet, apart from that master copy. And I, despite all my training, decided she would stay that way—blurred. The other reason was my guts after I met you. I came that day to your house because the Knightly's wanted me to make sure you were okay, but I wholeheartedly intended to take you down afterward. I was angry and out for blood. But then I saw you and talked to you, and, well, seeing you with your hands bloody and how your family operated, within a half an hour I knew you weren't the vindictive perpetrator I imagined in my head. You were a broken, angry, hurting kid who'd made a huge mistake."

Benji sat silent, staring at Paul with both admiration and confusion.

"I gambled that your father would cave without the video. If he didn't, I was in trouble. Especially without a master copy. It was stupid of me, professionally, but I knew in my heart it was the right thing to do. I planned this whole thing to tell the lead detective, about how telling your father we had a video was only a technique I was using to force him to confess. Thankfully, I didn't need to. That type of lying isn't easy for me and a good detective can normally smell a lie a hundred yards away. I think he would have smelled mine."

"Wow! I didn't expect that," Benji said.

"Yeah, well I didn't expect it either." Paul leaned back in on the bench and surveyed the sky. "It's beautiful out today. Almost time for fishing season."

Leah

Dear Glittery Diary,

 "Go Leah! You got this!" I heard Benji yell when I sprang from the platform into the pool. Lane four, it's my favorite lane so I won today. Tessa and Mrs. Knightly were in the stands right next to Benji, but, of course, Camille had a church meeting so she wasn't there. It doesn't bother me though; she's hardly at my swim meets or my horse riding competitions.

Oh, and, Benji says his dream is to buy me my own horse one day. "I'll name him after you if you do," I told him, which made him crinkle his face at me. I laughed at him. "Okay, how about I name him Glory then?"

"Much better," he said.

My dad hardly comes around anymore. He lives up in Brighton with a new girlfriend, in an apartment I've only seen one time. The last I saw him was two months ago when he came to have dinner with me and mom.

Just last night Benji sat me down and explained the real reason my mom and dad got a divorce—about what he was doing with a bunch of teenage girls. He said me being sixteen meant I was old enough to know what really happened. I'm not sure what to do with all the information, or how I feel about it. For goodness sake, Benji said my father even had a taxi company on tab just to pick up and then drop off the girls if they needed. (No wonder the basement always seems so eerie to me.) I guess I don't like knowing all of that stuff about my dad, but at least now I understand what happened. And now I understand why Benji never speaks to our dad, or why he never wants to see him again.

Before my swim meet this morning, while getting ready, I couldn't stop thinking about everything Benji told me, trying to find the silver lining—because that's what Benji and Uncle Scooby and the Knightly's would want me to do. Somewhere between searching the house for my swim cap and Benji calling, "Leah, we need to go, you're gonna be late," I realize I owe my love of swimming to that time in our lives. It was during the divorce "season," as Benji calls it, that my mom quickly enrolled me in a bunch of different extracurricular activities: horseback riding, swimming, ballet, summer camp, even the trumpet, which I failed at miserably, but she tried pretty much anything to keep me busy, and, now I know, distracted. It must have worked because I don't really remember the pain from that season, not the way Benji does.

Benji lives away on campus at Michigan State now, but he comes home every weekend to be with me for my swim meets and horse competitions—the two activities that have stuck with me. What sister can say their brother has dedication like that? I do miss him terribly during the week, especially because my mom is usually absent and busy with her own stuff so I'm alone a lot. "Crack face," Benji called her last night, making fun of our mom's makeup behind her back, which I think is mean and funny at the same time. Last week, he and I and Cassy were out to eat and he asked if I remember those calorie charts our mom used to keep on the refrigerator for me. I told him I remember it so much that whenever I see a teacher use a red pen to correct a paper I get a chill.

"Scarred by the red marks," Cassy had said.

"Yep," I agreed.

Now, I eat as I want because I burn everything up through swimming. I've still caught my mom's jaw tighten a few times when I choose something she doesn't approve of, for example, the third slice of pizza I ate last night. Though, I'm not sure why it still matters to her since if you stand Benji and me side-by-side I could wear his jeans. Apart from my boobs, and shoulders from swimming—my specialty is the butterfly stroke—I'm shaped like a tall, lanky boy. I have to add calories just so my clothes won't fall off.

Even though Benji left for college, I still sleep in his room. For some reason, it feels safer in there. I know that's silly, I'm not even sure of what scares me in my bedroom, but it never feels right to me. I remember once when I was eleven years old, I woke, curled in Benji's bed with him watching me. There was a strange look on his face as if he was about to break into tears. I hugged him and asked if he was okay. He said, "Yes, I was just looking in your eyes to make sure the light was still there." Then he kissed my forehead and said, "And it is."

Marula

Dear Journal,

Last night I was outside in the backyard of my house watching the fireflies dance with one another. My four-year-old daughter slid the patio door open and ran to me—barefoot and wearing a dress Aunt Tessa bought her for her birthday last week. In one hand, she carried a glass mason jar, complete with plastic wrap and a rubber band to make a lid, her other hand bounced and flowed through the air as if it were a ribbon attached to her arm.

"Daddy said I can poke the holes with this." She produced a kitchen fork from behind her back as if she were doing a magic trick. I could almost hear her heart saying, "Ta-da."

I'm twenty-eight years old and I still get a kick out of catching fireflies, especially with my daughter. The look of wonder on her face as she cups them in her hand and puts them in the jar, trying hard not to squish them, is priceless. Once, last year when she had less control of her grip, she got too excited and crushed one. She didn't stop crying until she fell asleep, still cupping the poor, dead firefly in her hand. This year it's obvious, she's far more careful with each one she catches.

"Fifteen minutes in the jar, okay, mommy. Only fifteen minutes," she says to me as if their time in the jar is a terrible pull on her heart and mind. She wants to see them light up—chasing them is great, but seeing them up close in the jar is her favorite part. But she hates the idea that they aren't getting home to their firefly family by being in the jar. Fifteen minutes is her rule. And I like her rule. I like the way her heart thinks.

Years ago I couldn't picture this part of my life. Not after Victor, or after the video. I remember not wanting to live. Not wanting to be in the ugly world anymore. And when things get hard, such as when my best friend lost a baby last year, sometimes I hear the whispers of the ugly world and I remember why I wanted to escape. It's not that it pulls me into its darkness anymore, it doesn't hold that kind of power, but it still exists, like a delicate spider web in the blackness waiting to catch an unknowing insect. I and it, we exist in this world because it's what made me who I am today.

I ran into a picture of Victor when I was eighteen. Through some strange internet six-degrees-of-separation, someone posted a picture of him and tagged our family. The person who had done the tagging had no idea what they were doing, or what happened to me, but never the less, there it was, my story, staring back at me. I remember looking at the image, into Victor's eyes. I remember how it re-shredded every part of my soul with shame. One image of him on a beach in Florida, a fishing pole with a fish dangling off the end of the line in one hand and in the other hand a bottle of beer, made me call up Tessa to calm myself down. She reminded me for the thousandths time, "It is not your fault, you don't need to carry the guilt. Release it, baby sister, release it again, and again, it's not yours to carry."

It took a lot of time for me to get the parts of my soul back that were shattered. It was as if every time Victor ever touched me, I was tearing off a piece of my soul and throwing it into the universe, believing the facade that I was giving it to him. And I innocently believed that he was giving me his in return. But that's how the deception works. Victor wasn't an obvious bad guy on the streets, who I or anyone else would place as evil. He was a good guy who traveled and helped people all over the world. When he told me how wise I was and how beautiful and perfect I was becoming it made me feel special and wanted, as if a hero wanted me. I believed I was going to be his forever love and it was merely a strange cosmic mistake that I was eleven, twelve, thirteen...

When he looked into my eyes and said he loved me, I believed him. When I saw the private signs he would give, signs that he was thinking about me— smiles from across the dinner table, and a special two-finger wave when he and my dad would board a plane or a car and go into the field for a few weeks—I believed him.

I didn't understand how someone being delicate and gentle, could be considered evil? How could someone not using force, be evil? How could someone looking you in your eyes be evil? To me, Victor and I shared a special secret. It was a grown-up secret.

But I was not the only secret he kept.

I was twenty, attending Michigan State, and it was early December when my father called me up from Indonesia. "Marula, baby, how are you?" He sounded like he was next door, which made my heart hurt. It had been two months since I saw him, and though my mother and Tessa were still in Ann Arbor, I missed them all, all of the time.

By his slight pause I knew this was not going to be an "I just wanted to say hello," call.

"Daddy, just tell me," I said, closing my laptop and laying back in my bed. I wanted to be in the softest place possible if I was going to have to brace myself.

"Okay, baby," he sighed heavily and it made a "whoosh" sound into the phone. "Victor has been arrested and the prosecutor is going after him this time."

Anger and confirmation and confusion had torn through me like a surgeon's scalp without anesthesia. I burned from the inside outward with pain. For months and months.

It took having my daughter before I really felt free. Seeing her innocence helped me understand what happened to me with Victor. In my young mind, it felt like love. And for my part, it was an innocent love because there was no reason to tell myself to close the doors of my heart to Victor and his advances. There was no experience beforehand to use as a gauge. It wasn't until I fell in true love with my husband, that I knew what unadulterated, unselfish, untainted love looked like.

"Mommy, mommy, isn't it the most beautiful thing!" my daughter chirped to me last night, holding the jar of fireflies. "Daddy, look, they're all lighted up like stars!" she proclaimed as my husband came from the house and handed me a glass of lemonade. I looked at his beautiful smile, his gorgeous curly red locks, the dash of freckles across his nose, and then to my daughter, her smile so much like Tessa's that you can't help but smile back, and I privately, quietly thanked God, again, for the day Benji released that video. It interrupted my life course, and forever changed it for the better.

Tessa

Dear God,

I was nervous and excited last night, the night before Benji's graduation. It took twenty hours' worth of plane travel to go from Botswana to Frankfurt to New York and finally to Detroit in order to make it back in time, but once I saw Benjamin Alexander Lockwood in his green and white cap and gown, his honors tassels hanging around his neck, I immediately knew it was worth it. He truly looked beautiful up there. And I could swear he'd grown since I saw him last, though later at dinner he swore he hadn't. Maybe it's because of the way he holds his head up now: tall and confident. It reminds me of Uncle Scooby. And of my dad.

Watching him up there, his smile bright enough to light up the conference center…well, after all of these months, seeing him still awakens a part of me that longs to reach out and touch his face, to trace the structure of his square jaw, to taste his lips. I still remember the teenage fumbling moment back in high school when he kissed me at the coffee shop. It all seems like years ago now, but I've never stopped thinking about it, or of him.

Benji and I have remained friends, but only friends, making regular monthly calls to catch up on life, to share our experiences, and check on each other's families.

Over the years Benji and I have dated other people, but none of them ever seem to last. Though, there was one girl for Benji, and a brief moment when I thought he was considering marrying Bethany—the girl he dated his junior year of college. But having a slice of pizza at Maria's during Christmas break, he told me that he and she never felt right for him. "Something seems to be missing," he had said.

(I had secretly hoped it was me that was missing).

During the year when they prosecuted Benji's father, my Uncle Scooby worked diligently to wipe the video of Marula off the internet. Sadly, we all know it will never truly be gone. But the good thing is she's merely a blurred internet face, hardly worth the watch for most pervs out there.

And Marula is doing well now, very well. She's met a guy at college and I think there might be wedding bells in their future. Especially because the way he looks at her is hardly describable: it's filled with admiration and wonderment as if she is the most beautiful thing God ever created. It's lovely to witness, actually.

And, of course, my sweet Leah is still the bright star she's always been. She's grown so tall that she towers me now, even hunching over to hug me.

Today, at dinner, she told me she still loves to plug in her music and do impromptu dance parties, even if it's only her doing the dancing. I missed her tons while I was in Botswana, and each time I found myself in the perfect sunrise or sunset I would think of her. Because that's exactly what Leah is like, a warm, beautiful, golden sunrise. And I'm ever so glad Benji saved her life path.

Benji

Dear God,

Today day I graduated with my Masters in Applied & Computational Mathematics, and Tessa and her family were in the front row next to Leah, Paul Schneider, and my mother.

I could hardly keep my mind on the ceremony seeing all of them there supporting me. And my favorite part wasn't the announcement of my name—with honors, I must add—or the handshake and presentation of my diploma, it was how the entire row of my people gave me a standing ovation, even causing my professors and a few fellow graduates to join in.

After the ceremony ended, and hugs handshakes and high fives were finished, only Tessa and I stood together. "I'm proud of you," she said handing me a small blue box wrapped with a red ribbon. Then she leaned in and gave me a heart hammering hug. (Oh, how I still miss her touch). I grew another two inches after high school so her face is barely to my chest and I had to hunch to squeeze her tight—but while I was there I made sure to inhale the familiar apple smell in her hair.

During our hug, off to the side, I saw Marula grin at Tessa and then thread her arm through Leah's and head off with the rest of our group toward the cars.

"Don't be late for dinner, the reservation is at four," Todd made sure to call back to Tessa and me, though I think he was secretly checking on us.

"Glad you could make it back for today. I'm really grateful. I missed you." I told her.

It's been a month since I talked with Tessa but a year since I actually seen her. She was gone the entire last year to study abroad in Botswana, and she was set to graduate with her master's degree next month same as me. She intends to follow in her father's footsteps at the U.N., though as a Human Relations expert rather than a field investigator.

"There isn't a plane or person that could have held me back from seeing this accomplishment," she said, hugging me again. "We are all so proud. And I missed you too."

An hour ago, alone in the night, tucked into my apartment, my boxes packed to move to D.C. to begin training for my new position as a criminal investigator in the Federal Bureau of Investigations Cyber Crime Division, I finally opened the small blue box Tessa gave me.

Inside was a necklace and a note:

Dearest Benji,

See, redemption is possible.

Now, let this be the last bullet you ever think about.

Love forever,

Tessa

Attached to the end of a leather rope necklace was the casing of a small bullet. Engraved on the bullet, in tiny writing it said, "Shoot for the stars."

Acknowledgements

I'd like to thank first and for most my amazing family, my husband and my children, for all of their cheering section support. (Especially on the hard days). Thank you for always nurturing my dreams and my heart. You are my necessary love nutrient in this life journey.

I'd like to thank my beta readers for their input and direction. They waded through my dribble and vomit writing in order to point me in the right direction with Benji. Thank you, Carolyn Lopez, for saying, "I already am proud." Those words made me keep going when I wondered if Benji, and I, had a future. Thank you, Ellen Plummer, for telling me that pee doesn't make sense. Such simple and priceless input sparked a whole new, and better, story line. Thank you, Dad, David Palmer, for the gift of technology and for saying that I have a great "career," ahead of me. That's a priceless word. Thank you, Irvin Hayes, for your invaluable "Jedi," teaching and your brilliant revenge idea. A grand thank you to my Mom, Patty Palmer, who reads and re-reads my stories until her eyes are tired and sore. Your input and cheerleading are priceless. Thank you, Beth Hayes, for our regular coffee time and for listening to my endless downloads over this story, and all of my stories, and for always believing in me. I'm trying to live tenaciously!

A word about the Author…

Kimberly J. Fuller grew up in a Military family, spending the majority of her upbringing in Europe. After high school, she settled in South East Michigan, met the man of her dreams and has called Michigan home ever since. A battle with cancer propelled her to reach for her writing dreams. During treatment, she finished her first novel.

You can find Kimberly's world and contact her here:
www.KimberlyJFuller.com

Benji, ~~The No One, The Loser, The Rejected~~, The Revenge Artist

ISBN 978-0-9857561-5-4

9 780985 756154